# THE SECRET OF THE ANGEL WHO DIED AT MIDNIGHT

## A DSS KATE SUTTON MURDER MYSTERY

### ROSY FENWICKE

**WONDERFUL WORLD**

*To Elizabeth Rosemary*

# PROLOGUE

GEOFFREY KNEW IT WAS COMING. The crunch of stones shifting under the intruder's feet gave it away. Then the whisper of disturbed air across the nape of his neck, milli-seconds before impact. He made no attempt to dodge or to escape; there was no point.

He was going to die.

It struck him as darkly amusing, that the stories about your life flashing in front of your eyes were true. Then it saddened him. These fragmented scenes scooting across the private cinema of his mind, would be the last things he would ever see.

He couldn't help himself.

He braced.

The spade delivered a catastrophic blow—the metallic clang resonating with the fillings in his teeth. As if in slow motion, he pitched forward, toppling face-down into the soft earth. The rough leaves caressing his cheek. The sweet heady aroma of crushed strawberries seeping through the fabric of his t-shirt, reminding him of summer puddings and tennis.

Suspended in a twilight consciousness, he waited.

The outcome as inevitable as taxes.

Dr Geoffrey Scott knew precisely what was happening to his brain. His middle meningeal artery, violently ruptured, now relentlessly pumped blood into the confined space of his skull, starving his brain-stem of oxygen, creating pressure where none should exist. Within moments, he would stop breathing, his heart would stop beating, his neurones would stop functioning—and that would be it.

How curious then, to experience the profound sense of relief now washing over him.

Life.

Unceasing toil.

The unmet demands.

The bottomless disappointment in Ava's eyes. His own bewildered reflection staring back at him in the mirror each morning—a man utterly perplexed by what he had become.

Yet, it hadn't always been this way. Happy memories of childhood, laughter, loving parents, loyal friends, adventures and travels, fun, love, joy and the soul-deep satisfaction of saving lives; these afforded him solace as he felt his heart fluttering erratically in his chest. Like a trapped butterfly desperately beating its wings behind a closed window.

Tentative footsteps on the gravel behind him. Laboured breathing, punctuated by grunts. The intruder leaning over him, scrutinising his face for signs of life.

Hoarding these last seconds of consciousness for himself, Dr Geoffrey Scott pretended he was already dead.

# CHAPTER
# ONE

THE FIRST TIME her phone rang, she was in the shower. The second, coming soon after, when her ears were still full of shampoo. It was the third call, eight minutes after the first, that she heard. Naked under her towel, she ran downstairs and grabbed her phone from the bench in the kitchen.

'Kate Sutton.'

'Sorry to call you on your day off,' said the operator. 'There's been a suspicious death in Martinborough.' She paused, her voice sinking with the weight of the information she was about to convey. 'It's Geoffrey Scott.'

'The doctor?'

'That's what I've been told. The fire crew and ambulance are there. DC Hunter is on his way. What do you want to do?'

'Did they say why it was suspicious?'

'His wife reported a head wound.'

It took five minutes for Kate to dry her short blonde hair, slap on some moisturiser and throw on a clean shirt and pair of trousers. She collected her vest, tossed her phone in her bag, grabbed her keys, and squeezed past the stack of boxes, containing twenty-five years of married life, in the hall.

From Masterton, the back route to Martinborough involves turning left at the roundabout on State Highway Two, onto East Taratahi Road at the end of which the driver makes a sharp right before reaching the Gladstone vineyards. From there, the two-lane road runs straight between hedged paddocks bypassing the towns of Carterton and Greytown. Then it dips to cross the narrow concrete bridge over the middle reaches of the Ruamahanga River, climbing again as it winds through gently rolling farmland before it finally reaches its destination.

It was seven-thirty on Sunday evening, another in a long spell of hot summer evenings that year.

A storm, as violent as it was sudden, had swept through the Southern Wairarapa an hour before, leaving behind clean air and a soft blue sky. Puddles pooled in ditches, but the road itself was dry; the rain having evaporated as soon as it hit the tarmac.

Free of traffic, Kate switched on her red and blues and floored the accelerator. She felt the Skoda Superb respond under her. On any other day driving faster than she should was her guilty pleasure, the moments of exhilaration a short relief from the constraints of her job as head of the Masterton Police Criminal Investigation Branch.

Not today.

When her marriage ended, Geoffrey Scott had been one of the few people who contacted her with an offer of help. It had touched her, because theirs was an infrequent work relationship. Based fifty kilometres away in the affluent town of Martinborough, his services weren't often required by the Masterton police.

The last time he assisted with a case was nine months ago. A suspected cot death. The mother had barricaded herself in the house, refusing to let anyone in. Geoffrey had spoken to her from the doorstep, calming her until she opened the door, then he stepped inside. Half an hour later, the door opened, and he emerged with his arm around the young woman as she carried her baby daughter to the waiting ambulance.

He had been kind and it was dread, not exhilaration that Kate felt now.

Promoted a year ago to oversee the two teams comprising the local CIB, Kate's team was responsible for investigating the more serious crimes. The other team, ably led by DS Will Beveridge, looked after whatever was left.

Will had not taken the news of her promotion well. With five years' experience on Kate, he had assumed the top job would be his. After a long silence and several even longer sessions in the pub, he reluctantly accepted the new arrangements.

With conditions.

The first, was that she was to keep her nose out of his business. The second involved a graphic description of what would happen to her if she didn't. So far, she'd never had to pull rank and interfere.

However she was still only a DSS. Murder cases had to be under the nominal oversight of a Detective Inspector stationed at district headquarters. As this was in Wellington, seventy-eight kilometres away on the other side of the steep and winding road over the Remutaka Hills, Kate was effectively left to her own devices. For the last twelve months, this arrangement had suited her perfectly.

This evening, as she drew closer to Martinborough and her first time in charge of a potential murder investigation, she wasn't so sure.

# CHAPTER
# TWO

SHE SLOWED the car to cross the bridge over the Huangarua River which marks the northern boundary of the town, then rounded a curve to crest a small rise. Here the transition from farmland to vineyards was striking—row upon ordered row of vines, their thick summer leaves a blanket of green in the evening sunshine.

Houses scattered along the road merged into suburbia as she neared the town centre. It hadn't always been this way. Thirty years ago, before the tablelands of the Ruamahanga River and its tributaries had been transformed into vineyards, Martinborough existed solely as a service centre for the surrounding farms. Back then, like the farmers themselves, the town struggled to survive. The wine industry changed everything, breathing new life into tired streets, drawing wealthy retirees, restaurants and boutique shops, accommodation and wedding venues in its wake.

A small village with a big reputation, Martinborough pulsed with life in the summer months when weekenders and day trippers ventured over the Remutaka Range to sample fine wines, linger over lunches, shop and play golf.

This evening, however, the long straight streets were deserted; the weekend visitors leaving early to avoid the forecast rain which had passed through an hour before. The locals were inside, preparing for the week ahead, blissfully unaware of the drama about to unfold in their midst.

As she approached the address Comms had sent through, she spotted DC Tony Hunter, currently the only other member of her team, waiting for her by the roadside. A fire engine, an ambulance, the SOCO van and several police cars, were lined up along the kerb. He waved her past them towards a space marked with two road cones, which he lifted out of her way as she pulled in.

Tall and thin with red hair and a pale complexion, Tony was in his mid-twenties. He'd transferred to Masterton from the West Coast of the South Island at the start of December, and despite it now being February—amid a scorching summer with almost no rain—his skin remained a translucent white beneath a dense sprinkling of freckles.

'It looks like the victim was hit on the back of the head,' he announced, before she could get out of the car. 'A couple of uniforms are talking to the neighbours. Nothing helpful so far.'

'Thanks,' said Kate. 'Where am I going?'

He pointed to the ribbon of white and red police tape hanging limply across a driveway on the other side of the road. 'Paul's here. He's with the victim at the back of the house.'

Kate followed his gaze down the drive. Partially obscured from the road stood a single wooden garage with a pitched roof. Beside it rose a two-storey house with an identical roofline. It was the final property in a row of established homes situated on one side of Palmer Grove, a quiet cul-de-sac at the edge of Martinborough. Across the street was a reserve of neglected native bush. A sign beside the entrance, defaced by graffiti, indicated that cyclists, pedestrians and dog-walkers were all welcome, with the proviso that dogs be kept leashed.

Tony jerked his head towards the fire engine parked near the corner and the fire-fighters in bulky uniforms clustered around it. 'I've got all their names and contact details. Can I let them go?'

She counted eight people, six men and two women. That added up to sixteen boots which had likely trampled through her potential crime scene. She closed her eyes when she thought of the contaminated evidence, but she had no reason to keep them. The news of the doctor's death would be widely known already, the shock overtaking the town like an unstoppable tsunami.

The fire chief waved. Not yet ready to listen to his version of events, she returned his wave before pretending to answer her phone.

'Yip, they can go.'

Tony marched off to tell them, passing a group of people congregated in the middle of the road on the way who she hoped were neighbours. It was too soon for sightseers.

Beyond them, parked off to one side under the overhanging branch of a Ngaio tree, was a gleaming black station wagon with discrete gold lettering stencilled on the door. The man sitting behind the wheel, caught Kate's eye and raised a hand in greeting. She nodded, surprised to see it was Bruce Murphy himself. His company, Murphy Funerals, held the contract for the police work in the district, but it had been ages since she'd seen the boss at a callout. It was odd him being here so early, until she remembered he was also the leader of the local business association. Undoubtedly concerned for the town's reputation, he'd want to know what was going on as soon as possible. She made a mental note to have a chat with him before she left.

By the time Tony returned, Kate had retrieved a couple of protective clothing packs from the SOCO van and pulled on a pair of overalls over her shirt and trousers. She fiddled with her gloves while Tony struggled into his suit, grunting as his lanky frame pulled the crutch uncomfortably high.

'Talk to me,' she said, when he was finally ready.

He took his notebook out of his vest and flipped it open as they crossed the road. 'The deceased is a forty-eight-year-old white male, Geoffrey Scott. His wife, Ava Scott, identified him. She is a thirty-eight-year-old white female and is in the ambulance behind us. Nothing major, she was in minor shock when the crew arrived. The paramedic looking after her, says she'll be fine.'

'I'll talk to her after I see the body,' she said, walking on towards the garage and the two cars sitting in front of it, one behind the other. The first car she came to, was a light blue Suzuki Swift. Old food wrappers and empty soft drink containers littered the passenger footwell. In the back, contents of an overnight bag spilled across the seat, alongside a folded drop sheet and a bag full of rags spotted with paint.

'Mrs Scott had returned from a weekend away,' Tony explained. 'It was raining, and she heard cats fighting in the back garden, so she went to intervene. That's when she found her husband. She thought he'd had a heart attack, so she started CPR. She kept it up, for around fifteen minutes, before she remembered she was supposed to call for help.'

Kate paused to peer through the windows of the second vehicle, a Ford diesel 4WD. It was even messier than the first car. An open brief-case lay in the front passenger footwell; inside it she could see the end of a stethoscope.

'Go on,' she said, as she followed him down the side of the garage, the path barely wide enough for single file. The gravel underfoot, still wet, had been well and truly churned up by the recent foot traffic.

'Comms sent through the voice recording. She was on the phone when she saw blood on the back of his head and panicked. According to the fire chief who arrived ten minutes later, she was hysterical.'

'Have you had a look?' asked Kate.

'I was waiting for you. The crew walked all around before the chief figured out it might be a good idea to secure the area. As you can imagine Paul is not happy.' He stopped abruptly and she nearly collided with his back. In front of them was a lovely garden surrounded by tall hedges, with white gravel paths between geometrically arranged raised beds. Standard laurels in the centre of each bed added to the formality of the space, though this was disrupted by the temporary pergola Paul had erected over the victim.

'Any witnesses?'

'None, so far.' He stepped aside to let Kate go ahead of him.

Hopping across the protective footplates, she approached the lead SOCO detective, Paul Roper. He was kneeling to inspect a spade lying beside the body.

'The murder weapon?'

'Could be.' He stood up. Balding, short and with the belly of a man who likes his beer, Paul was in his early sixties. By rights, he should have retired a year ago. Because there was no one with his skill and experience to replace him—and, more significantly, because there was nothing for him to do at home—he'd elected to stay on. 'Won't know for sure until I get it to the lab.' He scowled at the sky as if it was his enemy. 'Bloody rain.'

'What have you got?'

'Bugger all. First the widow moved the body, then the rain washed away most of the blood, then eight fire crew trampled through the place. One of them picked up the spade.' He shook his head in disbelief that anyone could be so stupid. 'I'm not going to be much help.'

'You always say that, and then you always find something,' she said.

'Not this time.'

'You say that too. Take me through what you think happened, then I'll get out of your way.' She nodded a greeting to Marsha, the police photographer, who was recording a video on the other side of the garden.

'It looks like he was bending over when he was hit,' said Paul pointing at a raised bed with a healthy crop of strawberries peeping out from under a cover of lush green foliage. 'See the leaves there are crushed. He's got a stain on the front of his shirt which matches the squashed berries. You've got that Marsha?'

The younger woman nodded and moved on.

'He didn't just fall and hit his head on the way down?'

Paul ignored the question. 'His wife said she found him lying face up on the gravel, so either someone moved him, or he rolled off the raised bed before he died. See here,' he said pointing to a patch of bare earth flanked by two piles of white stones. 'That's where she knelt to do the CPR. She pushed more gravel out of the way to lift his head. When Marsha's done, I'll get the intern to gather it up in sections and we'll analyse each stone for blood then DNA.' He rolled his eyes heavenwards as if appealing for divine intervention.

'What about the spade?' asked Kate.

'Haven't had time to examine it properly but I'd say the hairs on the blade belong to the victim. To answer your question, no, he didn't just fall.'

Kate turned finally to confront the body on the ground. No one ever looked good dead. Whatever dignity Geoffrey Scott might have possessed when he was alive, it had deserted him now. The waxy greyish pallor of his face accentuated his stiffened blue lips, which had peeled back to reveal a row of symmetrical teeth. His dull sightless eyes, their pupils fixed on some distant point, lurked behind half-closed lids.

A shudder rippled through her. It was hard to reconcile the man she'd known as a kind man and respected doctor in the community with this ungainly body splayed out on the gravel; his function now, a source of evidence for the investigation to come.

His faded polo shirt, undone at the neck, and pulled down to cover his chest wasn't long enough to conceal the mound of white, hair-covered belly rising above the band of his grubby black trackpants. Someone had placed the olive-green crocs he'd been wearing neatly together at the end of the raised bed—probably one of the fire crew. The SOCO team knew better.

'Tamsyn should be here soon,' said Paul. 'She had to find someone to look after the girls. Tim's working this weekend.'

Tamsyn Fraser was one of the country's best forensic pathologists. She was also Kate's best friend and tennis partner. They'd played doubles at the club this morning, as they did every Sunday, easily beating two older women from Featherston. Her daughters watched quietly from the sidelines, trusting their mother would fulfil her side of the deal and take them to MacDonalds afterwards. A treat, their on-call cardiologist father, wasn't allowed to know about.

'I guess you don't want to move him until she arrives,' said Kate.

'Correct. He's been moved enough. From the little bit I can see, the back of his head looks pretty bad.' He sighed, pushing up the sleeve of his overalls to look at his watch. 'If she's not here soon we'll have to set up the lights.'

'You will anyway,' said Kate. She stepped away from the body and surveyed the rest of the garden. 'Any ideas how the killer got in and out?'

'Give me time. I got here half an hour before you, so no, not yet.'

Knowing the pressure he was under, Kate let it go. 'I'm guessing he could have come through the hedge there.' She pointed to an area where the branches were more spaced out.

'Or he could have walked down the drive. Unless you're standing at the end, you can't see all the way in from the street. Add to that the storm, it being Sunday afternoon, and most people would have been inside.'

Kate sighed. He was right. It was unlikely she would find the one thing which would make her job easier—a witness. She turned to talk to Tony, but he had moved away to talk to one of the SOCO interns, a young woman whose curvaceous figure suited the overalls.

She called out to him. 'I'm going to talk to Mrs Scott. You stay here and do what Paul tells you. I'll be in touch about the arrangements for the morning.'

She performed one final three-sixty scan, fixing the details of the garden and the victim's body in her memory for recall later. Then she left, stepping across the footplates to go and talk to the grieving widow — the job all cops dreaded.

# CHAPTER
# THREE

THE PARAMEDIC CLAMBERED awkwardly down from the ambulance as soon as she saw Kate approaching. Arms stretched wide, she herded her away from the open back door and around the corner of the vehicle, to a place where they wouldn't be overheard. Sheila Comstock, Senior Officer, leaned her ample bosom towards Kate. 'She's still in shock, poor thing. If you want my opinion, I think you should wait until tomorrow before you speak to her.'

'I should have introduced myself. I'm DSS Kate Sutton from the Masterton CIB. While I appreciate your concerns, I do need to talk to her now. I promise I'll keep it short. I'd appreciate it if you could wait out here.' With a tight smile, she side-stepped Sheila's best intentions, returned to the back of the ambulance, climbed in and sat down on the stretcher facing Ava Scott.

The woman who slowly lifted her head to look at her reminded Kate of a wounded creature, suddenly thrust into a new reality she didn't quite comprehend. A small woman, she was swamped by the crinkly space blanket wrapped around her shoulders; her short dark curly hair framed large brown eyes leaking tears. With her upturned nose, tear-stained cheeks and youthful complexion, Kate thought she looked more like a lost child than a woman who had just found her husband bashed to death in their garden. Ava opened her mouth to speak but the words seemed trapped somewhere between grief and shock; she closed it again.

'I'm DSS Kate Sutton, Mrs Scott. I am leading the investigation into your husband's death. First, may I say how sorry I am for your loss.' She paused waiting for Ava to speak, then continued when she got no reaction. 'I'd like to ask you some questions, if that's all right?'

Ava managed a tiny nod. Outside, Sheila was huffing her disapproval—her paramedic's protective instincts projected through the walls of the ambulance.

Kate took her notebook and pen out of her vest. 'You found your husband after you got home, is that correct?'

Another slow nod.

'What time was that?' She kept her tone gentle but firm.

Ava's voice emerged as a painful croak. She cleared her throat to start again. 'When the rain started. I heard cats fighting. The neighbour's cat attacks Louie every chance he gets. Louie is my cat, he's old and can't fight back. It's horrible. Geoffrey must have left the cat door unlocked. I ask him not to, but he doesn't listen.' The present tense hung in the air between them, a reminder of how recently her husband had been alive.

Kate tried again. 'What time did you get home?'

'Have you seen him?' Ava scanned the street through the open door, her eyes wide with concern. 'He's called Louie. He'll be terrified.'

'I'll ask my team to look out for him,' said Kate. She waited as Ava nodded again before slumping back inside the blanket. 'Can you tell me what time you got home?'

'Seven, I think.'

Kate wrote this down, her pen moving steadily across the page. 'Did you see anyone when you got here? Anyone in the garden, or on the street?'

Ava screwed up her eyes to think. It made her look even more like a child than she already did. 'No,' she said. 'No one.'

'You were away for the weekend?'

'I go to my studio to paint most weekends. I sleep on the sofa.'

'Where is your studio?'

'In Featherston, in an old building off the main street. Phillip Marlow. He's my landlord. He lives in his shop at the front.'

'You don't mind if we check you were there?'

'That's why I told you, his name.'

'Is there anyone who might have wanted to hurt your husband?' Kate asked.

'No one,' said Ava. She said this forcefully. 'He's been the only doctor in Martinborough for twenty years. Why would anyone want to hurt him?'

'No threats?'

'I said no.' Ava pulled the blanket around her again, clearly irritated.

Kate decided to change tack. 'How long have you been married?'

'I'm thirty-eight. We got married when I was twenty-one, so we've been married for…' She freed her hands from the blanket and counted using her fingers, the simple mathematical task seemingly requiring all her concentration. 'Seventeen years. He's ten years older than me.'

'Was it a happy marriage?'

Two brown eyes flashed in the semi-darkness of the ambulance. 'Of course. My husband has just died, what do you expect me to say?'

Kate nodded, then took her time recording the answer in her note-book, not looking up until she heard Ava's breathing slow down. 'I'm sorry but you won't be able to return to your home for a couple of days, not until the forensic team has examined it.'

'What about my car?'

'We'll need that for a couple of days as well.'

'Sheila said that might happen. I called Mimi. She's coming to get me.' Her eyes drifted past Kate to the road. 'She'll be here soon.'

Kate recognised the name. Mimi was married to Bruce Murphy, the funeral director. Back when she was married to Matt, Kate had met the couple socially a few times. She knew them well enough to say hello to, but that was it.

'I won't keep you. If I could take your phone number, I'll be in touch tomorrow to arrange another time to talk. In the meantime, these are my contact details.' Kate handed her a card. Quickly she wrote down the number Ava rattled off, hoping she hadn't got it wrong. Understandably, Ava was in no mood to repeat herself.

Outside the ambulance Sheila was waiting for her; no doubt having listened to their conversation. Fretful, concerned, she motioned Kate aside. 'That poor woman, how's she going to manage?' She left no time for Kate to answer. 'Who would do this? He was such a wonderful doctor. Everybody loved him. You couldn't meet a nicer more helpful man.'

Kate put a calming hand on Sheila's arm. Surprised, the woman smiled, grateful for the gesture and covered it with her own.

'Will you wait with her until her friend gets here?' asked Kate.

'We're not supposed to.' Sheila sniffed. 'But that poor woman needs someone to look after her at a time like this.' Tsking, Kate's gesture forgotten, she climbed back into the ambulance and started fussing.

# CHAPTER
# FOUR

AFTER DISCUSSING IT WITH TONY, those in charge at Masterton, and DI Jack Anderson in Wellington, Kate set up the Incident Room at the Martinborough Town Hall. Renovated and modernised as part of recent earthquake strengthening, the large reception room to the left of the main hall was light, well-ventilated and private. There was enough room for the number of desks the extra uniforms, bussed in from stations around the lower North Island, would need. Best of all, there was the added bonus of a proper kitchen.

The advent of secure mobile connections to the police database had been a game changer. Before this great leap forward, Kate would have had no option but to use the spare room tucked away at the back of Masterton Station. Dark, and cramped, its windows opened onto the carpark, and it was so poorly ventilated that in summer, it felt like they were working in an oven.

It was lunchtime on Monday. Jack stood in the doorway of this brand-new Incident Room and surveyed the organised chaos. It was always like this for the first few days of an investigation: noisy, urgent, the atmosphere thick with adrenalin and, not that he would ever say this out loud, testosterone. He watched the staff getting to know each other as equipment was set up and workspaces delineated according to the tasks required. It was exciting and scary and for a few moments, it made him want to take off his jacket, roll up his sleeves and get amongst it. He took a deep breath and let common sense prevail.

Officially, he'd driven over the hill to assess the situation, make sure everything was being done correctly, before spelling out the budget Kate had to work within. This was not the only murder in his district and the latest funding cuts meant money and manpower were scarce.

He was under no illusions what this meant to the investigation. No stranger to the frontline, Jack had served his time in the Wairarapa, working first in uniform and then as a detective before taking up his current position at district headquarters in Wellington.

A young woman in uniform brushed past him, disturbing his train of thought. She hurried on to the front of the room where two murder boards, really just whiteboards on wheels, were set up. A 10 by 8 colour photo of the victim, with his name, Dr Geoffrey Scott, written underneath, was stuck front and centre on one.

It was surreal seeing the face of man he knew and had worked with for many years, occupying the spot reserved for victims. There weren't many doctors in the Wairarapa and Geoffrey Scott had been one of the good ones. When called upon he had been willing and able to help out at all hours of the day and night, no matter the situation. At first glance, Jack considered his death was as inexplicable as it was shocking.

A momentary vision of the pile of work waiting for him on his desk in Wellington flashed across his mind and was just as quickly dismissed. He was keen to find out what the team had discovered.

Six feet, five inches, his muscles defined by regular weight training, he cut an imposing figure as he wove between the desks to an area surrounded by wall dividers at the far end of the room. Whispers followed his progress as staff glanced up, nudging their neighbours and nodding in his direction. Outside the temporary cubicle he paused, his muffled tap on the divider almost knocking it over.

Kate stood up and motioned for him to come in. He looked at the rickety arrangement with distaste before he warily sat down in the plastic chair in front of her make-shift desk.

'It's fine,' she said, pre-empting his comments. 'It's better than the space in Masterton. Anyway, it's not for long.'

'That's what I like to hear.'

'You will be pleased to know, the council said we can use the space rent-free for as long as we need it.'

'Even better.' He unbuttoned his jacket and brought one large foot up to rest on the opposite knee. 'Fill me in on what you've got so far. Just the highlights.'

Kate tapped the keys on her laptop to read from her screen. 'You knew him. Geoffrey Scott, 48, white male, local GP. Born and brought up in Martinborough. His father was the doctor here before him. He's lived in the same house his whole life, apart from six years at Medical School in Dunedin and three years working in the UK. He returned to take over his father's practice after his parents were killed in 2001.'

'He told me. Their plane hit a mountain on its way to Zurich in November, two months after Twin Towers tragedy. It barely got a mention.' He motioned for her to go on.

'He married Ava Forrester when he was 32 and she was 21. She's the cousin of his best friend, Dan. They trained together. Dr Forrester is coming back to be with her and has agreed to look after the practice until they work out what to do.'

She paused and scrolled down to a summary of the SOCO findings.

'According to Tamsyn, he was killed by a single blow to the back of his head. She puts the time of death at between three and six PM. Witnesses saw him at the supermarket at one o'clock, where he bought bread and mayonnaise. His wife returned from a weekend away at around seven. She says it was right when the rain started so we can firm up the time. She found his body, did CPR for between fifteen and twenty minutes, then called for help.'

'Do we have the Comms recording?'

'Do you want to hear it now or later?'

'Now, if it's not too long.'

Kate tapped more keys. 'It starts at 7:10 PM.'

*'Fire, Police or Ambulance?'*

*'Ambulance.'* The woman's voice was shaky. *'My husband's had a heart attack. He's not breathing.'*

'That's her?' asked Jack. 'I've spoken to her a few times when I called Geoffrey at home, but I only met her once. Community fund raiser. She seemed nice enough.'

Kate nodded.

'*Your name and address, please*?' asked the operator.

They heard Ava gulping, then take a deep breath before she said her name and address. She sounded reasonably calm as she explained to come down the side of the garage to the garden at the back of the house. Then her voice wavered.

'*How long before you get here*?'

'*Ten minutes or less, Mrs Scott. In the meantime, can you do CPR*?'

'*I've been doing it.*'

'*Good. Keep it up and stay on the phone.*'

They heard teeth chattering, the pattering of rain hitting stones, and then a shoving sound and Ava grunting.

'*Oh God. Oh God, Oh God. No.*'

'*What's happened*?'

'*His head. There's blood.*'

'*The team is nearly there, Mrs Scott. Hold on.*'

'*You're not listening to me.*' This sentence was screamed into the phone.

'*I am listening, Ava. You're doing a great job. Try to stay calm. Let's focus on the CPR. Listen to me. I'll count with you. Ready? Together. One. Two. Three. Four.*'

'That's all.' Kate tapped a key, ending the replay. 'Do you think she sounds convincing.'

'Why do you ask?'

Kate shook her head. 'A feeling I got. It's how she was after. It could have been shock, but she was a bit snarky. Not your typical murder victims wife. I didn't get the feeling that she cared. She was more worried about her cat than about her husband.'

'People don't always act the way we think they should,' he said. 'Go on.'

'The fifteen minutes of CPR before she called, plus the rain, it was heavy and lasted maybe thirty minutes, effectively ruined the crime scene. Add to that the eight well-meaning volunteer first responders who trampled over everything in their great big fire boots. Worse,' she said, 'one of them picked up the murder weapon, turned it over and handed it to her mate before the fire chief yelled at her to put it down.'

'Which she did, but in a different place.'

'Correct.'

'How's Paul's blood pressure?'

'He's on new medication, so it's not too bad,' said Kate. She saw no need to tell Jack about his rant after she left. Tony had told her Paul had to go and sit in the van for ten minutes to cool off.

'Moving on. Ava's car was verified by CCTV travelling towards Martinborough on State Highway 2 just after six-thirty PM.'

Jack held up his hand. 'Before we get to that, does Paul reckon we'll get anything helpful from the crime scene? Any DNA, blood splashes?'

'He took away a wheelbarrow full of gravel, but he doesn't think it'll show anything. The rain was so strong it washed most of the blood away. Preliminary fingerprints on the spade match the fire crew and Dr Scott. No one else. You know how behind the lab is, it'll be ages before we get any DNA results back. Because he only found three sets of prints, Paul thinks the perp probably wore gloves.'

'No footprints?'

'Not on gravel,' said Kate. 'Nothing to indicate the killer's entry or exit points either.'

Jack sighed. 'Back to Mrs Scott. Where was she again?'

'She's an artist and has a studio in Featherston, where she spends most weekends. I've requested a photo ID from the road cameras to confirm it was her who was driving.'

'Good. Does she have an alibi for the rest of the day?'

'Tony is checking that with the landlord this morning.'

'What about the house?' he asked.

'The team's almost finished.'

'Have you been inside?'

'Not yet. I was hoping you'd come with me to look at it after the briefing,' she said. 'He was killed in the garden at the back of the house. It's surrounded on four sides by high hedges. No witnesses have reported seeing or hearing anyone in the immediate vicinity that afternoon.'

'No doorbell cams?'

'Wrong demographic. Boomers who aren't into tech.'

'That's a pity.'

'It's the last house on the street, and the only neighbour, June Whittaker, is an older woman who lives alone. She says she didn't see or hear anything. She was watching the races on TV with her headphones on when it happened. She's worn them ever since Ava Scott complained to the council about the noise.'

'Oh dear.'

'Indeed.'

She scrolled down, speed-reading through the information to find what she thought would be necessary for him to hear.

'It's a no-exit street. There's a bush reserve on one side of the road with a cycle, slash, walking track running through it. A bit rundown. A few of our guys did a quick reccy before it got dark last night. We're doing a proper search today. No results from the house-to-house interviews so far. We'll go over the job sheets tonight.'

'Do I know your DCs?' Jack asked.

'I've only got one now. Remember. Mary Jovani went on maternity leave at the beginning of the year, and you said I couldn't have a replacement. She had a girl by the way. Mother and baby well.'

'Did I send a card?'

'No idea.'

'I'll ask my PA to check when I get back to the office.'

'Tony Hunter is my one and only DC. He's new to the area. He's also young and hasn't had much experience but he seems keen to get ahead. This is his first murder. I'm sure he'll pick things up as we go along.'

'I don't know him.'

'He came up from the West Coast in December. He didn't get on with the desk sergeant down there and asked for a transfer. He was hoping for Auckland and was disappointed when he was sent here. Independent, smart, very ambitious, and he's read all the books.'

'Ah huh. And?'

'He's a touch arrogant.'

'Let me know if he needs a word.'

Kate shook her head. 'I'm fairly sure I can handle him.'

'The offer's there. West Coasters aren't known for their liberal attitudes to women.'

'If it's a problem I'll let you know, but it won't come to that. You taught me more than you know.'

He smiled, touched by her compliment. 'You were easy to teach.'

When Kate arrived at the station, fresh from police college eight years ago, Jack had been the DSS in charge of the CIB. Thirty-five and the mother of two growing boys, she was older than the other constables and quick to learn all she could about policing. After the requisite spell of frontline community work, she studied for her detective exams when shiftwork and parenting duties allowed, passing them at the top of her class. After six months as a Trainee Detective assigned to Jack's team, she passed four more exams and became a fully-fledged Detective Constable.

He had mentored her through her first investigations. She remembered his advice and had used many times since. 'It takes judgement,' he told her. 'Knowing when to come down hard on someone, but equally and more importantly, when to let well enough alone. Remember, if you don't muck it up, you can always go back and try again.'

When Jack moved to Wellington, it was his suggestion that she replace him. Will put it about that it was only because she was a woman and Jack was sucking up to his bosses and their DEI agendas. No one believed him, and once he and Kate had agreed on the terms of their arrangement, he soon shut up.

He cleared his throat. 'I sent through your budget for the investigation. You can see how tight it is. Keep it that way. Manage with what you've got because you'll need to make a good case if you want anything extra.

'Give me a break why don't you. You know this isn't a typical case. It was a fine weekend. Town was busy. There were a lot of visitors to the vineyards. It will take longer to track everyone down.'

'You've got twenty extra uniforms. That's it. You have to manage with what you've got.'

She swallowed back the sick feeling in her stomach.

'When do you plan to hold your first press conference?'

She had to bite her tongue, as she choked back the expletives, she usually used to describe the members of the fourth estate. 'Never?'

'You don't mean that. Get it out of the way. Do it this afternoon. Keep the news channels onside. You never know when you'll need them.'

'Fine,' she replied, knowing this was not a suggestion. 'Can't wait.'

'I had to work hard to convince the District Commander you were ready for this, Kate. Being able to front the press is part of being a lead investigator. Don't let me down.' His eyes met hers, his stern message not without a little kindness.

'I won't let you down.'

'That's what I told him.' He rose to his feet, smoothed his tie and re-fastened the buttons of his jacket. 'Good. Now, let's see this crime scene so I can go home.'

'You're not coming to the press conference?'

'It's your case, Kate. I'm here to advise and set the ground rules. You're the one in charge.'

# CHAPTER
# FIVE

'WE WORKED TOGETHER a lot over the years, but I never came to his home.' Jack climbed out of his car. He looked first at the Scott's house before checking out the rest of houses in Palmer Grove with the eye of an experienced investor in real estate. 'This must have been the first house on the street.'

'The Scott house is a well-regarded example of the New Zealand Arts and Craft movement of the early 1940s,' said Kate. 'I was married to an architect for twenty-five years, I should know. I've also seen the title deeds. His grandfather built it during the war. The family has lived here ever since.'

They walked across the road and up the gravel drive. 'It needs watering, but the garden's nice,' said Jack. He stopped. 'The house could do with a bit of work.'

Black paint peeled from the window frames on the upper storey, and tufts of weeds sprouted from the guttering along the eaves. A generously sized concrete terrace, partially obscured by an overgrown wisteria in full leaf, fronted the house with steps leading down to a lawn reduced to dusty yellow stalks by a lack of water.

'This way,' said Kate. She walked ahead of him to a side entrance. Concrete steps from the drive, led up to a covered porch. Gumboots and old shoes lay jumbled beneath an assortment of jackets and coats hanging from a row of hooks. Tupperware containers of food had been left next to the gumboots, some labelled, others anonymous in their generosity. Kate made a note to bring them inside before their contents exploded in the heat.

She opened the door and leaned in. 'Anyone home?' Getting no response, she went inside. Jack followed.

'At least it's cool in here,' he said. A fifties-era stove stood against one wall. Beside it, an old fridge. A pine table and six mismatched chairs occupied the centre of the room. Wooden cupboards and drawers lined another wall, some smudged with left-behind finger-print powder.

Jack pointed to the wire mesh door of a cupboard set into the outside wall above a chipped Formica bench. 'It's an actual meat safe.'

Kate wrinkled her nose at the smell of old milk rising up from the cat's bowl on the floor. Days-old, specks of dried cat food stuck to another bowl beside it. Louie must be starving, she thought, wherever he is.

'I can't believe Geoffrey lived like this,' said Jack. 'He was old-school. He wore a suit and tie. He was well-spoken and polite.'

'And yet…' said Kate.

'I have to see the rest of the house.'

This time Jack led the way and Kate followed. Next to the kitchen was a formal dining room, barely used, judging by the musty smell and the dust layering the surfaces of the antique table and chairs. A large semi-formal living room occupied one half of the front of the house. The air was thick and stale, caught in the back of her throat, making it hard to breathe. Side-by-side French doors, closed now, opened from this room onto the shaded terrace they'd seen from the drive. The furniture was old and worn out, the sofa seats and armchairs sagging under faded chintz.

Ornaments had been pushed out of the way to make room for books. They were stacked in piles on every available surface including the floor and they were all about art. Some looked expensive; the books bought from museums and design stores. Others were less so, instruction manuals and guides to various painting techniques. Each book bore the signs of having been read many times over.

Another wave of hot stuffy air overlaid with the faint rich smell of tobacco enveloped her when she pushed open the door on the other side of the hall. It was the original consulting room.

'That looks uncomfortable,' said Jack. He pointed to the examination couch pressed against one wall.

Kate looked up. 'There's no curtain. Women must have hated it.'

'It's like a museum,' he whispered. 'One that's been forgotten, then opened to the public so we can see how people lived last century.'

Taking the stairs two at a time, he poked his head into each of the three bedrooms on the next floor, finishing his tour with the solitary bathroom and its chipped pink fittings.

'They still slept in the same bed,' he said, going back to stand in the master bedroom. On one bedside table was a pile of gardening and medical magazines, and on the other, a book about Picasso. It was lying flat, spine up.

'Did Paul find anything useful?' he asked as he walked past her onto the upstairs landing.

'A box of personal papers. I've read some of them but they're just standard house stuff. Seen enough?'

'I have.' He led the way downstairs.

The contrast between the house and the garden could not have been more marked. Designed by a professional, it was pristine. Except for the bare patch next to the strawberry bed, the raked gravel gleamed white in the afternoon sunshine. There were no weeds, the raised beds were brushed clean. Even the plants stood to attention.

'Tamsyn is positive he didn't just hit his head as he fell?' asked Jack.

'He would have had to pirouette mid-air to get his head in the right position on the way down. Paul didn't find any hair or blood embedded in the wood, which would be consistent with an accident. They think he was bending forwards over the strawberries, there,' she said, pointing to the raised bed where the plump ripe berries poked out from under a mass of green leaves. 'The killer whacked him on the back of the head. He went down. There was dirt and bits of plant between his teeth and in his mouth. It must have been one hell of a blow.'

'Could a woman have done it?'

'They said it's possible, but she'd have to be incredibly strong. There's no doubting the intent. Tamsyn thinks the killer then tipped him onto the gravel, which was why Ava found him face up.'

'That's why didn't she see any blood?'

'It was still inside his skull. The bone was smashed to pieces, but the scalp, while crushed, was intact and held it in until she moved him when she did the CPR.'

'Nasty business. I liked the man. He was a good guy.'

'I didn't know him as well as you did, but he was always nice to me.'

'It's a beautiful garden.' Jack sighed and looked around it again, a tinge of envy in his voice. 'It must have cost a bit. I got a quote for landscaping at my place last year. Something this size, the quality of the materials, the mature hedging, the irrigation unit, this would be in the high forties.'

'Sixty-two thousand,' said Kate. 'Three years ago. The invoice was in the box Paul gave me.'

'Yet, he spent nothing on the house. My wife would divorce me if I did that.'

'She was into painting. He liked his garden.'

'No children?'

'None.'

'Right then,' he said clapping his hands together. 'I've seen enough. You clearly have everything under control. I'll leave you to it. Don't forget to breathe when you're talking to the press and look directly at the camera. Here's a hip for you. It worked for me. Think of it as a friend you can confide in.'

It didn't, she thought. You looked like a possum caught in head-lights, terrified you were going to be squashed flat any moment.

'Call if you need anything that doesn't cost money and keep me updated on progress.' Then Jack was gone. Leaving her alone in a beautiful garden with no gardener.

# CHAPTER
# SIX

JUNE WHITTAKER GRIPPED the edge of the bench and steadied herself. She should have known better than to stand up so quickly, especially in this heat. Dr Scott's warning, to stay hydrated and take things slowly, returned to her.

'It's fine now,' he'd said, unwrapping the cuff from her arm. 'But when you stand up quickly, your blood pressure drops through the floor. That's why you get dizzy. Old arteries and a weak heart. The blood can't get to your brain in time.'

He typed the numbers into her notes and swivelled around to look at her.

'There's nothing I can give you which will help I'm afraid. You're old. You're frail, and you're too thin.' He frowned. 'Stop smoking and eat more.'

'I stopped smoking twenty years ago. I told you that the last time I was here.'

'Don't be ridiculous,' he snapped. 'I would have written it down if you had.'

She opened her mouth to protest but closed it again. There and then she decided to change doctors. It surprised her because she didn't usually make a fuss, but she'd had enough. It wasn't the first time he'd been rude to her. She'd heard good things about a new doctor in Featherston, a woman. Maybe she could help.

At reception, she leaned across to Lily and keeping her voice low, asked her to send her notes across.

'Don't say anything,' she added. 'It's only because I'm getting old, and I'd prefer to see a woman for… you know.'

Lily did know. 'Leave it with me.'

'You don't have to tell him I've left do you? We're neighbours, and I don't want to get offside.'

Lily assured her no one needed to know.

That was six months ago. Her new doctor was nice, but she had insisted June take medication, and it wasn't helping. Maybe it was even making things worse.

Gradually the wooziness settled. She let go of the bench and dropped a couple of teabags into the pot. That way, she'd only need to add the hot water when her guests arrived. She consoled herself with the thought she had every right to feel funny. What with him being murdered next door.

Normally calm and level-headed, June hated that she felt scared. She lived alone. She had no one to protect her if the killer came back. Yesterday, the policeman had been very nice but telling her to stay inside and lock the doors and windows wasn't going to work, not in this heat. She'd suffocate.

The checkout operator at the supermarket hadn't helped when she popped in to buy a packet of biscuits. 'Just think,' she said. 'The killer walked right past your window. I don't understand how you didn't see him.'

'I didn't see him because there's a hedge between me and the Scott's. Besides, how do you know it was a man? It could have been a woman.'

A cold wave of fear washed over her as she pictured the killer walking down the drive, only a few feet and the hedge away from her living room window. She'd only popped in to buy a packet of biscuits.

She was worried she was going to be next. Maybe locking her doors and windows was a good idea, after all. Not all of them; the windows high off the ground could stay open so the air could circulate.

She had felt relatively safe when the police were next door. Sunday night and most of Monday morning, they had tramped up and down the drive, in their white overalls, talking quietly to each other, making her feel she wasn't alone. Then around lunchtime, they packed up and left.

June kept a lookout for Ava, so she could go over and pass on her condolences. Her car was there, but she was nowhere to be seen. Then she overheard an officer say that Ava was staying at the Murphy's.

This made June feel even more isolated and alone. She had no one to stay with. No family and the only friend she could ask, had a cat. June was allergic to cats. No matter what the nice policeman said about calling 111 if she saw anything, Martinborough was a tiny village. Surrounded by vineyards it was a long way from the nearest police station. She'd be dead before they got to her.

Arthur would have known what to do. He would have said something comforting and made her laugh like he did whenever she felt anxious. She tried to remember the sound of his voice as he held her and murmured in her ear that everything would be all right, but she couldn't. He was gone, a heart attack three years ago. She would have to get through this alone.

Now, she was about to be interviewed again. The head detective was coming with the lovely young man she spoke to yesterday. She glanced at the clock. With five minutes before they were due to arrive, there was enough time for her to watch a replay of Saturday's last race at Te Rapa. Sunbeam Dancer, one of several horses she followed, had come up lame in the home straight, and she wanted to check the damage for herself. She put on her headphones and watched the horse in slow-motion, concentrating on what the jockey on the next horse had been doing, sure that there must have been a foul.

# CHAPTER
# SEVEN

'SHE IS EXPECTING US?' asked Kate. There had been no answer to several loud knocks on June's front door.

'I texted to say we were on our way,' said Tony. 'Wait here. I'll check around the back.'

A minute later, Kate heard the clunks of a lock turning, then a bolt being scraped into its barrel. June opened the door, her lined face and tightly permed hair highlighting the apprehension in her eyes. Tony was standing behind her.

'I'm so sorry,' said June. She looked flustered and apologetic at the same time. 'I was watching a race, and I don't hear a thing when I'm wearing my headphones.'

'Not to worry.' Pleased to find her at home, Kate smiled. 'I'm Detective Senior Sergeant Kate Sutton. You met DC Hunter yesterday.' She stepped inside, standing back while June made a show of re-locking the door.

'Is that yours?' Kate asked. She pointed to a five-iron resting against a delicate white and gold entrance table.

'No, that was Arthur's,' said June. 'He was the golfer, not me.' She ushered them into her living room, directing them to two chairs on either side of a table. It was situated under a large window which looked out onto a tall hedge and the sky above it.

Two pink velveteen upholstered armchairs took up most of the middle of the room. They faced a giant TV which hung on the wall above a closed off fireplace. The sound had been muted. On the screen, led by their grooms, silent horses paraded around a leafy enclosure next to a grandstand.

On the table beside June's chair was a glass of water, the remote control, a pile of racing books, a pen and a set of bulky headphones.

She sat down then swivelled her chair ninety degrees to face them. 'Do you know who did it yet?' she asked.

'That's why we're here,' said Kate. 'We need your help.'

'I'm not sure there's anything more I can tell you.' She flipped the bottom of her blouse over the top of her trousers, her busy eyes watching Tony as he took out his notebook then opened it on the table.

'You have a lovely home,' said Kate. She meant it. The faded wall-paper and tired carpet must have been cosy once. 'Do you live alone?'

June nodded. 'Ever since Arthur died.'

'Arthur was your husband?'

'My partner. We didn't see the point in wasting money on a wedding. Not at our age. He died three years ago. Heart attack.'

'I'm sorry,' said Kate.

'So am I. He was a good man.' She paused. 'I suppose everyone says that when they lose their soulmate.' Her eyes turned to a framed photo of her and Arthur on the mantlepiece, then, with a sigh, returned to focus on Kate. 'You haven't come here to talk about me. What do you want to know?'

'You were here on Sunday.'

'I was. The Hawera Races started at eleven, and I had bets on every race. I like a bit of a flutter; it's the only vice I have left.'

Kate returned her tentative smile with a grin. 'Good for you. This is the only TV?'

'This is the only TV,' repeated June.

Kate liked her. She was quick and didn't fluff about with her answers. 'Do you always use headphones to listen to the races?'

'Always. Ever since Ava complained to the council about the noise.'

Kate ignored the eye roll which accompanied this statement. 'Can you hear anything else when you're wearing them?' she asked.

'Nothing.' June hesitated. 'I take them off between races though.'

'Did you see or hear anything unusual at the Scott's house on Sunday afternoon?'

'I don't remember anything unusual. I heard Dr Scott get in his car, drive away and come back. That was before the second race at one o'clock. He was gone about ten minutes.'

'How did you know it was him?' asked Kate.

'He drives a diesel.'

'You heard the car, but did you actually see him driving it?'

'No. But it was him. I've lived here long enough to know who's driving what car and how. He does it the same way every time, slowing down a few seconds before the end of the drive, before he reverses onto the road. She never slows down. It's lucky we don't have any foot traffic.'

'By she, you mean Ava?'

'Yes.' She tucked her hands together between her legs and leaned forward, her brow furrowed, as she concentrated on Kate's questions.

'Did he come back before or after the race started?'

'After.'

'You're sure?'

'Definitely. I had my headphones off, and I heard their back door close. I heard it open again, and he went down to his garden at the back.' She paused. 'I don't spy on them. I just hear them.'

'It would make our job a lot easier if you did spy on them,' said Kate. Her attempt at humour went over June's head.

'He's up and down that path so often, I really don't take much notice.'

'Was it any different on Sunday?'

June strained to remember. 'Later, maybe. It was quieter than usual, but I put that down to the storm. I was standing at the window looking at the sky, and I heard him walk into the house and shut the door.'

'What time was that?'

'Just before half past four. The seventh race starts at four thirty.'

'That's very helpful,' said Kate. She checked to make sure Tony was writing everything down before giving June a tight smile. 'Take us through what happened next.'

'There's nothing to tell. I always watch the six o'clock news at seven, so I can fast forward through the ads.'

'Wearing your headphones?'

'That's why I didn't hear the rain. I remember shivering and when I looked out the window, it was bucketing down. That's when I took my headphones off. It was so loud I couldn't hear myself think. The noise on the roof is terrible. The tiles were cracking, so I replaced them with corrugated iron last year. I wish I hadn't.'

Kate nodded for her to go on.

'It was when I was closing the windows, that I saw Ava's car in the drive, parked behind his. She must have gotten home while I was watching the news. Next thing, I hear a siren, the fire engine arrives, and the crew are running down the drive.'

Kate turned to look out the window but could only see a wall of green hedge. 'How did you see them?'

'There are gaps in the hedge if you know where to look. But I couldn't see much so I went upstairs. I've got a good view of their garden front and back from my spare bedroom.'

Kate and Tony exchanged glances. 'What happened then?'

'I went over to see if I could help. The fire chief, Marty, told me there was nothing I could do and to go home. I was leaving when I heard Sonja, she works in the hardware store, say that Dr Scott was dead, and the police were on their way. I was in shock because it took me back to when Arthur died. Then the Hills, who live two doors up, came out of their house, and they asked me what had happened.'

'Before the crew arrived, did you see anyone going into the Scott's house or anyone leaving? Anyone hanging around you didn't know?'

June frowned. 'What do you mean?'

'Anyone who doesn't live on the street? Or anyone at all?'

After a moment June shook her head. 'No one.'

'If you do remember anything or anyone, please call me.' Kate reached over and handed her card to June.

Tony looked up from his notebook. 'How long have you been neighbours with the Scotts?'

June picked up the glass of water from the table beside her and took a careful sip. 'Me? Not long. This was Arthur's house, his family home. I come from the other side of town, near the sewage ponds. He lived here with his mother. After she died, he asked me to move in with him. That was twelve years ago.'

'You must know them quite well,' he said.

'Not really.'

'Oh?'

'They keep to themselves. I went over and introduced myself like a good neighbour should. Ava didn't want to know. She was distant. I didn't go back.' Her eyes flicked momentarily to the TV and the start of a race.

'What do you mean, distant?' asked Tony.

'Arthur said she used to be an artist. He said artists are temperamental. In my book, that's no excuse for being rude.' She folded her arms across her chest. 'Dr Scott's mother was a proper doctor's wife; she couldn't do enough for you. That one! The only person she has any time for is Bruce Murphy's wife, Mimi. Although, when I think about it, not so much lately. Not since Mimi went to rehab.'

'Why did she go to rehab?' asked Kate.

June made a drinking sign, followed by a realistic imitation of a drunk. Kate couldn't help smiling.

'Were the Scotts happily married?' asked Tony.

June had warmed up to her audience and made a face as if she was working out what she could and couldn't say. Everyone thought Geoffrey Scott was a wonderful doctor and had a happy life. She wasn't going to be the one to ruin the illusion.

'I don't want this to come back to me. Understand?'

Tony and Kate nodded.

'She yells. She slams doors, and she sulks. When my windows are open in summer, I hear what she says to him. Arthur called it her 'love language'.' She tweaked the speech marks with two fingers of each hand. 'How he puts up with her, I'll never know. I never heard him. Only her.'

'Recently?' asked Tony.

'When I come to think of it, no. She's quietened down. She goes away every weekend. When she is at home, he is down in his garden.'

'Is there anything else you think we should know?' Tony asked.

June's eyes widened; her hand covered her mouth in horror. 'I'm so sorry,' she gasped. 'I had the tea things all ready, and I haven't offered you as much as a glass of water.'

'That's all right, we appreciate you talking to us,' said Kate. Tony closed his notebook and tucked his pen into the spine while Kate got to her feet. On the TV, a mass of horses streaked across the finish line at once, the numbers on their saddles a blur.

June, who'd turned back to watch, clapped her hands with delight. 'A win and two places.'

'How can you tell?' asked Kate.

'The numbers are at the bottom of the screen,' she explained. Using her arms, she pushed herself upright, staggering slightly, before steadying herself by gripping the back of the chair. They waited, then June led them to the front door.

In the hall, Kate pointed to the golf club again. 'I know you're frightened, but that won't help. Not if an intruder gets to it first.'

'I won't let that happen, Detective,' said June. 'I'm stronger than I look.'

You'll need to be, thought Kate, taking in her frail appearance. 'If you see anything suspicious call us, and if you're worried, lock yourself in the bathroom and wait until we get here.'

'I will,' said June.

'You've been a great help Mrs Whittaker,' said Kate as she stepped outside.

'Miss Whittaker,' said June. 'I never married. Find him soon, won't you.' She closed the door, and they waited on the steps, listening as she locked it behind them.

# CHAPTER
# EIGHT

'*CALL TAMSYN.*' Kate recognised her eldest son's scrawl on the Post-it note on her fridge. It was a running joke that Toby had the worst handwriting in the family, or it had been when they still lived together. Matt, who was pedantic about anything visual, had tried to teach Toby how to craft his letters when he was young, but when there was no improvement, had given up.

Her son had arrived at the beginning of the weekend with a pile of dirty washing. He announced he was staying for a week to organise his stuff before heading back to university. He dumped the dirty clothes beside, not in the machine, then he disappeared off to the pub with his mates.

Tonight, the only evidence he'd been there other than the note, was the empty milk container in the fridge, a pot lined with a layer of baked beans in the sink, and another pile of dirty laundry beside the washing machine.

At least Toby made a pretence of wanting to spend time with her. Reuben, her youngest son, hadn't contacted her since his first visit to her new house. Her texts went unanswered, and he didn't pick up if she called. What could she do? She couldn't force him to talk to her.

At their old family home, Reuben enjoyed unlimited access to the contents of the fridge, the swimming pool and the tennis court. And with Matt and Carla at work all day, he and his mates had the run of the place: blissful freedom for an eighteen-year-old boy.

It had nearly destroyed her when he blamed her for the break-up of his family. That it was Matt who had run off with another woman, didn't matter.

'You're always at work.' Reuben yelled when together they told him the news. 'You should have been here, at home, looking after your family. Looking after me.'

His words had hurt her badly, but at the same time they made her angry. Unable to fight back, she held her peace, waiting for Matt to say something. She was still waiting.

In two weeks, Reuben would follow in Toby's footsteps, leaving Masterton to study engineering in Christchurch. She had hoped to find some way to restore their relationship before then, but time was running out.

Tonight, as it was every night, the townhouse was silent. Now and then, the muffled sounds of her neighbour's stereo floated through her upstairs window but that was it. She wasn't used to the quiet and she wasn't used to being alone.

She had spent the last twenty-five years bringing up two active boys and running around after a career-driven husband. How often during those years, had she wanted five peaceful minutes to herself? Five minutes when she didn't have to referee a fight, supervise home-work, cook, clean, or ferry the boys backwards and forwards to their various activities. She used to dream about what it would be like to tidy up a room, and have it stay tidy. Fantasise about going to the supermarket and not have the food gone by the next day.

There was truth in the saying, '*Be careful what you wish for.*' Now she had more peace and quiet than she could ever want, and she didn't like it. It was unnatural. She wasn't prepared for it and she had no idea what to do with it. Her adult life had been a constant round of other people's demands on her time. She had no idea what her own demands, her own needs might be. Her personal life, apart from her weekly tennis game, was non-existent. Her work was all she had left.

She poured herself a glass of wine, heaved open the doors to her tiny garden and went outside. Warmed by the day's sunshine, the pavers of her tiny patio felt like a Mediterranean holiday under her bare feet. She put her glass on the table and sat down to call Tamsyn.

'Hey,' she said, her phone on speaker. 'There was a message to call you. If it's about tennis next Sunday, I'm going to have to cancel.'

'Me too,' said Tamsyn. 'No, this is business. It's about the postmortem.'

'I thought it went well,' said Kate. She sipped her wine and waited for Tamsyn to tell her what she had to say.

'It's the same cause of death, blah, blah. But there was something else, I didn't tell you at the time. I need to get it checked before I can be certain of my diagnosis. It could be just an incidental finding, but it could be relevant to the case. Can you talk because it'll take a few minutes to explain?'

'Take all the time you need,' said Kate. She sipped her wine, savouring the feeling of the cool liquid slide down her throat.

'The frontal and temporal lobes on the left side of Geoffrey's brain don't look normal. They're smaller than the lobes on the right side.'

'Meaning?' asked Kate.

'I think Geoffrey Scott may have been suffering from the early effects of dementia.'

'Rubbish, he was only forty-eight. And he was a doctor.'

'This may surprise you Kate, but doctors suffer from the same conditions as other human beings. If I'm right and he's got the type of dementia I think he does, then he would have been able to work. Just not for much longer. This type develops more slowly than Alzheimer's. It's called frontotemporal dementia, or FTD for short.'

'Catchy,' said Kate. She wasn't being rude, but it was challenging to fit dementia into her own impression of the man.

Tamsyn continued. 'The symptoms sneak up on people. And their families. The frog in the hot water story springs to mind. There is usually a gradual loss of inhibitions, often years before any obvious memory loss. Odd bouts of rudeness, drinking or eating to excess, gambling, unusual behaviours, are excused or put down to stress.' She paused, and Kate heard the sounds indicating that Tamsyn was also drinking a glass of wine.

'You need to check with Ava and ask if she noticed any changes.

Ask the staff at the medical centre too. Did he make any mistakes he wouldn't normally make, that sort of thing?'

'I'm seeing her tomorrow,' said Kate. 'She hasn't been very helpful, but I'll ask. What is it you need to get checked?'

'There's a lab in Auckland that will run the panel of histochemical tests I need to confirm the diagnosis. I want to send them samples of his brain for analysis.'

'Why not just go ahead? You're the pathologist. You don't need my permission.'

'It costs three thousand dollars, plus the courier fees.'

'Whew, that's a lot of money.'

'Can you afford it?'

'No.' Kate paused. 'We have the cause of death. How will a diagnosis of dementia help the investigation?'

'What if the dementia was past the early stages? What if he said the wrong thing or offended the wrong person, or worse, made a mistake with a patient? Think about it. What if he gave someone the wrong treatment and the person or their family found out? It might be a reason for someone to kill him.'

'It's possible,' conceded Kate. 'It's still a lot of money.'

'I know. Paul said budgets were tight.'

'Tighter now.' She sighed, knowing what Jack's reaction to the request would be. She wondered how she could get it past him without drawing attention to the cost. 'You're sure?'

'As much as I can be, but without confirmatory testing, my opinion won't hold up in court.'

Kate took another deep breath, playing out various scenarios in her mind. So far, all she had was a victim. Nothing else. No motive, no evidence, no suspects, no explanation. She might be grasping at a very expensive straw, but it was something. 'Do it,' she said finally.

'It'll go off first thing in the morning. The results will be back on Friday. You won't regret it.'

Tamsyn paused. Another sip of wine. 'How are you getting on? Have you unpacked those boxes yet?'

'I was all set to do it after tennis on Sunday, but then I got the call. I can't believe how much stuff I have. I'm tempted to take the whole lot to the dump.'

'Unpack first, then biff it. That's what we did when we moved here. I found things which now I'm pleased we kept.'

Kate's glass was empty, and she went inside for a refill. 'Okay. But it's going to have to wait until after this investigation is over.'

'You'll do it when the time is right.'

'That's just it,' said Kate. 'I can't imagine when it will ever be right. My whole life is in those boxes, everything is a reminder of what we had. I'm not sure I can put myself through it.'

'You sound like you need a hug,' said Tamsyn. 'Do you want me to come over? Tim's home, so I can.'

It was all she needed to feel less alone. Tamsyn's offer was genuine and from the heart. 'You enjoy your family time. I'm fine.'

'You're sure? I can bring chocolate.'

Kate managed a laugh. 'No, I'm fine, but hey, thanks. Knowing you're there if I need you, helps. It really does.'

# CHAPTER
# NINE

'WOW,' said Tony. He slowed the car to a stop at a set of imposing gates on a hill overlooking Martinborough. 'I'm definitely in the wrong job.'

It was late on Tuesday morning, Day 2 of the investigation. Kate looked up from her phone to see the Murphy's house, its profile dominating the horizon—the clean white lines of its bold design simultaneously complimenting and contrasting with the surrounding countryside. Rows of dusty green vines ran in straight lines down the hill from the house to the flat farmland which was dotted with sheep and cattle. Below, behind them and to the left, the streets of Martinborough, set out by its founder like a Union Jack, radiated from a central square planted with mature trees. In the distance, the silver ribbon of the Ruamahanga River snaked across the plain, while the sawtooth lines of the Tararua and Remutaka Mountain ranges, snowless at this time of year, shimmered blue in the noonday heat.

'How did he get so rich?' asked Tony.

'He wasn't born with money, if that's what you're thinking,' said Kate. 'His father was the local undertaker, lazy and a bit of a bastard by all accounts. He forced Bruce to leave school early to help in the business. The story goes that in two years, Bruce had taken over every funeral director's business in the lower North Island.'

Tony nodded appreciatively.

'That was only the start. See those vineyards,' said Kate. 'He owns them, or rather his company Murphy Enterprises owns them.'

'All of them?' gasped Tony. 'No way.'

'Twenty-five years ago, when the wine business was still getting established, it was tough to make a living out of farming. Still is. He approached the local landowners and offered them cash for any land close to town. Then later, he bought the town.'

'No way,' he said again. The admiration in his voice was genuine.

'The shopkeepers own their businesses, but he owns their shops. He owns the hotel, the motels, the restaurants, the lot. That's why he's the head of the local business association. Partly to keep them in line and partly because no one is brave enough to stand against him. If people are too afraid to come to Martinborough, who do you think has the most to lose?'

'He does.'

'Correct,' said Kate. 'He and Mimi, to a lesser extent, run their companies together. In 2008, when the economy went into freefall, they had stored away enough cash to buy property all over the country and in Australia.'

'So why do they stay here? In little ole' Martinborough. They could live anywhere.'

'Rude,' said Kate. 'Very wealthy people enjoy living in the Wairarapa. James Cameron, Peter Jackson—the movie directors—they have houses here. Bruce travels for work but he always comes home to Martinborough.'

'It is a fabulous house.'

'It's even better inside,' said Kate. 'I went to the housewarming. My ex was their architect.'

'Tell him he did a great job.'

'I will if I ever talk to him again,' she said, only half laughing. 'Come on, get moving. We've got a wife to interview and a killer to catch.'

Bruce greeted Kate at the door with open arms, but she pulled back, thrusting her hand out instead. This was work, not a social visit.

Not hiding the amused look on his face, he took her hand and gave it a gentle squeeze. 'Good to see you again, Detective. Pity about the circumstances.'

'This is my offsider, DC Tony Hunter,' she said, standing back to let the two men shake hands. Despite his height advantage, Tony looked uncomfortable, as if he were meeting an idol. Bruce, who was shorter and solidly built, was the more confident. Even at a first meeting, his personality was large enough to be overwhelming.

'Geoffrey Scott and I were school friends.' Bruce directed this to Tony rather than Kate, as he showed them into his home.

'I'm sorry for your loss,' Tony replied. His foot caught on the step, and he blushed furiously as he stumbled before regaining his footing. They walked down a vast hall, lit by sunlight streaming through a sloped glass ceiling. It took them into an enormous living area, which occupied most of the front of the house and which opened onto a terrace. Sitting outside, drinking coffee under the shade of a bright yellow sun umbrella, were Mimi and Ava, their oversized sunglasses covering half their faces. Behind them a pool, its dark green depths, looked inviting on such a hot day.

'Mimi, why don't you see if our guests would like coffee,' suggested Bruce.

'That's very kind, but it won't be necessary,' said Kate.

'Are you sure? She does a perfect flat white, don't you, darling?' Mimi was half out of her seat when Kate said, 'We're good.' She lowered herself again, sitting with one leg tucked under her. Unlike Ava, who wore a pair of denim dungarees over a red singlet that had been washed too often, Mimi looked clean and pert in her Lululemon shorts and strappy t-shirt. Her dark-blonde hair hung in curls over her shoulders, and her makeup, lip-gloss included, was flawless. Kate thought Mimi looked as if she had just stepped out of a 'housewife of somewhere' set. She felt Tony shift awkwardly beside her.

'What can we do for you?' asked Bruce.

'We've come to see Ava,' said Kate. 'But it would be helpful if we could talk to each of you while we're here.'

'I must be off, I'm afraid,' he said, collecting a set of keys and his sunglasses from the kitchen counter. 'Local business association meeting. I'll let them know you're on the job. And' he said, fixing his eyes on her, 'that this won't be like last time. Talk to Mimi. She isn't doing anything.' Without waiting for a response, he turned and, rattling his keys over his head in place of a wave, was gone.

Kate took a moment to let the Bruce Murphy whirlwind settle, then turned to Ava. 'The forensic team is finished with your house. And your cars. Sorry, it took so long. But it means you can go home.'

Ava looked at Mimi. 'I don't want to be there by myself. Can I stay with you until Dan arrives?'

'Of course. Stay as long as you like.'

Ava slipped her sunglasses down her nose and peered up at Kate. 'I suppose you want to talk to me first.'

'If you don't mind.'

'Use the library,' said Mimi, collecting their coffee cups. She followed Ava inside. 'It will be cooler in there.'

The beautifully crafted bookshelves in the library were devoid of books. In their place were family photographs and a few ornaments, civic awards mainly. The sorts of trinkets business leaders exchange with other business leaders to mark ceremonial occasions. The long table in the middle, with chairs on either side, took up most of the space. Paintings hung on the walls; each one painted by a named artist who commanded high prices. They were mostly modern, apart from a small but very expensive Goldie.

Aside from the art, she couldn't help but be drawn towards the floor-to-ceiling window at the end of the room. When she looked onto the valley below, she felt as if she was standing on the edge of a cliff. She imagined Bruce standing here at night, looking out over his lands and subjects with a proprietorial air, swirling his best pinot noir in the correct glass, warming it with his hand until it was ready to enjoy.

Tony interrupted her thoughts with a tactful, 'Ah hem.' Tearing herself away from the view she went back and sat next to him on one side of the table.

Ava sat in the chair opposite. It had been less than two days since Geoffrey's murder, and Kate thought she already looked thinner. The lines on her face were more pronounced, their definition not helped by the dark rings under her eyes. Maybe she was upset after all.

'We'd like to record this if that's all right with you,' said Kate. She took out her phone and placed it between them.

Ava waved a hand.

'We have the postmortem results if you want to hear them.'

'I get the feeling you're going to tell me no matter what I say.'

'Your husband was killed by a blow to the back of the head,' said Kate.

'It wasn't a heart attack.'

'No.'

'He'd put on so much weight lately, I was sure that's what it was.'

'Heart attacks are more common,' conceded Kate.

Ava flicked her a look of gratitude.

'Describe your husband for me.'

Ava rolled her eyes as she craned her neck to stare at the ceiling. 'He was a good doctor. Everyone said so. He worked hard, always putting his patients first. He built the health centre ten years ago so he could provide a better service. That's why we didn't do up the house; all the money went into the centre.'

'You were okay with that?' asked Tony.

'It was his money.'

'Not many wives would feel that way,' he said.

'I'm not any wife. It was his parents' house. I never liked living there.'

'What will happen to the health centre now?' asked Kate.

'Dan, my cousin, you know he's coming, don't you? He's agreed to look after the practice until the new owners take over.'

Kate raised her eyebrows. 'New owners? Have you sold it already?'

'It sounds bad when you say it like that, but yes, I've sold it.'

'How?'

'Is that important?' asked Ava.

'It is if you're the one benefiting from the sale.'

'I am, if you must know. It's not Lotto money. I wish it were then I could run away to the south of France.' Seeing the look on Kate's face, she sighed wearily. 'Geoffrey was going to sell it last year. The buyers were lined up to sign on the dotted line. He changed his mind at the last minute.'

'Do you know why?'

'No. It was his business not mine.'

'Why did he want to sell in the first place?' asked Kate.

'No idea. Thank you for doing the press conference by the way. That's how they found out he'd died. They phoned first thing this morning with another offer. It's better than the last one because now they can bring in their own doctor.' She ended with a soulful look. 'Every cloud…'

'I'm glad it's worked out for you,' said Kate.

Ava, her chin jutted forward, glared at her. 'The money will keep me in paint and canvasses, that's all.'

'Paint can't be that expensive,' said Tony.

'It's not cheap. A tube costs about sixty dollars. I use one or two a day, you do the maths. I also sold because I'm not a doctor and I have zero interest in running a medical practice.'

'Fair enough. Tell me about your painting,' said Kate.

'I thought you wanted to know about Geoffrey.'

'I'd also like to hear about your painting.'

Ava tipped her head back and shook her hair, her short, dark curls bouncing around her face. 'I'm an artistic genius,' she said, laughing. 'There. I've said it. But it's true. I have always been talented. When I was sixteen, I won a scholarship to a prestigious art school in London. No point in telling you the name because you won't know it. Anyway, I went when I was eighteen. I was too young. A bad man took advantage of my naivete, and I came home. I only started painting again last year.'

'It sounds like you had an awful experience.'

'I did.' Ava paused. 'It was terrible, and if it hadn't been for Dan, who came over and brought me home, God knows what would have happened.'

'That's the doctor coming to help at the practice?'

Ava nodded. 'We're each other's only living relative. He introduced me to Geoffrey after it happened. We were married a year later. Geoffrey worked so hard that I never saw him. He didn't like holidays. If I'd known he was like that beforehand, I'd never have married him. That sounds horrible, doesn't it? But you have no idea how lonely it was to be stuck in that fifty's mausoleum of a house with no one to talk to.'

'You didn't join any groups?' asked Kate.

Ava snorted. 'Like what? The country women's institute? I've got nothing in common with people like that.'

'You could have worked.'

'Doing what? I've got no qualifications. Painting was out of the question. My confidence was shattered. I had flashbacks if I smelled paint.'

'What did you do?'

'I'm no good at sport, and I couldn't have children, not after what that bastard did to me. Geoffrey was devastated when we found out.' She broke off to stare out the window, to let what she'd said sink in.

For such a traumatic subject, thought Kate, her little speech was too polished: said as if she'd practised the pauses and soulful looks in front of a mirror, maybe honed the sadness to play on the heartstrings of others.

'Anyway,' continued Ava. 'We got over it, or I did. And he let me buy as many art books as I wanted. I read each one over and over again and thought about what I was going to paint, if I ever found the courage to start again. Last year, I found a studio and it all came back.'

'Did your husband like your work?' asked Tony.

'He wasn't interested. You had to be either sick, injured, or a plant for him to show the slightest flicker of enthusiasm. Lately, not even that.'

'He'd changed?' asked Kate.

'He wasn't the man I married that's for sure.'

'How?'

'He was never a barrel of laughs, but he used to be fun. Last year, he was no fun at all. Worse, he got fat, and it didn't bother him. He used to go for a run now and then, but that stopped.' She leaned back in her seat, her hands stretched in front of her on the table, one finger tapping the wood to a rhythm only she could hear. Kate knew she'd have to hurry if she was going to get through the list of questions she wanted to ask.

'A patient complained about him,' blurted Ava. 'He was shocked someone would do that. He insisted it was a misunderstanding, but I think there were others. Michelle Parker, the practice manager, knows more about them than me.'

'When was this complaint?' asked Kate.

'Last year sometime.' Ava fiddled with a nail, flicking a sliver of paint out from under it. 'Ask her. He started eating junk food. He tried to hide it. I don't mind an occasional packet of potato chips, but he ate two or three at a time. Big bags. If I said anything, he sulked.'

'Your landlord confirmed you were at your studio on Sunday, but I'd still like to check it out.'

'Be my guest. All the paintings are for sale. Let me know if you see one you like. It's in an old garage behind the shops on the main street in Featherston, I don't know the number.'

'Thanks. We're almost done,' said Kate. 'Have you thought of anyone who would want to hurt your husband? Did he have any enemies? Anyone with a grudge against him?'

'Apart from the person who complained about him, no. No one. I've been thinking.' She paused, giving Kate a sideways glance. 'Could it be the same person who killed that French girl?'

Kate sat very still. It wasn't appropriate to tell a grieving widow she was talking a load of bollocks. 'We've got no evidence linking the two events and I'm not looking for any.'

'Just a thought. You never found the person who killed her did you?' Ava moved to get up. 'Is that it? Are we done?'

'Almost,' said Kate.

Ava groaned and sat down again.

'Dr Fraser has sent a sample of Geoffrey's brain tissue to a laboratory in Auckland. She thinks Geoffrey might have been suffering from a type of dementia when he died.'

Ava stared at her, open-mouthed. 'You're joking, right? He was forty-eight. He wasn't old enough to have dementia.'

Kate started to explain but Ava held up her hands.

'I don't want to hear it.' She shook her head, her curls bouncing in a frenzy around her face. 'I want you to stop. I can't listen to you any more.'

She rose then, pausing when she got to the door. 'What was that girl's name again? The one you didn't find.'

'Juliette,' said Kate. 'Juliette Bisson.'

With a toss of her curls Ava was gone.

# CHAPTER
## TEN

KATE REACHED for her phone and turned it off. She sat for a moment. Ava was unlike any other woman she had met. Coquettish, erratic, vicious even. A part of her felt sorry for Geoffrey and what he'd had to put up with.

Tony broke the silence. 'I remember reading about it. How long ago did she disappear?'

'Three years this month.'

'It must have been hard, when you didn't find her.'

'It was, but it was worse for her father. He went back to France not knowing what happened to his only child. He died six months later.'

'That's tough.'

'It was.'

She put her phone in her bag and stood up. 'Let's concentrate on this case, shall we. You stay here and take Mimi's statement while I go to the health centre and talk to this practice manager, Michelle something.'

'Parker.'

'That's her. Call me when you're done, and I'll come back and pick you up. What?' she asked when she saw the look on his face.

'I've never done an interview alone before.'

'Sure you have.'

'Not in an actual murder investigation.'

'Think of it as part of your training.'

He shifted in his seat. 'You've seen what she looks like. Wouldn't it be better if a woman spoke to her?'

'I'll pretend I didn't hear that.' She slung her bag over her shoulder. 'I've seen your results. You aced this section in the final exam. Remember PEACE?'

'Yes.'

'Do that.' She left the room without looking back.

Tony swallowed nervously, got up from his chair and stretched his arms over his head, then lowered them and leaned on the back of the chair. Should he wear the suit jacket as it made him look professional? Or leave it off so he looked relaxed and used to this sort of thing? The door opened before he could decide, and Mimi walked in. The shorts and strappy top were gone, and she was wearing a t-shirt and unisex designer track pants in their place. It was a label he coveted but couldn't afford. Decision made. Jacket on. She sat down, waiting while he got organised.

'DSS Sutton had to go to another appointment, so I will be conducting your interview.' He took his time, writing the name, date, time and location at the top of a fresh page in his notebook, then drew a line down one side.

'That sounds very formal,' said Mimi. Her green eyes twinkled at him from under her dark-blonde fringe as she picked up a curl from her shoulder and twirled it around a finger.

He didn't return her smile. 'Where were you on Sunday afternoon?' he asked.

'At home by the pool. I came inside when I saw the clouds rolling across the valley.'

'Can anyone verify that?'

'Bruce was working in his study. We facetimed the girls around four. They're in Canada, skiing before they go back to uni. We spoke for an hour. It's on my phone if you want to check.'

'We can do that later,' he said, putting a reminder in his notebook to follow it up. 'Tell me about Geoffrey Scott.'

Mimi smiled again and this time he smiled back.

'He was decent,' she said. 'A dedicated doctor. A wonderful asset to the town. Polite. He helped a lot of people.'

'That's how he was professionally. I'm more interested in what he like as a person?'

'Sorry, I should have realised. I've known him a long time, almost as long as Bruce. I was two years behind them at school. Not that they knew I was there for the first ten years. They ignored me until I became interesting.'

'Sorry?' said Tony.

'Puberty. Girls get interesting, and boys get interested.'

Sweat soaked the armpits of his shirt. He was pleased he'd left his jacket on. 'I understand.'

'They were best friends at primary school, they did everything together, then Geoffrey went away to boarding school. One Christmas, he brought Dan Forrester home. Dan's parents worked overseas, so he was all alone and Geoffrey felt sorry for him. Bruce's nose was well and truly put out of joint. They worked it out though. You know what it's like. Teenagers.'

He nodded, not sure where this was leading but too unsure of himself to stop her.

'We lost touch when they went to medical school. Bruce and I started going out and we got married. Geoffrey only came back from England because his parents died. I don't think he would have otherwise. He felt obligated to take over the practice, you see. It's a small town, people weren't as well off as they are now, and no one else wanted to work here.'

'Thank you,' said Tony. He wrote in silence then looked up. 'How was he recently?'

'Recently?' She paused, looking serious as she considered her answer. 'Distant. He didn't talk as much. Not even in the surgery. You'd tell him what was wrong, he'd send the prescription to the pharmacist, and you were out the door before you knew it. I didn't mind, but it annoyed Bruce so much, he transferred to a practice in Wellington.'

'Even though they were friends?'

'They weren't though. Not by then. They hardly saw each other.'

'How was he getting on with Ava before he died?' he asked.

Mimi laughed. 'How long have you got?'

'I don't need details. An impression is enough.'

'They barely spoke. Strangers sharing the same house.'

'Did you ever see them arguing?'

'Not for a while. That's just it,' said Mimi. 'They used to go at each other like crazy over the smallest thing. When I first got to know her, I was shocked by what she said to him. She yelled, slammed doors, threw things. He just brushed it off and laughed. They always made up. I would never have dared to speak to Bruce the way she spoke to Geoffrey.'

'Did either of them have anyone else in their lives?'

'Not that I know.'

'Did he have any enemies?'

'He was a lovely man. He got on well with everyone. That's why this is so shocking.'

He didn't quite understand where the next question came from or why he asked it. It didn't fit into the PEACE plan he'd prepared in his head.

'You were in rehab,' he said. 'When was that?'

Mimi's eyes narrowed. 'How is that related? I don't have a problem talking about it. But what's it got to do with Geoffrey's murder?'

'Background information,' he said.

'Hmmm.' She tapped one painted fingernail against her chin. 'June Whittaker needs to mind her own business.'

'It helps us build a picture of the people around Geoffrey,' said Tony. Inside he kicked himself. It had been going so well, and one rookie overstep looked like it might alienate a friendly witness. But it was out there now. He couldn't and wouldn't back down. He'd look stupid if he did. He waited.

'Rehab is probably overdoing it,' said Mimi eventually. 'I went to a spa on the Gold Coast, detoxed, and since then, I haven't felt the need to drink alcohol.' She pushed back her chair and stood up. 'If that's all? I have an appointment in town that I'd forgotten about, and I don't want to be late.'

It was obviously a lie, but Tony had no option. The interview was over whether he liked it or not. My own fault for not sticking to the plan, he thought, sliding his business card across the table. 'Here's my number if you think of anything.'

Mimi swept up the card and left the room. He slumped forward, his head on his arms. He'd stuffed up. What an idiot. Humiliated, he called Kate, hoping she'd come back and collect him as soon as possible. He didn't want to stay here any longer than necessary. That's when his day really hit the fan. His call went straight to voice message.

# CHAPTER
# ELEVEN

KATE SAT IN HER CAR, staring at the front of the health centre. She'd learned nothing significant from Michelle. Like everyone else, the practice manager only had good words to say about Geoffrey Scott. As to her whereabouts at the time of his murder, she was at home, alone with her cat. She was more upset than others she'd spoken to, but Kate put the tears down to her having worked closely with the man for ten years.

Whatever, Kate was getting tired of hearing what a wonderful person her victim was and how everyone had loved him. Random killings were unusual in small towns like Martinborough. People were murdered for a reason. Not that she was victim-blaming. Far from it. But someone had hated the good doctor enough to kill him. They'd done it efficiently, at a time when they knew there'd be no witnesses and they'd taken care not to leave any evidence behind. She was about to start the car when her phone rang. She answered, expecting it to be Tony.

'There's a man in the trees across the road.'

It took a few seconds for her to work out she was listening to June Whittaker. 'June? What's wrong?'

'There's a man standing across the road staring at the Scott's house. He was here last week.'

'Can he see you?' asked Kate.

'Not now. I did as you said. I'm in the upstairs bathroom with the door locked.'

'Stay on the line, don't hang up. I'm on my way.' Kate hit the ignition button, spun the car around, floored the accelerator and sped down the road. No lights, no siren; she didn't want to scare anyone off. On her way, she called Comms, requesting backup and a dog team to meet her at June's place. A minute later, she braked as she neared the street on the other side of Palmer Grove, parked, got out and let herself into June's back garden through a gate in the fence. The unlocked back door opened when she turned the handle.

Upstairs, she tried the bathroom door. It was locked. 'It's me,' she whispered.

'Thank goodness,' said June.

'Where is he?'

'You can see him from my bedroom window. He's across the road in the reserve, next to the sign.'

Keeping out of sight, Kate sidled across the bedroom and peering around the edge of the curtains, looked down onto the reserve. She didn't see anyone. Taking the stairs two at a time, she yanked open the front door and ran across the road. Partway down the path into the bush, she stopped to listen for footsteps, for the sound of twigs snapping underfoot, branches being pushed out of the way, anything. Plain old heavy breathing would do.

She heard the distinctive call of a korimako somewhere deep in the reserve but that was all. She waited a few minutes then decided it was pointless and walked back to the sign. A full-grown Rimu tree stood behind it. She searched around its base and saw plenty of scuffed footprints in the dust but nothing definite. The usual scattering of empty vape cartridges but they were old, their plastic faded by time and sunshine.

She was crossing the street back to June's house when two marked cars swung around the corner. She waited as they pulled up on either side of her, windows down.

'What's up, boss?'

'My witness saw someone in the reserve. A guy. Can you take a look for me and report back?'

'Sure thing.' Windows up, they moved off and parked their cars near the sign. Four uniformed officers got out and disappeared down the path. A Ute with a dog box on the back arrived next and drew up beside her. Nathan, one of only two dog handlers in the district, looked up at her from the driver's seat for instructions.

'Thanks for coming,' she said. Hearing Kate's voice, Brutus got up and turned around in his dog box, his tail thumping the metal walls with delight. A sucker for dogs, it took all Kate's willpower not to smooch the big Alsatian every time she saw him. Luckily, Nathan understood and ignored her when she gave his partner an occasional furtive head tickle.

'There was a murder there on Sunday afternoon,' she said pointing to the Scott's house. 'The neighbour called to tell me she saw a man standing by that sign in the reserve, watching their house. She thinks he was here last week. I've been over and didn't see anyone. Do you mind taking Brutus through to check?'

'Only because it's you, and Brutus needs the walk,' said Nathan.

'Thanks, I owe you one.'

'You owe me more than one, mate.' He pulled the Ute over behind the other cars.

'June, I'm back.' Kate called from the front door.

Upstairs, the toilet flushed and June still adjusting her trousers, emerged from the bathroom onto the landing at the top of the stairs. 'Did you get him?'

'There was no one there. My guys are checking the reserve now. You're sure he was watching the house and not just taking a walk?'

'He was there all right. And he didn't want to be seen.'

'He can't have disappeared in the time it took me to get here,' said Kate, walking upstairs to meet her. 'Show me again where you saw him.' They entered June's bedroom and June pointed to the same area Kate had been searching.

'I looked. Didn't see any sign of him.'

'Anyone home?' It was Tony.

'We're up here,' called Kate. She turned to June, 'You don't mind, do you?'

'I'm glad I made my bed.'

'How did you know I was here?' asked Kate when he walked in.

'I called Comms. They caught me up. Mimi dropped me off on her way to an appointment.' He nodded to June. 'Afternoon Mrs Whittaker.'

'Good afternoon, DC Hunter.'

'Tell us what he looked like,' said Kate.

'Youngish. Definitely under forty. He was wearing a black hoodie and black track pants. I mean, who wears clothes like that on a day like today?'

'Was he big or small?' asked Tony.

'He was muscley with big shoulders. He was wearing hunting boots, or they could have been work boots. Black ones and the laces weren't done up. I thought he'd trip over them.'

'Did you see his face?' asked Tony.

'He had his hood up. He might have a beard. I can't be sure.'

'You say he was here last week,' said Kate.

'Last Thursday. I came back from the supermarket and saw him. He was standing in the same place, and he was staring at the Scott's house. I should have said something, shouldn't I?'

'Was he there long?' asked Tony.

'I didn't take any notice then. It wasn't until I saw him today that I remembered.'

'Did he see you?'

'I don't think so,' said June. She suddenly looked worried. 'I've heard of people casing houses before they come back and rob them. You don't think that's what he was doing?'

'It's possible,' said Tony.

'I went over and didn't see anyone. The guys are having a look and Nathan's taking Brutus through the reserve now.'

'If he's there, they'll find him,' said Tony.

June saw him roll his eyes at Kate and tensed. 'He's real. I didn't make him up.'

'We're not saying you did,' said Kate. She glared at Tony, who gave a slight shrug, again seen by June. 'Our problem is that you're the only one who's seen him. When my guys return from their walk-through, I'll get them to check with the neighbours to see if they've seen anyone.'

'They're at work during the day,' said June. She looked from Kate to Tony. 'I'm telling you; he was there.'

'Why don't you make a cup of tea,' said Kate. 'While we go and see if they found anything.'

As soon as they reached the street, Tony turned to Kate. 'It's obvious she's making it up. A lonely old lady sees a perfectly innocent guy taking a walk, panics and calls the police. It's a tale as old as time.'

'I think you're wrong,' she said. 'June isn't silly.'

When they entered the reserve, it was to see Nathan, with Brutus on the leash, coming back to meet them. Brutus wagged his tail when he saw Kate, then promptly sat on her foot, his big tongue lolling pink against his fur as he panted in the heat.

'Anything?' She kept her voice low so June wouldn't overhear their conversation. Brutus leaned into her fingers as she scratched him behind his left ear.

'We had a nice walk, didn't we boy? It's a beautiful reserve. That's it. I'm going to have to love and leave you, Kate. We've got a call in Featherston to get to. Come Brutus.' She'd half expected this but that didn't stop her feeling disappointed.

'What do you want to do?' asked Tony.

'You don't believe her,' said Kate. 'But I do. She's sensible, she's not the type to panic. Get video surveillance set up. If this guy comes back, I want him on film. I'll go and get June's permission for the camera and explain what we need her to do. I'll see you back at the town hall. We've got a lot to discuss before tomorrow morning's briefing.'

'I'm about to go off shift,' said Tony.

'Too bad,' she said. 'This is a murder inquiry; we work when we have to. See you when you're done here.'

# CHAPTER
# TWELVE

MIMI HANDED Bruce his first cup of coffee of the day, then checked the temperature of the water in the pan. 'I talked to the girls again. They're coming home next week. A couple days here to sort out their gear, then they're off to Christchurch.'

Bruce looked up from his phone. 'Will you go down and settle them in?'

It was six o'clock on Wednesday morning. He was dressed in a blue jacket, white shirt and cream chinos. He was sitting at the kitchen bench. The sun had come up an hour ago. From the intensity of the light striking the marble worktop through the windows he could tell it was going to be another very hot day. He wondered if he should ditch the jacket.

Mimi was still in her nightgown, her hair tied in a loose ponytail at the nape of her neck. She always waited until Bruce had gone to work before getting dressed. That way she could take her time. Earlier when she'd checked, Ava was fast asleep. It had taken a lot of persuasion, but she'd finally convinced her friend to take a sleeping pill and was pleased to see it had worked.

She cracked an egg and tipped it into the water. Bruce ate two eggs on toasted rye bread every morning. This 'breakfast of champions' hadn't changed in all the years they'd been married.

'I should go down to Christchurch,' she said, cracking the second egg. 'The agent said she looked over the inventory when we settled on their apartment. It doesn't hurt to double check.'

'It doesn't. You can take them shopping if it's not all there,' said Bruce. He was on his phone and wasn't really paying attention. He brought up his emails and scrolled through them, deleting as he went. Finished, he looked up. 'How did it go yesterday with the detective?'

'Fine.'

'Where were you? That sort of thing?'

'That sort of thing. I said I was at home with you.' The toaster pinged. She took the rye bread out and put it on a plate. It was a constant battle to get him to pay attention to his diet and lose weight. She passed his plate to him, watching close-mouthed as he slathered half an inch of butter on each slice of toast before he handed it back to her. Then she lifted the eggs out of the pan, laid them carefully on top of the bread and passed the plate back.

'Pepper.'

She passed him the pepper mill, then refilled their cups with coffee from the machine.

'You told her I was here with you on Sunday?'

'I just said that.' She paused. 'I got the young detective. Not Kate. He was a bit flustered. I don't think he's done many interviews before. I had to drop him off at June Whittaker's place. She saw someone lurking in that reserve across the road from the house. You know what she's like. I bet it was a false alarm. She's always been a bit anxious.'

Bruce didn't look up. He grunted a smile, pretending he'd heard her when it was clear that he was more interested in his food than June Whittaker. He was a loud eater, with the ability to clatter his knife and fork on a plate when he'd finished, more loudly than anyone Mimi had ever known. Early in their marriage his table manners had annoyed her so much that one day, unable to bear it any longer, she told him not to make so much noise. It was the first and last time she ever tried to correct him. The bruises went away, but the memory of his threats did not.

'Ava suggested we get takeaways and have dinner at her place tonight. Dan will be there. What do you think?'

'Okay,' he said looking up. 'But I'll be late. They've called an emergency council meeting to discuss my idea of the sculpture park. You remember I told you about it last night.'

'I was asleep.'

'I woke you up. Never mind, let me practice my pitch on you.' He sat up straight and fixed his gaze on her. 'Essentially, the town's image is taking a bit of a battering, and we need to find a new reason to bring the punters in.' He interrupted himself to explain. 'I thought we could donate Hector's Rise to the council and build a sculpture park there.' She nodded and he carried on. 'It will take a year to get planning permission and get the works installed. By then, the police will have either got their man, or woman,' he paused so she could laugh then carried on. 'The public will have forgotten about this nasty business. We need to be ready to move on to something new. Something magical.'

'Like a sculpture park,' she said, finishing for him. She smiled brightly feeding his enthusiasm back to him.

'Exactly.'

'I'll ask Ava if she wants to be the curator,' he said.

'Excellent idea. It will give her something to look forward to.'

Bruce returned to his eggs, and she held out one hand for his cutlery as soon as he'd finished, whisking his plate away with her other hand.

'Where's Danger-Doc been this time?' he asked.

'Don't call him that. Ava said the Northern Territory. Dan does locums overseas, it's good work.'

He laughed. 'I'm having you on.'

He was only half-laughing. She knew he'd never forgiven Dan for ruining his friendship with Geoffrey. In public, her husband hid his feelings beneath a façade of male cheeriness, but at home, she saw the anger behind his snarky comments. Anger which he sometimes took out on her.

She put the plate in the dishwasher and returned to their previous conversation. 'What did Martin say about Murphy Enterprises donating Hector's Rise?'

'What he always says. Have you thought it through?' He paused.

'The more I think about it, the better it gets. We'll donate the land to the council. It's useless for anything else. The accountant can swing it through this year's tax return as a charitable donation. If we play our cards right, and if the council doesn't dither about making a decision, we should be open in time for the Wellington Arts Festival next summer.'

'I'll ask the PR team to develop a strategy,' she said. 'But they'll need to keep everything on the down-low until after they catch Geoffrey's killer.'

'That's my girl,' said Bruce. He climbed off the stool and gathered up his phone and keys. 'Walk with me to the car.'

Outside, he took her in his arms and rocked her gently from side to side. 'You're the best thing that ever happened to me.' He murmured this in her ear, his breath irritating the tiny hairs on her ear lobe. 'I couldn't have achieved any of this without you.'

'I thought the girls were the best thing that ever happened to you,' she replied.

'You came first. You always will.' He followed this up with a kiss on her forehead then half-released her. 'I'd better go. It'll be good to see old Dan again. Text me when he arrives.'

His hands dropped from her sides, and he climbed into this year's Porsche 911 Turbo. It was the only make and model of car Bruce ever bought. One for him and one for Mimi, a standing order with the dealer. He pressed the ignition, and the engine roared into life before settling into a low burble while he checked the controls. Then his foot hit the gas pedal, and the car fishtailed, spitting gravel behind him, until he got it under control. He was off, full speed down their drive. Mimi stood listening to the mechanical whine of the engine protesting at having to slow down when he reached the gate. She only relaxed when the car disappeared over the brow of the hill.

# CHAPTER
# THIRTEEN

WEDNESDAY MORNING and the Incident Room was full to overflowing, the extra uniforms occupying most of the chairs. It was standard practice in a murder investigation, to bring in staff from outside the district. It avoided embarrassment and elicited more information that might have been otherwise forthcoming if it was a stranger asking the questions. Being a nark is bad enough, without the added risk that your friends and neighbours might find out, because a local cop later lets something slip at the pub.

Kate stood in front of the whiteboards. 'Quiet everyone,' she finally yelled when no one paid her any attention.

They settled and the noise levels gradually reduced to zero.

'First,' she said. 'Thank you all for your excellent work. Investigations are team efforts, and you're proving to be a fantastic team.' There were a few smiles. More importantly, she had their attention.

'Every household in Martinborough has now been canvassed for information. The job sheets are waiting to be analysed. I'd like a volunteer with IT experience to do this today.'

Eyes dropped to the floor as people shuffled in their seats, not wanting to be the one picked for such a tedious and time-consuming task.

'You,' she said, pointing to a Senior Constable in the third row. 'You look like someone who's good with computers.'

'No one better,' said the guy sitting next to him, earning a punch in the arm for his endorsement.

'What's your name and where are you from?'

'Abel Potter. Hawkes Bay.'

'Right then, Abel. Pick someone to help you and get to it. Have the summary report on my desk by the end of the shift.'

'Yes, ma'am.'

'Paul, where are you?' She searched the sea of faces until she found him. 'Stand up and introduce yourself. Give the team a rundown of your findings.'

At the back of the room, Paul got to his feet. There were more shuffles as people turned in their seats, craning their necks to see him. The room warming up, and she hoped he'd be brief.

'Detective Sergeant Paul Roper, SOCO team leader. Not much to report, I'm afraid. We worked with Dr Fraser and can now confirm the spade belonging to Dr Scott is our murder weapon. That's it. Marsha's excellent photographs are up there on the board and can be downloaded along with the video of the scene. On the designated terminal over there.'

'Thanks Paul,' said Kate. She looked around the room. 'Questions?'

'The lack of evidence points to this being a pre-meditated murder, doesn't it?'

'Who said that?' asked Kate. A hand shot up, and she recognised a young woman constable, new to the Masterton station. 'You are?'

'Constable Sophie Taylor, ma'am. If it was pre-meditated, that means there was a motive. This was not a spur-of-the-moment killing.'

'While I agree with you, Sophie, it's too early to be definite about anything. We have to keep an open mind.' She paused and wiped a bead of sweat from her cheek. 'I'm also aware of how stuffy it is in here, so if you don't mind, we'll move on. Tony, can you update us on June Whittaker? I want everyone to know that if she calls, you're to drop what you're doing and go.'

Hemmed in by people sitting on either side of him, Tony got awkwardly to his feet. He opened his notebook but didn't read from it.

'June Whittaker, Dr Scott's elderly neighbour, reported seeing a man in the reserve 'staring' at the Scott house. Four uniforms and the dog handler searched the area, we found nothing to indicate anyone had been there or was where she said he was.'

Kate interrupted him. 'What DC Hunter is trying to say is that a credible witness saw a person of interest on two separate occasions near the Scott house. A video camera has been installed in case he comes back. If he does and June Whittaker calls, you are to take her concerns seriously and attend immediately.'

She stared at Tony, who was still standing. 'That was what you wanted to say, wasn't it, DC Hunter?'

Tony stared back at her. No one moved.

'That's all,' said Kate, dismissing him. He flipped his notebook closed and sat down.

'We have completed the first round of interviews with people who knew Dr Scott personally. Not a lot to tell you, I'm afraid. There are some alibis which need to be double-checked, and DC Hunter and I will do that in person this morning.' She looked at him to confirm the arrangement she'd made with him before the meeting started, but he ignored her.

She was puzzled. What possessed him to act this way in front of everyone? The sooner she brought the meeting to a close, the better. She remembered Jack's offer, but Tony's insubordination, though public, was so far, a one off. It was too soon for a 'wee chat'. Besides, she'd met men like Tony before; he'd only double down if she showed the slightest sign of weakness.

'One last thing, and it's important,' she said. 'It's Dr Scott's funeral tomorrow. It's in the hall next door, so this room will be locked for most of the day. You've been divided into teams, I understand?' She waited. More nods and murmurs.

'I want a record of everyone attending the funeral and everyone in town tomorrow. This will be a big job, as I understand it will be a big funeral. Those of you in plain clothes for the day mingle and listen. I want to know what everyone says. It doesn't matter if you think it's trivial. I want to know.'

There was a shuffle of paper as people wrote her instructions in their notebooks.

'Who's at the cemetery?' she asked. A couple of hands, including Marsha's, went up. 'Good. I want a video of everyone at the graveside, everyone inside and outside the cemetery, anyone watching from afar, and I want to know who they are and what they're doing there.'

Another pause while they wrote in their notebooks.

'Those of you in uniform, look smart. Clean shirts, ironed. The town will be heaving with press. I want them to see you all looking and behaving like the professionals we are.' Their groans were more for effect than real. Police officers liked their uniforms and took pride in wearing them. As the upholders of law and order in their communities, there wasn't an officer among them who didn't believe their work was a righteous cause.

'Remember,' she said. 'Good police work is about the boring stuff. Small details trip up perpetrators. Routine work and the long, slow plod to the correct conclusion. It's not the romantic shoot 'em-up stuff you see on TV. We're better than that.'

'What do you say to the reporter who says this is New Zealand's first serial killer,' a voice from the back called out.

'Who said that?' asked Kate.

'Me.' A youngish man with a thin brown moustache stood up. He was in uniform and wasn't afraid to meet her gaze.

'Firstly, surprise, surprise, but the press hasn't done its homework. New Zealand's first serial killer was a man called Hayden Poulter. He killed three sex workers in Auckland, admittedly more by accident than premeditation, in October 1996.'

She paused.

'Secondly, if the reporter is lumping Dr Scott's murder in with the disappearance of Juliette Bisson three years ago, then he, she, or they is drawing a very long bow. Juliette's body was never found. She disappeared, but there's no proof she was murdered.'

'But—'

Kate held up her hand. 'Thirdly, give me one fact linking the two events?'

'I don't have one. But—'

'There are no buts. You have a reporter flying a flag to sell papers, not caring that he might terrify the good people of Martinborough in the process. When I say we are to behave as professionals, I mean it. We deal in evidence, not the fevered imagination of a cub reporter who's watched too much CSI.'

In the silence which followed, the young man at the back of the room sat down, slinking low in his seat as those sitting beside him leaned away.

'Now,' she said. 'Does everyone know what they have to do?'

'Yes, Ma'am.'

'Then do it.'

She spun around, walked into her cubicle and sank into the chair behind her desk, her palms sweaty, her heart beating a tattoo in her chest. Being the boss in her first murder inquiry wasn't turning out quite the way she expected.

# CHAPTER
# FOURTEEN

MID-MORNING, and they had only passed one car on the twenty-minute drive to Featherston. Tony kept his eyes fixed on the road ahead. He's a careful driver, but too cautious, thought Kate. He also hadn't said a word since leaving Martinborough.

On her part, Kate couldn't be bothered to make small talk. Not after he'd publicly misrepresented June at the briefing and thereby attempted to undermine her judgement. It wasn't her job to teach him manners. She was his boss, not his mother. If he wanted to remain on her team, he'd better understand that, or she'd personally put him on the plane back to the West Coast.

She tuned out the callers to the talkback show on the radio, preferring to gaze out the window. The paddocks, dusty yellow instead of their usual green, were bare of stock. What rain they'd got on the afternoon of the murder had been too heavy and too short to break the drought; the sun-baked earth had shrugged it off.

Even Kate, born and brought up in the suburbs of Masterton, knew more rain was needed if the farmers were to survive. It was fine for the vineyards; at this time of year, the endless sunshine helped mature and fatten the grapes, but they were a much smaller portion of the local economy. Conscious that each day she didn't catch the killer was another day that the tourists and their dollars stayed away, she tried not to feel swamped by the unrealistic expectations of others. No thanks to Tony, the gnawing self-doubt she had suffered from, during the Bisson investigation was back. Leaning against the door, she settled into her seat and closed her eyes.

———

They found Ava's studio in an old garage at the back of a falling-down shop on a corner of the main road running through Featherston. The town, lying in the shadow of the Remutaka Range, had once been a stopping-off place for road and rail travellers on the journey north. No longer, and as a consequence, the town had fallen into a general state of disrepair.

Recently though, there had been signs of a revival in its fortunes. Young families had moved in to take advantage of the affordable housing and its proximity to the capital city on the other side of the hill, as the bush-clad range was euphemistically known. The slow gentrification taking place, gave Kate hope that one day the town might also rid itself of its criminal element, the low-level drug dealers and gang members, who had moved into the same cheap houses.

Tony turned the car into an overgrown lot at the back of the studio and turned off the engine. 'I'll get the landlord,' he said, and was gone before Kate could get out of the car.

Five minutes later, he was back. A thin man, hollow-chested and unshaven, wearing baggy shorts, a t-shirt and sandals, followed him.

'Phillip Marlow.' He shook Kate's hand and looked her in the eye.

'DSS Kate Sutton. You've met DC Hunter.'

'We spoke on the phone,' said Phillip. 'I'm not sure what else I can tell you.' His perfect diction and deep voice did not match the elderly beach-bum vibe.

There was no shade at the back of the building, and Kate could feel the sun searing a path down the part in her hair. She wished she'd brought a hat. Poor Tony, with his pale complexion and buzzcut was suffering more than she was, something Phillip and his dark mahogany tan didn't seem to notice. He stood balanced on one leg, his right hand shading his eyes, the other on his hip, dressed for the heat, seeing no need to rush, just happy to have someone to talk to.

'We'd like to take a look at Ava Scott's studio,' said Kate. 'Did you bring a key?'

'Well,' he drawled. 'I can let you look, but I can't let you inside. Not unless you've brought a search warrant or something in writing from Ava giving her permission.'

'She's been through a lot lately,' said Kate. 'I don't want to bother her if I can help it.'

Phillip took his time considering this, and the sun continued to beat down on their heads. Kate felt a blister forming on the tip of her nose. 'Okay,' she said. 'Fine. What if we look from the doorway?'

'You won't go in?'

'We will not go in.'

'That's all right then,' said Phillip. He fished a key out of the pocket of his shorts and unlocked the door, giving it a push before stepping back and out of their way.

Kate leaned over the threshold and looked inside. The space was bigger and much lighter than it appeared from outside. She understood why Ava had chosen it. A row of canvasses leaned against the opposite wall. Each one, an explosion of colour and form, which Kate had to tear her eyes away from in order to check out the rest of the studio.

Nearest the door was a bench, on it, a kettle and mini oven. A toothbrush and tube of toothpaste stood upright in a glass next to the sink. Right angles to the bench and door, was a long sofa covered in rugs, a sleeping bag slung across the back, and a pillow with a head-shaped dent in the middle at one end.

In the centre, where the light from the windows on both sides converged, stood a large easel on a drop cloth spattered with dried paint.

'It's pretty basic,' said Tony.

'And hot,' she added. 'There's no insulation. I bet it's freezing in winter.'

Behind them, Phillip coughed the wet hacking cough of a smoker, then spat a gob of phlegm into the base of the downpipe next to the door. 'Seen what you came to see?'

'Thanks,' she replied. 'Is there somewhere out of the sun we can talk?'

They followed him to a café around the corner. A staff member staring listlessly at a cabinet full of unsold muffins and cakes brightened when Tony walked in to order their coffees while Phillip and Kate found a table outside. Phillip fished around again in his pocket and brought out a packet of cigarettes. He slipped one out, straightened it between two fingers, and put it between his lips. He lit up and took a long deep drag. 'That's better.' He turned away and blew the smoke behind him, away from Kate.

Tony returned, unloaded three coffees from a tray onto the table, and sat down.

'Right,' said Kate. 'You say Ava was at her studio all day?'

'She was,' said Philip.

'Where were you?'

'What time?' asked Phillip.

'All day.'

'I live at the back of my shop.' He pointed to a second-hand bookstore beside the café. There was a closed sign in the window. Below it the books lay in dusty piles beneath another sign which read 'Phill's Books'. 'I sleep in on Sundays. Get up around ten.'

'Was Ava in her studio when you got up?' she asked.

'She's here every weekend.'

'Did you see her?' She sipped her coffee, waiting for him to answer.

'I heard her music. She plays it when she paints. I don't usually mind it being so loud, but I had a migraine on Sunday. She turned it off when I banged on the wall. Does that work for you?' He took another drag on his cigarette, this time directing the smoke under the table.

'My mother had migraines,' said Kate. 'They used to put her in bed for days.'

'Me too, but the injections help if I use them in time.'

'Did you use one on Sunday?' she asked.

'I did. I went back to sleep and woke up around two feeling fine.'

The gnawing feeling in Kate's stomach just got worse. It wasn't when the murder occurred, but the three-hour gap in Ava's alibi was still relevant. Tony should have asked these questions when he first spoke to the guy. Keeping her voice calm, she asked if Ava was still there at two.

Phillip tapped the ash off the end of his cigarette while he thought about it. 'Not sure, but I know I saw her around five-thirty when she left.'

'You can't state with absolute certainty Ava Scott was in her studio between ten in the morning and five that afternoon?'

'Put like that, no.'

Tony tensed beside her, his pen poised above the notebook. Apart from placing Ava at her studio at five-thirty PM, Phillip Marlow's alibi for the rest of the day didn't stack up. Annoyed so much time had been wasted, she drank the rest of her coffee and stood up to leave. Tony hurriedly followed.

'Call me if you think of anything.'

She handed Phill her card. He took it, squinting as he read her details. Then he waved her off with a casual salute. Phillip Marlow didn't get up. Legs crossed, he sipped his coffee and lit another cigarette.

In the car on their way back to Martinborough, Kate phoned the Incident Room, relieved when it was Sophie Taylor who answered. She needed someone she could trust to do what she asked.

'Hey Sophie, I want you to check the CCTV footage for State Highway Two and any other roads between Featherston and Martinborough between ten AM and six PM on Sunday afternoon. Yes, again. Yes, Ava Scott's car. You've got the number plate.'

'Don't worry, we all make that mistake once,' she told Tony after she ended the call. 'It's easy to do.'

He slowed their car, to let an elderly man driving a beaten-up Toyota out of a driveway. Then he followed it so slowly, Kate thought it would be quicker if she got out and pushed the car back to Martinborough.

'I know. I would have checked the alibi myself if you hadn't. I would have picked it up.'

She left it at that. He obviously didn't understand the importance of his mistake. Hoping that a change of subject might improve the atmosphere in the car, she asked if he liked the paintings. He took her question seriously as if his opinion actually mattered.

'They are excellent. She's incredibly talented, and I love the sunset theme.'

It dawned on her that he was right about the sunsets. Maybe he did know what he was talking about.

'What will she do with them?' he asked.

'She said they were for sale, so I presume she'll sell them. I'd buy one but I don't have a wall big enough.'

Frustrated by his slow driving, she leaned forward to peer around the car in front. 'Put your foot down and pass this car after that truck goes by.'

She suddenly needed to get back. Ava's alibi had been blown apart. She finally had something to investigate. The gnawing feeling in her stomach was gone.

# CHAPTER
# FIFTEEN

MATT'S CAR was parked outside her house when she got home. She'd been at the funeral all afternoon. The last thing she needed now was an argument.

Packed tight with sweaty mourners drinking more than they should, the rugby club rooms had no air-conditioning. Rumours about the murder, each one more outlandish than the last, did the rounds in the fetid atmosphere, escalating fear and anxiety to new heights. She listened patiently to anyone who wanted a private word. She explained they were doing everything they could before adding that they weren't getting much helpful information in return. This state- ment was met with cold stares then exhortations to do more. Of what they couldn't or wouldn't say. The words, fruitless exercise, barely described it.

She was tired. She had sore feet and a hoarse voice from speaking over the noise of too many voices contesting to be heard in too small a space. All she wanted to do was to have a cup of tea and sit down with her feet up. Maybe watch a film on Netflix to settle her brain.

She didn't want to fight about stuff, money, or any of the usual topics Matt used to needle her. After twenty-five years of marriage, he knew exactly which buttons to push. Well aware that she wasn't perfect, Kate sincerely believed her ex-husband was worse.

Unfortunately, the cursory wave she gave him before she drove into her garage and lowered the door didn't put him off. She only had time to kick off her shoes and switch on the kettle before she heard his knock on the door.

'It's been a long day. What do you want?'

'You look tired Kate. From what I hear, it's a tough case.'

'It is.' She hoped her curt reply was enough to make him understand she wasn't inviting him in. 'Can whatever you've got to say to me, wait?'

'You're working too hard.'

'As you never fail to remind me.' She sighed, hoping he'd hurry up, say what he had to say, then leave. According to Matt, it was her work, not his, which had been the problem in the marriage. He'd told her this right after informing her about his affair with his business partner. Poor Carla. She wasn't the reason Matt wanted a divorce. No, it was Kate's work that had ruined their marriage. Twenty-five years and she should have known. It was always her fault when something went wrong. Never his.

'Maybe this will help,' said Matt. 'I've brought someone to see you.' He stepped back from the door, and like a showman, held out his arms as if introducing a special guest. Her father peeped around the corner of the house.

'Dad?'

She almost didn't recognize him. Jim Sutton had grown a beard and changed his glasses since the last time she'd seen him. Five years ago? Six? She couldn't remember. He looked frail when he stepped into the open. His legs were thinner, his shoulder bones sticking out like a wire coat hanger beneath the fabric of his shirt. The only thing that hadn't changed was the size of his belly and the way it hung over the top of his shorts.

'What are you doing here?'

'More to the point, Kate, what are you doing here?' He waved his arms at the front of her townhouse.

Matt backed down the path. 'I thought you'd be pleased. I'll leave you two to get reacquainted. Jim, I've put your bags beside the garage.

Remember, you're coming over for a drink and catch-up with the boys on Saturday. Kate, Carla says you're welcome to join.'

As if I would, she thought, watching him scuttle back to his car, his arm waving farewell over his head.

'Aren't you going to invite me in?' asked her father 'I urgently need a pee and a drink in that order. Gin if you have it, but I'll take vodka or wine if you haven't.'

He shooed her inside, saying he'd get the bags later. Standing in the kitchen, she listened to him perform a quick inspection of her new home. He opened doors, checked inside cupboards, and even bounced on the bed in Toby's room before—she stopped listening then—using the bathroom.

Jim Sutton had devoted his life to his one true passion. Photography. He was good at it. When Kate was growing up, his work always came first. He would be off to his next assignment at a moment's notice, never staying long enough to appreciate what he was leaving behind.

That he saw nothing amiss with his fathering of his only daughter didn't help her come to terms with his absences. Once, when she was fifteen, she asked him if he loved her. He was genuinely shocked that she didn't think he did. It had taken years for Kate to accept his assurances. Once she did and her anger went away, their relationship improved.

Notwithstanding, his sudden reappearance tonight had caught her off guard; her emotions now a whirling mess of happiness, doubt, distrust, and irritation mixed with sheer relief that he was still alive. Her adult-self lived in a state of low grade anxiety that one day she would receive a phone call from some obscure corner of the world, informing her that he was injured, or sick. Or worse, dead. Always with the expectation that she was going to be able to do something.

He joined her in the kitchen, and she pointed to the cupboard above the fridge. 'The gin's in there,' she said. 'Toby gave it to me for Christmas.'

'Tonic?' His hand shook as he reached for the bottle.

She took a single serve can out of the fridge and put it on the bench.

Next, she fetched a tall glass, and loaded it with ice cubes from the freezer. The gin nearly missed the glass, his tremor was so bad. He added a smidgeon of tonic then paused, ignoring the clink of ice and the liquid sloshing over the rim onto his hand, to ask if she was having one.

'I'm having tea,' she replied. Her sniff was unconscious, but they both heard it.

Focused on pouring the hot water over her teabag and swirling it around to release the flavour, she looked up to find his glass was nearly empty and her father more relaxed.

'You haven't unpacked.' He gestured towards the boxes. 'This isn't a permanent arrangement?'

'It's permanent. You've met Carla.'

'I have. I can see why Matt likes her. But she's not his wife.'

'As of two months ago, neither am I,' said Kate. She caught the floating edge of the teabag with her fingernails then tossed it in the bin. She took the milk out of the fridge, smelled it to check it was okay and added it to her tea.

'Why didn't you tell me?' he asked.

'Mum sent you an email.' Cradling the cup in her hands, she leaned against the bench.

'I delete most of my emails. Must have missed it.' He poured himself another gin, adding a splash of tonic for effect. A small, familiar knot was forming in Kate's stomach. It was the same old dance. The only question, how many more glasses would he drink before he collapsed into oblivion?

'Do you delete your work emails too?' she asked.

'Of course not.'

'Just Mum's then?'

'You know what she's like,' he said.

Kate was way past the stage of getting caught up in the turmoil of her parents's marriage. She changed the subject. 'Matt said you have bags. Does that mean you're planning to stay?'

'If I'm welcome. I won't if I'm going to put you out.'

'That depends. Toby's using the spare room at the moment, but he's hardly ever here, so I guess it will be all right. How long are you planning on staying?'

'A couple of weeks.' He socked back another hefty slug of gin. 'It's only until I get my next assignment. I've pitched a project to the Guardian about pearling in Western Australia. I'm waiting to hear back from the editor.' He put his glass down. The tremor in his hands had stopped. For now, she thought, looking at the level of gin left in the bottle.

'Do you have any money?'

'Why? Do you want me to pay rent?' This amused him. The sound of his laughter, accompanied by the twinkle in his light blue eyes, reminded her of happier times. When he didn't drink so much. Like this, balanced halfway between being desperate for a drink and being blind-drunk, he was the father she had loved as a child. She could tolerate him like this. She could even make up a bed for him in the spare room.

For now, she thought, she could manage the dutiful daughter act. When never once had he ever been the dutiful father. Later, after she cooked him dinner and after he finished the bottle of gin, when she heard him snoring loudly in the other room, she called her mother to let her know he was back.

# CHAPTER
## SIXTEEN

HIS SNORING KEPT her awake most of the night. That, and seeing him again. Then, just as she had fallen asleep, her phone rang. It was six AM, and daylight streamed through the chinks in the undersized curtains left behind by the previous owner. She scrabbled to answer it so as not to wake her father. He was not a morning person.

'He's back.' It was June. 'He's seen me.'

Kate sat up and pushed her hair off her face. 'Did you turn on the camera like we showed you?'

'Not yet.'

'Do it, then lock yourself in the bathroom.'

'Please hurry, I'm scared. I don't know what he's going to do.'

In the pile of dirty clothes in the corner, Kate found trousers and a shirt she'd only worn once. She pulled them on, shoved her feet into her trainers and laces undone, ran downstairs. She remembered her sleeping father only after she'd slammed the door. Tough, she thought, as she backed out of the garage. Mindful of her neighbours, she didn't switch on her siren until she exited the street.

With the wee-waw blaring and her red and blues dancing across the front of her car, early morning motorists pulled over, clearing a path for her as she sped through the quiet streets of Masterton. South of town she hit State Highway 2, where she slowed to an impotent crawl. Road cones were everywhere. Drivers had nowhere to go when they heard her siren. Swearing, she swerved onto the shoulder to get around them, knocking over several of the orange beasties on the way past. A sharp left turn towards the Gladstone wineries, and she was free. Her foot flat to the floor, she flew down the narrow road, braking sharply to make a hard right onto Ponatahi Road. This was the back way to Martinborough, and the only traffic at this hour of the morning was an occasional tractor.

She called Comms to let them know where she was going and asked them to tell Tony and Nathan to meet her there. She'd hung up before she remembered it was Tony's day off. No matter, it would be good for him. It would keep him on his toes. That done, she sat back and enjoyed the adrenalin rush as she accelerated into then out of the corners on the winding road ahead. All thoughts of her father, gone.

She slowed down when she reached the outskirts of the town, and turned off the lights and siren. As before, she parked a block away from Palmer Grove. The key was under a pot of geraniums on the back step. She let herself in and called softly to let June know she was there. A relieved whimper from the bathroom indicated she'd been heard.

In June's bedroom, she stopped. The camera was lying on the floor, still running. Kate stepped over it and looked down onto the reserve. As before, there was no one there.

She reached down and turned off the camera, her disappointment physical, like a punch to the stomach. There'd be no footage of June's mysterious man. No proof that he existed let alone an image she could use to track him down. Thoroughly deflated, she walked across the landing to the bathroom.

'It's safe. You can come out.'

The lock turned, and June stood in the doorway. Pyjamas and an open dressing gown hung from her bony frame. She looked expectantly at Kate. 'Did you see him?'

'He wasn't there. What happened to the camera?'

'I went back to turn it on like you said, and he saw me. I got scared and knocked it over. Then I was terrified that he'd seen the camera, and I couldn't put it back. I ran into the bathroom and hid.' She reached across and put a hand on Kate's arm. 'I'm so sorry. I know how much you were depending on me.'

'You did the right thing.' Trying not to let the old lady see just how let down she felt, she turned away. 'I'll go downstairs and wait for the others. You get dressed. I'll come back when we've decided what to do.'

'I've ruined it, haven't I? No one will believe me now.' Tears popped into her eyes, and she swiped them away with the back of her hand. 'I'm sorry, I was scared, and I panicked.'

'You did what you could. You're safe. That's what matters.'

Out on the road Tony was talking to Nathan, who was sitting in his Ute, his elbow resting on the open window.

'Nathan's got another call to go to,' said Tony. 'One with a definite sighting.' Kate ignored the sarcastic tone in his voice. For now, she wasn't going to call him on it. Not in front of Nathan. Not in public.

'I'll stay if you really want me to,' said Nathan. He looked past Tony to Kate. 'From what Tony says, I don't see much point.'

'Go,' Kate replied. 'Apologies for wasting your time.' She tapped the roof of the cab and got a bark from Brutus in reply. Someone liked her. With a heavy heart, she watched Nathan turned the car around at the end of the road and drive away. Behind her, Tony was huffing and puffing, desperate to have his say.

'Look.' He held out his phone so she could see the video of June's wallpaper. 'I bet she knocked it over on purpose,' he said. 'I've done a quick scroll, and this is all we got. Yesterday, I spoke to the Hills who live next door. They haven't seen anyone hanging around. Not this week, not last week.'

'Maybe they missed him,' said Kate, pushing his phone away from her face.

'Highly unlikely. They walk their dog every morning at six. Through the reserve and back around the street to their house. If anyone had been there, they would have seen him.' He paused as he pocketed his phone. 'You know what I think?'

'Tell me.'

'She's lonely, and she's scared,' he said. 'I get that, and I feel sorry for her. Truly. But she loves the attention, and she doesn't understand she's wasting valuable police time. You need to talk to her.'

'And say what?' asked Kate. 'You want me to tell her she's seeing things and not to bother calling us again.'

'I wouldn't put it like that, but something along those lines, yes.'

'Let's do it together then shall we,' said Kate. She started across the street, turning back when he didn't follow her. 'Come on. What are you waiting for? Telling little old ladies, they're seeing things is as much a part of the job as catching crooks.'

When they returned to the house, they found a man kneeling beside June's chair. He stood up when he saw them.

'I'm Dan Forrester. I'm staying next door.'

This man might be the same age as Geoffrey Scott, but where Dr Scott had let himself go, Dan was broad shouldered. He had a flat belly and tanned complexion, he looked healthy, in the prime of life. Taller than Tony, his grey hair was cut short around his face, and he had the sort of smile which made you want to sit down and chat. Kate thought he was the best-looking man she had ever seen.

'I came over to see if I could help.'

'I'm DSS Kate Sutton,' she said. They shook hands. 'This is DC Tony Hunter.'

'Find anyone?' he asked.

'No,' said Tony. 'This is the second time we've been.'

Kate knelt beside June. 'How are you feeling?'

'Better.' She looked up, first at Dan, then Tony. 'I'm sorry to make such a fuss. I haven't had this many visitors since Arthur died.'

'You got a better look at him this time,' said Kate. 'Describe him for me.'

'He was behind the tree when I pulled back the curtain. I looked down as he looked up and we saw each other. We both got such a fright. I hid.'

'This time, you saw his face?' prompted Kate.

June nodded. 'I did. That's the funny thing. I know him from somewhere. I've been trying to remember, but it won't come.'

'Was he wearing the same clothes as last time?'

'He was wearing army trousers, the camouflage ones, but it was the same hoodie.'

'Anything else?'

'I already told you about the beard. He's got brown eyes and dark hair.'

Kate, keen to relieve the pressure on her knees, stood up and stretched her legs. 'Tony, ask Denise to come and talk to June. It would be good to have a composite.'

'What's a composite?' asked June.

'You've seen it on TV. Denise is a police artist. With your help, she'll put together a drawing which looks like the man you saw.'

'I'll do anything.'

'Do you mind if Tony resets the camera in case he comes back?'

Her hand flew to her mouth. 'Do you think he will?'

'It's possible,' replied Kate.

'Then do it. I promise I won't knock it over next time.'

After Tony had gone upstairs, Dan moved towards the door. 'We're close by if you need us.' He nodded to Kate and left, his exit leaving a huge man-sized hole in the room. Her sigh was involuntary.

'He's very good looking, isn't he?' said June quietly.

'He is indeed,' said Kate.

'He's single and he's not gay, in case you were wondering.'

'I wasn't, but good to know,' said Kate, trying not to smile.

'You could do a lot worse,' said June.

Kate put her hands on her hips and stared down at her. 'Are you trying to fix me up?'

'Maybe,' said June. She winked.

Tony thumped back down the stairs and stood impatiently in the doorway. 'Ready?'

'Ready.' On her way out, she noticed the golf club was still leaning against the table. 'Do you want me to put this away?' she asked June.

'No, dear, I'll do it.' June got up from her chair and waved. 'Thank you.'

'Bye,' said Kate.

They waited, listening as once again June locked the door behind them.

# CHAPTER
# SEVENTEEN

MICHELLE PARKER HAD NEVER LIKED Dan. He had irritated her from the very first moment she met him. Mature enough to understand that beautiful people can't help the way they look any more than a genius can help being smart, Michelle's dislike was born of her own inadequacy. She had lived her whole life in Martinborough, and when he was around, she felt like a lesser human being. Her inferiority was personal.

Because Dan Forrester was a man of the world. An international man of mystery, Geoffrey had once called him to his face. They had both laughed, but Michelle knew Dan was only being polite.

He was sophisticated in a way she would never, could never, be. Not that he ever did or said anything to make the disparities obvious; his innate good manners wouldn't allow that.

Three years ago, he had filled in at the practice, so Geoffrey and Ava could take the holiday that Ava had insisted they take. She coped then by telling herself that it was only for a couple of weeks, after which, she would never have to see him again. She held her tongue, smiling when he smiled, agreeing with everything he said. At night she went home and screamed her rage into a pillow.

Now, here he was. Back in her life, on the day after Geoffrey's funeral. It was the worst of all possible circumstances.

She welcomed him with gritted teeth and a forced smile. 'You remember Lily, our receptionist?'

'I do. You were on work experience the last time I was here.' His smile was sickeningly genuine. 'It's good to see they made you a permanent member of the team.' Michelle nearly gagged when the silly girl blushed as she stammered a greeting.

'And this is Alex McLeod,' said Michelle. She swivelled around to the clean-shaven young man standing behind her. 'Alex is our practice nurse. How long have you been here now?'

'Nine months,' said Alex. He spoke with a soft Scottish burr. 'I'm from Edinburgh originally, but I met a Kiwi lass, and here I am.'

'Which part are you from?' Dan asked.

Alex's face lit up. 'Costorphine, do you know it?'

'I was there last summer. I used to run through the park and up to the tower in the mornings before work.'

'Then you probably ran past my mother. She walks her dog there in the mornings.'

'It's a small world,' said Dan.

Of course he ran past Alex's mother, thought Michelle. What part of the world hadn't he run past someone's mother? She moved between them, consciously breaking the connection. 'Your first patient is booked for nine o'clock.' she said. 'You're working in Geoffrey's room. It's pretty much the same, but I do need to update you on some things before you start.' She was already walking away when she said this. Dan exchanged raised eyebrows with Alex, then turned and followed her.

'His old papers are in the bottom drawer of his desk.' She stood just inside the door, pointing at the drawer as if he'd never seen a desk before. 'Your log-in hasn't changed, but you'll need a new password. The Post-it notes on the bottom of your screen are messages from patients. It's up to you whether you call them back.'

She frowned. 'A solicitor called Aiden Cooper has phoned a couple of times. He won't talk to me. Insists on talking to a doctor. His number is on your desk.' She drew herself up to her full height. 'This time, remember to fill in the codes at the end of a consultation. It makes the audit so much easier and it's more work for me if you don't. I don't see why I should make up for your shortcomings.'

Having got the matter off her chest, she left.

Geoffrey's room was the same as consulting rooms the world over. A desk, three chairs, a computer, an examination couch, various instruments and on the bookshelves, papers and old medical magazines lying in disorderly piles next to out-dated photographs of family members. Framed degrees plus or minus a painting or photograph of the university attended to get those degrees, the only decorations.

As soon as he sat down and tucked his feet under the desk, Dan felt the walls closing in on him. How anyone could work in the same room, day after day, year after year, was beyond him. Geoffrey had laughed in disbelief when Dan told him how he felt. He was equally bewildered about Dan's chosen way of life: travelling the world, never staying in one place long enough to really get to know anyone. The different attitudes had caused a rift in their friendship, one they never openly discussed but which was there just the same.

Dan remembered yesterday's funeral and the town hall full of people coming to pay their respects to his friend. That so many people had come to honour the man was a testament to a life well lived. Or was it? How do you judge a life? Dan was at peace with the likelihood that his own funeral, if he had one, would be a paltry affair. His body buried, sans mourners, in an unmarked grave in some corner of a foreign cemetery—if he was lucky.

He went through the rigamarole of creating a new password, logged into the computer and brought up the morning's appointments. A quick glance confirmed his suspicions. The same names from three years ago were still here, most likely with the same complaints. It was eight fifty-five. He had a few minutes to spare and decided to call the lawyer.

'Cooper, Collins and Associates,' answered the receptionist.

'Dr Dan Forrester from Martinborough Health, Aiden Cooper asked me to call.'

'I'm sorry, but Mr Cooper is in court today. Can one of the other partners help you?'

'I don't know. I'm returning his call.'

There was a pause while keys were tapped. 'He'll be in court today and all next week. Can I take your number and get him to call you back?'

He gave her the number for his cell phone and was about to hang up when something occurred to him. 'Tell me, what sort of law does Cooper Collins practice?'

'Our clients generally have a health background,' said the receptionist. 'Doctors, dentists mainly. We act for the defence society.'

'I see,' he said. 'Thank you.' He sat for a moment, staring at the monitor. Had a patient made a complaint? Is that why the lawyer insisted on speaking to a doctor? If that was the case, then he felt sorry for his friend. Geoffrey, meticulous about his work, would have been mortified, if alive.

The desk phone buzzed. Dan hit the speaker button.

'Mr Jones is here, Dr Forrester.'

'Thank you Lily. Send him in.'

After that, his morning passed quickly. A steady procession of run-of-the-mill coughs and summer colds, medication and diabetes reviews: a nasty case of shingles in an otherwise fit young mother raised alarm bells, so Dan sent her for blood tests, prescribed anti-virals and organised to see her again the following week to monitor progress.

After the last patient left, he checked with Alex to make sure he didn't need him, then let Lily know when he'd be back. His soul lifted as soon as he walked out the door. Usually, he went for a run at lunchtime. Last night, after the funeral Ava had asked if he would come back to the house instead.

'The police want to interview me again,' she said. 'They won't tell me what it's about, but this will be the third time.'

'They'll be tidying up loose ends.'

'I don't care. Please say you'll be there.'

'Of course I'll be there. You're my cousin. I'd do anything for you.'

# CHAPTER
# EIGHTEEN

IT WAS day five after the murder and finally Kate had a lead. It was too soon to call it a breakthrough, but it might be and that was all that mattered. Not to mention the boost in her mood when she watched Tony's face as they replayed June's video back at the Incident Room. Slowed right down, from the very beginning, frame by frame. First shock, which was followed by disbelief and then finally and only after he'd seen it three times, did he grudgingly concede, that he'd been wrong.

June's watcher was there for all to see. Kate made sure everyone saw him, several times. The old woman's state of mind was no longer in question. They all saw the man she had described standing exactly where she said he had been standing, under the Rimu tree. Vindicated in front of everyone, she graciously accepted Tony's mumbled apology.

There was, however, a problem. The watcher had been caught as he was turning away from the camera, the edge of his hoodie obscuring his face. From the tiny bit of him she could see, Kate surmised he was younger than fifty. He had dark hair, and he did have a beard. He was probably white, but she couldn't be sure. There was just enough to send the image through the facial recognition software. If he was on the police database, they might get a match and his details, though privately, Kate wasn't hopeful of a result.

The video wasn't the only good news that morning, there were other results. The report from the accountants had come through. Geoffrey Scott's practice income barely covered the wages and the overheads at the health centre.

'I thought doctors earned a lot more than that,' she said to Byron. He was the senior accountant at a firm in Masterton.

'They do in the cities. They also work fewer hours and take less responsibility. I hope Martinborough appreciated him.'

'His funeral was packed,' she said. 'Standing room only at the town hall.'

'Well, there you go. If you turn over to the next page, you'll see he also had the Scott Family Trust to fall back on.'

Kate flipped several pages to get to the bottom line. Ava would be inheriting a healthy five million dollars. That was before any money from the sale of the practice was added to the total. At thirty-eight, she was set up for life if she was careful and didn't spend too much. This left Kate wondering whether five million dollars and an old house was sufficient motive for murder. Having met the woman, her gut instinct told her it wasn't, but she couldn't discount the possibility altogether. She reminded herself that people have killed for less.

As is often the way, the analysis of Geoffrey's phone records and laptops, landed on her computer at the same time as the financial report. It had helped that neither Geoffrey nor Ava used social media. Although Ava had recently purchased a domain name, *AvaScottPaintings.com.* There was no website attached to it. One thing stood out in the phone records. It was the number of texts Geoffrey sent to his practice manager, Michelle. He sent them at all hours of the day and night and usually received an immediate reply.

She looked at Tony who was sitting on the other side of her desk. 'It fits with the feeling I had when I spoke to her,' she said. 'They were closer than your average boss and employee.'

'Do you think they were, you know… ?' He winked.

'Possibly. She claimed he promised her a lump sum when he sold the practice. She dressed it up as payment for her hard work setting up the computer systems.'

'Do bosses do that?'

'Not that I'm aware.'

'Now that the sale's definitely going ahead, will she still get the money?'

'There's no mention of Michelle or a payment to her in his will,' said Kate. 'Ava is the sole beneficiary.'

'Maybe Michelle found out and that's why she was upset.'

'Could be. We won't know until we know.' She closed the file on her computer. 'What have you got for me from the funeral?'

'The guys haven't finished analysing it yet. So far, though, everyone checks out. Except for this man.' He passed Kate an 8 x 10 print. The photo had been taken a long way from its subject. In the enlargement, his features were grainy and indistinct. 'This person doesn't match to any of the names we took.'

'He's wearing a black hoodie,' said Kate. 'Remind you of anyone?'

'We won't know until we know, will we?' He smiled and Kate smiled back.

'I'm off to see Ava Scott. I want to show her the footage from the CCTV. While I'm gone, get the image of June's watcher blown up and put on posters. Send the troops door to door to see if anyone knows him. Oh, and get the media team to write a press release asking for any information about him. Make it very clear that he's a person of interest and not a suspect.'

'Will do.' He paused. 'I forgot to tell you. Bruce Murphy called yesterday after you left. He's had to go to Auckland for business. He asked if you could come to the house on Saturday instead of today. I said that wouldn't be a problem. I hope that's all right.'

Her face fell. 'Saturday's my day off.'

'I'm sorry,' said Tony. 'That's my bad for not checking the roster. I'll send him an email and explain.'

She could see from his face that he wasn't in the least bit sorry. It was payback for making him work late. 'I don't mind. Leave it,' she said. 'I need to get it out of the way.'

'Oh, and boss,' said Tony.

'Yes?'

'He said any time after eleven.'

# CHAPTER
# NINETEEN

DAN SHOWED Kate into the living room. Ava didn't get up. She stayed perched on the edge of the ancient sofa, her hands between her knees, looking, Kate thought, like a little bird. She had changed her t-shirt, but the dungarees were the same ones she'd been wearing at the Murphy's.

Thankfully, the French doors were open. The stale air Kate associated with her last visit was gone, replaced by the gentlest of breezes carrying with it, the heady smell of roses from the garden. She sat down in an old armchair, hoping Dan didn't notice when she sank unexpectedly into its depths. If he did, he didn't react as he moved to sit beside Ava.

'It was nice of you to come over to see June this morning,' said Kate. She dug around in her handbag and brought out her notebook.

'What's this about June?'

'You were asleep. June saw a man across the road. She called the police, and I went over to see if I could help.'

'What man?'

Dan, his eyebrows raised, deflected the question to Kate.

'He was hanging around the reserve,' she explained. 'She's seen him there before and we're following it up.'

'What was he doing there?'

'We don't know the answer to that yet?' said Kate.

'Is it the killer?'

'I don't know,' said Kate.

'You mean it could be. How many times has she seen him?'

'This morning would be the third time.'

'Third? That's awful. What does he look like?'

'This is what we've got so far,' said Kate. She passed her phone across to Ava who squinted at the image, before showing it to Dan.

'It's a man in a hoodie. It could be anyone.'

'I agree,' said Kate. 'It's a start.'

'What if he's the killer?' asked Ava. 'What then? Do I get an armed guard? Three times is a lot. Why would he come back so many times?'

'Let's leave the police to do their job, shall we?' said Dan, handing the phone back to Kate.

'Easy for you to say. I'm here alone during the day.'

'Go to your studio then.'

'I will.'

'Sorry to interrupt but there are some matters which I still need your help with.' Kate held up her phone. 'Do you mind if I record this?'

Ava shook her head.

'Has the sale of the practice been finalised yet?'

'What does that have to do with anything?'

'It's background information.'

'It has, as a matter of fact.' She nodded at Dan. 'The final settlement goes through next week, Friday.'

'What will happen to the staff?' asked Kate.

Ava looked puzzled, then shrugged. 'I assume the new owners will keep them on.'

'Does that include Michelle?'

'Probably. How would I know?'

'When I spoke to Michelle, she said Geoffrey had promised her a lump sum payment for services she had provided. He promised her this money from the sale of the practice. Did he mention anything to you about it?'

Ava stared at her for a beat longer than necessary. She recovered and straightened her shoulders. 'I don't think so.'

'Is that something he would do?'

'How would I know? Sorry,' she said. 'Let me get this straight. An employee says my husband was going to give her money, and you believe her?'

'Why would she say it if it wasn't true?' asked Kate.

'Duh,' said Ava. 'I wonder!'

'Perhaps Michelle was more than an employee?'

'Perhaps she was,' replied Ava.

Dan stunned looked at Ava. 'You mean … Geoffrey and Michelle were… ?'

Ava threw him a pitying glance.

'How long have you known?' asked Kate.

'Why? What does it have to do with the investigation?'

'Your husband was in a relationship with another woman, and you knew,' said Kate.

'It doesn't mean I killed him.'

'So why not tell me?'

'Pride, I suppose,' said Ava. She looked at Kate, staring her down. 'You, of all people, should understand.'

Dan gasped and laid a restraining hand on Ava's knee. She pushed it away. The red-hot heat of embarrassment, stained Kate's face. Of course, Matt's infidelity would be common knowledge in such a small community. She swallowed, composing herself, bringing every ounce of professionalism to her next question. 'When did their affair start?'

Folding her arms across her chest, Ava glared at her.

Kate waited.

'When I started painting again,' she said eventually. 'Nine months ago.'

'Did you say anything?'

'What do you think?'

Kate waited again.

'I didn't see the point,' said Ava. 'Is there anything else? Because I'm done with this.' She moved to stand up, stopping when Kate raised a hand.

'Actually, there is. I want you to look at this video.'

She opened her laptop and turned it around so Ava and Dan could see the screen. 'I've slowed it down to make it easier to understand,' she said. 'Note the date and time in the top corner.'

She studied Ava's face as she watched the video of her car passing the camera on State Highway 2 between Featherston and the turn-off to Martinborough. The time stamp said it was 3:31 PM on Sunday.

Kate pressed pause and brought up a photo of Ava, her face clearly visible behind the wheel. 'You told me that you were at the studio all day.'

'I forgot. I left for a short time.'

Kate started the video again. She sped it up, then slowed it down to show Ava driving her car back towards Featherston, this time in the other direction. 'You turned around and returned at 3:36 PM,' said Kate. 'Why was that?'

'Because the tube of Cadmium Red I was going home to get, rolled out from under the passenger seat. I must have dropped it in the rush to pack up on Friday night. I didn't tell you because I didn't think it was important.'

'On the two previous occasions when I asked if you left the studio, you said you hadn't. Yet, here's proof that you did.'

'I didn't go home. Surely that is the point. I left to get some paint. I found it and I turned around and went back to my studio,' said Ava. 'Big deal.'

'Is there anything else you have forgotten to tell me?'

'Nothing.'

Kate waited.

'I didn't kill my husband because he was screwing his practice manager, if that's what you're getting at. Because let me spell it out to you, Detective. I didn't care then.' She stared hard at Kate, her lips set in a tight line. 'I don't care now. Our marriage was over a long time ago.' She looked at Dan. 'Don't you look so shocked. You knew.' She turned back to Kate. 'Is there anything else because I'm tired, and Dan has to get back to the surgery.'

Kate reached across and turned off her phone. 'You've been very helpful. I should be getting the results of those tests back this afternoon.'

'What's this?' asked Dan.

'The pathologist thinks Geoffrey had dementia,' said Ava. 'I think she's the one with the problem myself.'

'What sort of dementia?'

'Enough. Stop!' Ava held up her hands. 'I'd like you to leave now.'

Kate levered herself out of the old chair, slid her laptop into her bag and slung it over her shoulder. 'Thank you for your time, Mrs Scott.' She saw herself out.

# CHAPTER
# TWENTY

IT WAS SATURDAY MORNING. Her alarm trilled annoyingly beside her head. Kate yawned and reached over to turn it off. She closed her eyes again, hoping the scratchy feeling beneath her eyelids would go away before she interviewed Bruce.

Thanks to her father, she'd barely slept. When he wasn't snoring, he was turning on all the lights before he stumbled to the bathroom. She'd counted five flushes before she finally dropped off to sleep. Only to be woken when he came into her room and prodded her leg. She opened one bleary eye and looked at the shadowy outline at the end of her bed.

'You're kidding. Right?'

'I love you,' he said. His words were slurred.

She sat up and turned on the light. She was relieved to see him wearing pyjamas. She took the glass out of his hands and sniffed the contents. As she suspected—straight gin. 'It's four-thirty in the morning Dad. Go back to bed.'

'We need to talk,' he said, swaying sideways. 'I love you. You know that don't you? I didn't leave you and your mother because I didn't love you. I left because she and you,' he pointed a shaky finger at her, 'you never asked me to stay.'

Flinging back the covers, she got out of bed, and held out her hand.

Reluctantly, he gave her the glass. Scooting past him, she tipped the contents down the sink in the bathroom.

'Now go back to bed,' she said.

'But—'

'I don't want to hear it.'

'You're tough, Kate. Has anyone ever told you that? Because if they haven't, they should.' He swayed again as he pushed himself off her bed. 'You're just like your mother.'

'Go back to your own room and go to sleep.'

'We're alike you and me.'

That stopped her. 'We are not.'

'Take a look in the mirror sometime and ask yourself how much you love your job.' He paused, a leary grin on his face. 'Ask yourself why Matt really left you. Between you and me,' he beckoned her closer, 'it wasn't because of Carla.'

'How would you know. You weren't here.'

'I know you. You may not like it, but you feel the same way about your work as I do about taking pictures. It's a drug and you're an addict.'

Outside a blackbird, the first of the early risers, started its morning song. A grey tinge infused Kate's bedroom with light. Her father's eyes drooped, his head sagged onto his chest. She caught him just as he was sliding off the bed, and supporting him around his waist, she walked him into the spare room and dropped him on the bed. He grumbled, and rolled over, instantly asleep.

It took ten minutes for Kate to quell her outrage at his comments and breathe normally. Another ten minutes to relax enough to fall asleep.

An hour later, she woke to her alarm. She lay there, listening to him snore, practising how to ask him to leave, then she hauled herself out of bed.

# CHAPTER
# TWENTY-ONE

CLEAN-SHAVEN, his well-cut hair combed back over the top of his head, and dressed in expensive, designer casual wear Bruce greeted her at the door to his home. Bright-eyed and brimming with energy, he was the epitome of a successful man. He made Kate feel underpaid and dowdy.

He led her into the library where his laptop was open on the table, a pile of papers beside it. As before, her eyes drifted to the window. It was nearly harvest time and since her last visit, the vines had been covered in nets to keep the birds from eating the ripening grapes. Instead of rows of green, white lines stretched beneath her, like bandages rolling down the hill.

'I've got a Teams meeting in twenty minutes,' said Bruce. Startled she turned away from the view. His huge watch on his left wrist, rattled as he made a show of checking the time. 'Coffee?' he asked.

Kate shook her head. 'Thank you but no. This won't take long.' She sat opposite him at the table and took out her notebook.

He spoke before she could ask her first question. 'To save us both a lot of time, I was here all day on Sunday. Working. For my sins. Mimi was here too, as you know. We spoke to the girls at 4:00 PM for about an hour.' He leaned back his fingers interlaced on the table in front of him.

'Thank you.' She said this intentionally slowly, then paused, not looking at him, giving herself time to regain control of the interview. 'I'll check Mimi's phone before I go.'

'I've printed off the minutes from my Teams meetings for that afternoon.' Bruce took a single sheet of paper from the top of the pile next to his laptop and slid it across the table. There was a list of times, and beside each one, the names of the people who had joined each of the meetings. It only took a quick glance to see that he'd been busy until four o'clock. He had restarted his meetings at six, stopping for the day at eight. It was an impressive work schedule.

'I've checked,' he said. 'Everyone is fine with you contacting them.'

'Very helpful, thank you.' She folded the paper in half and moved it to one side. 'Describe your relationship with Dr Scott,' she said. 'I understand you were old friends.'

'Since school,' he replied.

'You stayed close?'

'Lately, not so much. We saw each other socially, but this was more because Ava and Mimi are friends. He was busy with patients, and I'm one of those sad bastards whose business takes up every hour of every day. As you can see.'

'You travel a lot with your work, don't you?'

'Too much. And before you say anything, it's not as glamorous as you might think.'

'I understand it's quite tiring. Why haven't you moved to Wellington, to be closer to the airport?'

'And leave Martinborough? Never! I owe this town too much. I'm one of those people who believe in giving back to the community. In fact, as soon as you find the killer and this ghastly business is over, I'm building a brand, new sculpture park.' He got up and walked to the window, beckoning her to follow. 'There,' he said, pointing to a hill on the horizon.

'Where?'

'See that ridge past the line of trees on the other side of the river,' he said. 'It's called Hector's Rise. We've owned it for ten years and never known what to do with it until now. I'm donating it to the council. I'm going to ask Ava to curate the artwork, when she's recovered from this awful business.'

He paused.

'We're hoping to open in March next year in time for the Wellington Festival of the Arts. It will be something positive to bring people back to Martinborough.'

'That's incredibly generous,' she said. She meant it. 'Martinborough is lucky to have you.' Before he could say anything else, she returned to her seat, leaving him no choice but to do the same.

'We're calling it the Geoffrey Scott Memorial Sculpture Park.'

'How fitting. The man I knew was quite humble, but I'm sure he would be honoured. When did you say you last spoke to him?'

He smiled then cleared his throat. 'If I remember correctly, he and Ava came for dinner last winter so that would be eight months ago. I had business associates from Australia staying, and I thought they would enjoy each other's company.'

'Did they?'

'Actually, Geoffrey was quite rude. He'd got it into his head that because they owned a winery, they had something to do with the alcohol problems among Aborigines. He wouldn't let it go. In the end, I had to ask Ava to take him home.'

'That must have been embarrassing,' said Kate. 'Was he usually like that with people he didn't know?'

'That's what was so odd. The Geoffrey I grew up with had perfect manners. His parents were the same and he went to a private school where they beat courtesy into the boys with a stick.'

'Did you speak to him again?'

'Only in passing.'

'You're the head of the business association,' she said. 'You hear things. Did he behave that way with anyone else?'

'You think that's why he was murdered?'

'It's possible,' she said.

'There were some unfortunate happenings at the health centre— Geoffrey talking out of turn in front of people in the waiting room. That happened a few times.'

'Can you remember the names of the people he spoke to?'

He shook his head. 'Let me think on that and get back to you.'

'Of course.' She took the enhanced photo of June's watcher out of her folder and slid it across the table. 'Do you recognise this man?'

Bruce slipped on his glasses and studied it. 'Is he your suspect?'

'June Whittaker saw him standing outside the Scott's house before Geoffrey was murdered.'

He picked up the photo to take a better look. 'When was it taken?'

'Early yesterday morning,' she said. 'We have a camera set up on her property. June has a panoramic view of the Scott's property from her house, and she's been invaluable. She's starting to remember more details from Sunday.'

Bruce looked up and shook his head. 'Sorry, I don't know him, and I know most people around here.' He slid the photo back across the table and checked his watch. 'I don't mean to rush you, but if there's nothing else, I have some preparation to do before my meeting.'

'That's all I wanted to ask. Thank you,' she said. 'Unless there's something you'd like to ask me?'

Bruce cocked his head to one side. 'I don't think there is.'

'If Mimi's home, I'll check her phone before I go.'

'I should have said before, but she's in Wellington for the day.'

'No problem. It's just a formality. I'll text her and arrange a time to meet up.'

Bruce moved to stand, but she held up her hand.

'You're busy,' she said. 'I can see myself out.'

He sat down again, his eyes already focused on his screen as she reached the door.

'Jonathon,' she heard him say, his tone suddenly upbeat. 'It's been a while! You're—'

The door shut, sealing off the sound of his conversation.

# CHAPTER
# TWENTY-TWO

IT WAS SEEING the ice cream signs that made Kate realise she hadn't eaten anything all day. Hungry and hot, she parked her car, got out and walked across the grass, past the war memorial in the middle of the square, to the truck parked on the side of the road.

Any other Saturday and the square would have been full of picnicking families and visitors to the town, everyone sitting in the shade of the hundred-year-old oak trees. The only other time she remembered it being this quiet was after Juliette disappeared.

Eighteen and a recent arrival from France, Juliette Bisson worked six days a week in a vineyard, with the intention of earning enough money to fund the rest of her travels. Unlike the other student workers, she rarely went out at night, which meant she wasn't well-known in the village. Every night at ten o'clock, she phoned her father in Robion, a small town in the South of France, to let him know she was alive and well. One Friday night in February three years ago, she never made the call. The next day, her father contacted the police station in Masterton and asked if someone would check on his daughter. No one did.

He called the station every day for the next five days. Getting no response, he called the French Ambassador in Wellington, who called the Minister of Foreign Affairs, who called the Police Commissioner, who called the Masterton Station. That afternoon, a police officer went to the house and found the doors open, and the place deserted. There was no sign of a disturbance and no sign of Juliette. The only thing missing from her belongings was her phone. Six weeks later and not having found a body despite an extensive search and after pleas to the public for sightings hadn't resulted in any leads, they couldn't even be sure she was dead.

The investigation was scaled back, and Kate drove Juliette's father to the airport to put him on a plane back to France. At the entrance to customs, he made her promise she would find his daughter, the hope that she was still be alive, burning bright in his eyes when she said goodbye.

Six months later, he died of a suspected heart attack without ever finding out what had happened to his only child. It was Kate's first major investigation as a detective and the failure to find Juliette still haunted her, especially when she came to Martinborough.

Luckily, the ice cream truck was a memory-free zone. It hadn't been here three years ago.

'Salted caramel, double scoop, if there's any left?' she asked the server.

'That's a good one,' said the young woman, looking down at her. 'Two weeks ago, there was a queue all the way back to the war memorial. Today, no one. The sooner the police do the job they're paid to do, the better.' Kate smiled and tapped her card on the machine to pay, then she walked over to a picnic table to eat her ice cream in peace.

'Hey boss, that looks good.' Sophie slung a leg over the seat opposite Kate, sat down and pushed her sunglasses to the top of her head.

'You should get one.'

'Can't. I'm in uniform,' said Sophie.

'I promise not to tell,' said Kate. She took in the slicked-back hair and the blue shirt stuck to the young woman's sides. 'When did you last have something to drink?'

'An hour ago,' she said, waggling an empty water bottle. 'I stopped for a refill when I saw you, so I thought I'd say Hi and see how you were getting on.'

The kindness in her voice almost melted Kate's heart. 'I was on my way to see Michelle Parker when I decided to get an ice-cream. How about you? Any response to the leaflets yet?'

'Nope. But I'll keep trying. Someone will know him.' She replaced her sunglasses and stood up. 'Nice chatting.'

'And you,' said Kate. She licked her ice cream and watched the best young officer in the station show the photo of their suspect to the woman in the ice cream truck. And get her water bottle refilled at the same time. Licking the drips of salted caramel running down the back of her hand, she wiped off the stickiness with a tissue and threw the last of her cone into a rubbish bin. It's amazing how a little sugar and a friendly face can lift the spirits, she thought as she walked back to her car.

# CHAPTER
# TWENTY-THREE

MICHELLE LIVED on the opposite side of town from the Scott's, in a row of single-story flats, each with its own low-wire fence, wooden gate, and concrete path to the front door. Michelle's battered Toyota was parked outside. As she drew up behind it, Kate saw a curtain in the window of the flat next door to Michelle's twitch and then fall back into place. Neighbourhood Watch in action.

She must have been waiting for her because the door opened without Kate having to knock. Michelle stood to the side in the narrow entrance to allow Kate to squeeze past and enter the living area. A tiny kitchen at one end was separated from the living room by a tall bench with two stools underneath it. The colour scheme, pale lemon and cream, suited the small space. Cream linen curtains hung on either side of a glass sliding door that led out to a paved area and beyond it, a dusty green lawn stretched to an unpainted wooden fence.

'I'm sorry to bother you on a Saturday,' said Kate, after Michelle gestured to her to take a seat.

'I'm not doing anything, but I thought I'd already answered all your questions,' said Michelle, sitting opposite her. A grey cat walked in, jumped up, turned a circle, and settled in her lap to sleep. 'This is Gertie,' said Michelle, running her hand over her back. A loud purr cut through the silence.

'She sounds happy,' said Kate. She took out her notebook, opened it to a fresh page and filled in the details. 'You said Dr Scott's last holiday was three years ago.'

'That's right.'

'Did he take any breaks? I only ask because being a GP in a small town must have been quite stressful.'

'Geoffrey managed his workload so he didn't get burnt out if that's what you're getting at,' said Michelle. 'We went away to conferences at the weekends. I suppose you could call them breaks.'

'You both went? Why was that?

'His experience as a sole rural practitioner put him in demand as a speaker. I went to talk to the other practice managers. Also, I helped him manage the technical side of his presentations. Geoffrey wasn't good with computers.'

'Did Ava go to any of these conferences?'

Michelle laugh-snorted. 'She hated that kind of thing, so no.'

Without looking up, Kate asked the next question very carefully. 'Did you ever share a room while you were away?'

For a moment, she thought Michelle would deny anything had happened between them, but then she relaxed, stroking Gertie's fur with one hand. 'He was going to leave her.' She said this quietly but with dignity.

'Did you love him?'

'Yes, and he loved me.' Her voice wavered slightly, but she held back her tears.

'Does anyone else know?' asked Kate.

'He said we had to wait before we told people.' She paused, and then the words rushed out. 'We were at a conference in Queenstown nine months ago. I was tired of waiting for him to make the first move and I only reserved one room. The hotel was fully booked when we got there, so there was nothing he could do.'

'You trapped him.'

'I did. And it was wonderful. He had so many plans for us. We were going to leave Martinborough and travel. He wanted to show me all the places he'd been to when he was young. Then, when we got back, we were going to set up a practice somewhere new, maybe try to have children.' The look of surprise on Kate's face made her laugh. 'How old do you think I am?'

'Sorry,' said Kate. 'It's me. Not you. My kids have left home. The thought of having a baby at our age feels strange.'

'I'm thirty-nine. How old are you?'

'Older, forty-three. Sorry, I just assumed.'

'I know I look old, but I'm still young enough to have babies. Geoffrey always wanted children. He was devastated when Ava refused to have any. But if we couldn't have our own, we were going to adopt.'

'Sounds like you had it all mapped out,' said Kate.

'I thought so,' said Michelle.

'Until when?' asked Kate.

Michelle shuddered, waking Gertie, who jumped off her lap and stretched, arching her back before walking past Kate on her way to the kitchen. 'What does it matter now? I'm never going to have children.'

'You said that he promised you money. I'm sorry to be the one to tell you, but there was nothing about this in his will.'

A single tear dropped onto her lap. 'That's not his fault. He didn't have time to change it.'

'What will you do?'

'What can I do? I've got no money, a big mortgage and selling this place would leave me with nothing. I've got no friends, no family,' she said, tears welling up in her eyes. 'Geoffrey was the only person who ever loved me, for me.'

She wept then, in loud gasping sobs. Kate sat very still, knowing that Michelle needed her presence. Not poorly chosen words said in a clumsy attempt to make her feel better. For now, at least, that was impossible. If the last year had taught her anything, she had learned that grief, like water, has to run its course, and the more freely it can do that, the sooner it goes away. Gradually, the sobs eased, and Michelle fumbled a tissue from a box on the coffee table, blew her nose and wiped her eyes.

'Sorry.' She looked at Kate. 'For nine months I felt like a normal woman if you can understand what I mean. I was like everyone else, I had a relationship. He loved me, and I loved him. I didn't care that he was married; I know that sounds awful, but I was happy and I really,

really didn't care.' She pressed the tissue into each eye, then tossed it on the table and pulled another out of the box. 'I hate being alone.'

'What are you going to do?' Kate asked the question again.

Michelle blinked. 'Stay here and work. There's nothing else I can do.'

'I don't believe that,' said Kate. 'You're a professional woman. You've been a practice manager for over ten years; you've presented at conferences. I bet you've put something away for a rainy day. You're not the type who fritters away everything you earn. And besides, thirty-nine is young enough to start over.'

'So you're a life coach now?' snapped Michelle.

Kate froze. Then a moment's reflection told her Michelle was right. Her police persona had slipped; the non-judgmental, non-interfering, live and let live face that she put on when she joined the force. In its place, an unqualified agony aunt she didn't recognise. She'd snuck in probably because she was tired and because the woman's loneliness had triggered something inside her. A need to take action, perhaps, to be in control, after sitting back for too long, letting other people's dramas dictate her future.

'My apologies,' said Kate. She changed her position to sit side on to Michelle. 'Not long now. You said there hadn't been any complaints about Dr Scott?'

'What I said,' replied Michelle, 'was that Geoffrey had the usual issues you get in a people-facing job.'

That was definitely not what she had said, but Kate let it go. 'I understand there were several occasions when Dr Scott was rude to patients. He also talked about their problems in public. Are they what you would call usual issues?'

Michelle leaned forward. 'Who told you?'

'Is it true?'

'Once,' she admitted. 'It was at the end of the day. There was hardly anyone there, and Geoffrey may have let slip things that were better said in private. He apologised.'

'The Health and Disability Complaints Commissioner wasn't involved?'

'He apologised.' Michelle's face was set.

'Tell me again where you were on Sunday afternoon,' said Kate.

'I know I said I was here, but I was wrong. I got the days muddled. I actually went to the movies.'

'Oh? What did you see?' asked Kate.

'*Anyone But You.*' It's pure fantasy, but I like Glen Powell.'

'Which cinema?' asked Kate.

'The Roxy in Masterton, the four-thirty session.'

Kate wrote down the details. It would be easy enough to check. She took the photo of June's watcher out of her folder and passed it to Michelle. 'Have you seen this person before?'

'It's not a great shot, is it,' she said after she'd looked at it for a while. 'I've seen him before but can't remember where.'

'Take your time,' said Kate.

Michelle opened her mouth to speak, then closed it again and passed the photo back to her. 'Sorry, I can't remember. It could even have been someone who looks like him. Why do you want to know?'

'He was seen outside the Scott's house. Once before Geoffrey's murder and twice after,' said Kate.

'June saw him, didn't she? ' said Michelle. 'She was always spying on them. She used to pretend she wasn't, but Geoffrey caught her looking down on him from the window in her spare bedroom. She was the reason he didn't let me come to his house. He was worried she'd tell Ava.' She picked up the photo again. 'Isn't it annoying when you know you know something, but it won't come? Can I keep this?'

'Please,' said Kate. If only Michelle could remember. It was frustrating to be so close and still so far away. Suddenly, she wanted to be outside in the fresh air, free and away from this tiny room filled with cheap furniture and broken dreams. She closed her notebook, put it in her bag and thanked Michelle for her time, adding that she would see herself out.

And stepped into the warm sunshine under a clear blue sky. There was still time to enjoy what remained of her day off. She remembered Jim and figured that if she hurried, she might just make it back before he got too drunk to hold a decent conversation. Disregarding the curious glances from Michelle's neighbours, Kate got in her car and headed for home.

# CHAPTER
# TWENTY-FOUR

THE SOUND of men laughing greeted Kate when she opened the door.

'Hey, Mum,' said Toby. He got up from the table to come over and kiss her on the cheek. 'Dad cancelled, so Jim suggested we have the barbecue here. Hope you don't mind.'

'Of course, she doesn't mind,' said her father. He winked at her and raised his glass of beer in a mock toast. 'Just say the word when you're ready to eat, and I'll put the meat on.'

'Hey Reuben,' she said, dumping her handbag on a chair. 'Good to see you.' He was sitting with his back to her and hadn't moved, not even looking around, when she came up behind him, put her hands on his shoulders and kissed him on top of his head.

'Be polite and say hello to your mother, boy,' said Jim, his tone surprisingly firm.

'Hello to your mother,' parroted Reuben. He shrugged her off him, squirming to get away.

It was the most she'd had from him since his one and only visit to her new home, just after she bought it. Then he had looked in horrified disbelief at her tiny garden before hot-footing it out the door with some excuse about going to the beach.

Toby had gone through a similar silent phase at the same age, grunting when anyone spoke to him, but he'd got over it and moved on. Reuben was different. His silence had a sullen quality, which Kate found hard to overcome.

If she and Matt had been on regular speaking terms, she would have asked him if their son was acting the same way with him. But that horse had bolted. Rather than listen, Matt weaponised her concerns, automatically blaming her for any problem before pooh-poohing her suggested solutions. There were times when she wondered if she had ever really known her husband.

She put Reuben's shunning of her down to his being at home during the collapse of their marriage. Toby, away at university had escaped the drama. It had been impossible to shield Reuben from the hissed arguments and the words she wished he hadn't heard. Like the time when Matt confessed he was in love with Carla and Kate hurled a full cup of coffee at his head. She missed, thankfully, but the look on her son's face was forever seared into her memory.

Whatever, Reuben blamed her more than Matt for the breakup of the family. He said he loved her and deep down, she knew he did.

She understood he didn't have the words to express how he felt, and she knew she should be the grown-up, but she was alone, she was vulnerable, and his silence was deeply hurtful.

She was absolutely delighted he was here now. It was a huge step forward, and strangely it was her father she had to thank for bringing him back to her.

'I'll get changed,' she said. 'I don't suppose you carnivores have thought about a salad?'

'Real men don't eat rabbit food,' yelled her father. She climbed the stairs, listening to her boys egging him on and laughed. Tonight, her new place actually felt like a home. She tossed her work pants and shirt back into the dirty pile, making a mental note to put them in the washing machine before bed, and pulled on a pair of shorts and a sweatshirt. The pair of bright orange plastic Birkenstocks that Toby had given her for Christmas sort of matched, and after a hot day spent in shoes, the air around her toes felt like a tonic.

Toby and Reuben had taken it upon themselves to man the barbecue downstairs. Reuben listened attentively to Toby's wisdom on surviving at university as they turned the sausages and a line of hefty steaks. There was enough food to feed the starving poor in three countries. Jim was busy setting the table.

'Thanks for inviting them, Dad. It's the first—, ' she broke off and turned away.

'About time then,' he said. 'You're all as stubborn as each other, you know. Especially that Reuben. He got your mother's temperament, poor kid.'

'Leave Mum out of it,' said Kate, laughing.

'Surely I'm allowed one shot across the maternal bow,' said Jim, standing back to admire his work. 'Wine glasses. Where are they? I've got a Dry River Pinot to go with the steak. To say thank you.'

'For what?'

'For having me to stay. National Geographic came through. I leave tomorrow. Toby is driving me to the airport in the morning, and Reuben might come too. He hasn't decided, but I've got my fingers crossed.'

'Why don't you let me take you?' asked Kate. She eased one of the boxes from the middle of the stack and carried it into the kitchen. Inside, she found the wine glasses she'd been looking for wrapped in newspaper.

'You've got a murderer to track down,' said Jim.

'Yeah, but I'm not so busy I can't take a morning off to drive my father to the airport.'

'Really? And what if something happens while you're away?'

'The team would cope,' she said. She stopped and thought about it. They probably wouldn't, but her offer was genuine.

'It's nice of you, Kate, but it's decided. Besides, I want to spend time with my grandsons.' He looked horrified as she picked up the glasses. 'You're not putting them on the table without washing them, are you?'

'They're clean.'

'Wash them,' he ordered. 'In hot water. And pour me a gin. I'm getting gassy from all the beer I've been drinking. I'll go and check the boys aren't burning the sausages.' He stopped at the door. 'The salads are in the fridge, and there's a fresh baguette in the cupboard. I've bought ice cream and strawberries for pudding.'

'Why are you doing this?' she asked, but he was gone when she looked up from the sink.

That night, after the boys had left to return to Matt's and Reuben had deigned to hug her, Kate went to bed happy for the first time in months. Her father had behaved. He hadn't drunk too much, his presence smoothing some of the wrinkles in her relationship with her boys.

After the last year's tumult, she closed her eyes, knowing everything would finally be all right. She felt her body grow heavy, sinking with relief into the mattress and was just drifting off when she heard the first snore. Her eyes snapped open. There was no point in fighting it. She picked up her pillow, tucked her duvet under her arm, and went off to sleep in the car.

# CHAPTER
# TWENTY-FIVE

SUNDAY WAS another of Kate's scheduled day off and she was determined to take it. She played her usual doubles game with Tamsyn at the club in the morning. They scored their first win against a couple of girls from Carterton who moaned they only lost because they were injured. Tamsyn's raised eyebrows as they walked back to the club-house spoke for both of them.

'Sorry I didn't get back to you on Friday,' said Tamsyn. They were sitting on the steps of the veranda in the shade, drinking bottled iced coffees. 'There was a machine malfunction at the lab. His results should be back tomorrow.'

Kate nodded as she wiped the sweat off her forehead, draped the towel around her neck, then slugged back half the bottle of coffee. Their opponents might have been 'injured', but the match went to three sets before Tamsyn and Kate finally clinched the win with a tiebreak in the third. She was physically exhausted.

'You've got a suspect already. Well done,' said Tamsyn.

'He's a person of interest,' corrected Kate. 'He's not a suspect yet.'

'Still, it's only been a week. Good work.'

It was the tiny boost to her ego that Kate needed. She could have kissed her friend but made do with buying her another cold drink and a muffin instead. A table came free, and they sat there, idly watching the rest of the games, talking about kids, fathers and shopping. It was a welcome break from the grind of the investigation.

'I'm here if you need me,' said Tamsyn. 'Promise you'll call me if it gets too much.'

'As you're the only person in the Wairarapa who would understand, I might just take you up on that,' said Kate.

'What do you want to do if the test comes back positive?'

'You're a doctor, so it would be better if the news came from you. Ava gets weird whenever I mention it.'

They parted in the carpark, Tamsyn giving Kate a quick hug.

On her way home, she dropped into the supermarket to re-stock, buying all of her sons' favourite foods just in case they called in to see her after their trip to the airport. Back at the house, she loaded up the washing machine, took a shower, and put on her shorts and a t-shirt before she tidied up the mess from last night. She found a cold sausage on the barbecue and ate that for lunch.

All the while, the thought of unpacking the boxes percolated in her mind. When it came time to do it, she couldn't summon either the energy or the courage. Far better, she thought, to catch up on sleep than unpack a bunch of stuff she didn't have room for.

———

Refreshed after her ordinary day doing ordinary things at home, Kate walked into a subdued Incident Room on Monday morning. A couple of uniformed officers were entering the final details from the weekend's job sheets into the computers. They greeted her with barely a nod as she skirted past their desks. Others were on calls. One officer stood, staring blankly at the whiteboard as if the answer to who killed Geoffrey Scott was suddenly about to appear. She left him to it.

The rest of the morning was spent in her makeshift cubicle, tidying away loose ends and catching up on paperwork. She printed off the transcript of her interview with Bruce Murphy and got it ready for him to sign when she saw him next. She sent Michelle's alibi to Tony for follow-up. That left Mimi's phone to check. She'd do it herself when she next saw her.

She reflected on Saturday's conversations. Two very different people, their only link—a relationship with her victim. Bruce, confident with the potential to be overpowering, had been the leader of the business association when Juliette went missing. Back then, he preferred to deal with Jack—the boss—not Kate, the lackey. Like most men with money, prestige and power, he was used to getting whatever he wanted when he wanted it. She liked his plan for the sculpture park. It was a good idea. She just hoped she'd caught the killer before it opened.

Michelle was a totally different kettle of fish. Kate recognised the saying as one of her mother's, which reminded her she should phone and let her know Jim had left. Maybe not. Lee would expect a visit and right now Kate didn't have time.

Her thoughts returned to Michelle, a woman confident only in her work environment. Even there, she was fragile. One of life's victims, Michelle seemed blinkered to the possibility of anything positive happening to her in the future.

Suspicious of everyone until one day she had fallen in love with her boss. When her love was returned, she saw a different, happier future for herself. Kate didn't blame her for seizing it with both hands. But fortune failed her as it always had. Her one love murdered, she was alone again, her misery palpable. Left with nothing but memories, and the lines of suffering permanently etched into her face, there was nothing Kate or anyone else could do to help her.

She turned to the next report in the document stack on her computer. The plea in the media for sightings of their person of interest had resulted in a flurry of calls to the dedicated line. So far, nothing, but she lived in hope the exercise wouldn't be a colossal waste of time and resources.

Jack Anderson must have been thinking the same thing somewhere in Wellington. When she answered her phone, she could tell he was hoping she would report a string of positive developments.

'So that's it,' she said when she'd finished. 'Day eight of the investigation, and that's where we are. Geoffrey's test results are back today.'

'Remind me.'

'If they're positive, and he does have FTD, it could point to a motive.'

'For that amount of money, it damn well should. The commissioner's on my back. I can't emphasise enough how tight budgets are. You've got the extra staff until the end of the week, then they go back.'

'That's not long enough.'

'Yours isn't the only murder in the district.'

'There's tight, and there's tight Jack. You're strangling me.'

'It's not my call. I stood up for you, but I was overruled.'

'How am I supposed to get a result with no staff? This is the Bisson investigation all over again.'

'Except then,' said Jack. 'It was me and my reputation which were on the line. Every government department is cutting back. That's not going to change, so deal with it. And before you yell at me again, understand I have every faith in you to do your best and solve this case.'

'Flattery doesn't replace twenty extra coppers.'

'I know, but it's free. Take it.'

As soon as the call ended, her phone rang again.

'I was right,' said Tamsyn.

'I'm pleased someone is.'

'Bad time?'

'You could say that. My extra staff are leaving at the end of the week. Funding cuts.'

'This will help. You didn't waste your money. Geoffrey definitely had FTD.'

Kate stared at the fabric inside her cubicle wall, idly noting where it had pilled when someone rubbed against it, as she considered the implications of the diagnosis. 'Someone must have noticed. There had to be signs.'

'I know, but it's subtle. It comes on gradually.'

'Did he know?'

'Intelligent people have ways of compensating when their mind gets away from them, often without realising they're doing it.'

'If you say so,' said Kate. 'You saw how many people were at the funeral; imagine how betrayed they will feel when they find out he shouldn't have been practising.'

'If he made mistakes, they need to be made public for the sake of his patients,' said Tamsyn. 'You can't keep it a secret.'

'When do you want to tell Ava?'

There was a muffled knock on the wall of her cubicle, and she looked up to see Tony beaming from ear to ear. She held up her hand, signalling him to wait. 'I've got to go. I'll get back to you, okay?'

'Later today is good for me.'

'I'll be in touch.' Kate ended the call and looked at Tony, who positively bounced into her cubicle. 'Whatever this is, it better be good,' she said.

'There's a guy on the phone,' said Tony. His voice was fizzing with excitement. 'He says he knows who our man is.'

# CHAPTER
## TWENTY-SIX

VIEWED through the observation window of Interview Room One, Logan Benson was of medium height. In his late twenties, he had the lean, muscular physique of a man who lives off the land. His shoulder-length sun-bleached hair was dark at the roots, the same colour as his beard, and he wore a black woollen singlet, dusty shorts, and thick socks. He'd left his boots outside.

As his evidence would be crucial, Kate decided to conduct a formal interview at the Masterton Police Station, where a video would record what he had to say. Restlessly yawning and fidgeting, Logan was neither impressed by nor comfortable in the tiny room.

'Don't close the door.' His voice bordered on panic when Kate and Tony entered the room. 'I'm claustrophobic.'

As the air-conditioning was on the blink, Kate was more than happy to comply and left the door ajar before she sat down next to Tony. It was a typical police interview room, windowless apart from the dark oblong mirror at one end, behind which everyone knew observers monitored proceedings. Along with four chairs, two on each side of a central table bolted to the floor, there was a moveable cabinet which contained the recording equipment, and a video camera trained on the room's occupants.

When they were preparing for the interview, Kate suggested Tony take the lead. Happy to do so, he bristled with the importance of the task. Seated in front of the witness, he opened his folder on the table. 'We'd like to video the interview if you don't mind,' he said and pointed to the camera.

Logan shrugged. 'Do what you have to do.'

Tony pressed a button on a remote control, and the lights in the cabinet turned green. He stated the day, date, time, his name and rank and Kate's name and rank. Then he looked at Logan. 'Please state your full name and date of birth.

'Logan Alexander Benson, 21$^{st}$ of August 1996.

Tony placed the photo of June's watcher on the table between them. 'Do you know this man?'

'Yip,' said Logan. 'That's my mate, Ludo Wilkins. He's wearing my hoodie. See that nick at the bottom edge?' He pointed to a tear where the hood met the shoulder seam. 'That's how I know it's mine. My Jack ripped it when we were playing.'

'Your Jack?'

'My Jack Russell, Maddie. I live in the bush up behind Featherston; I'm a possum trapper and also get the occasional pig. I've got three pig dogs apart from Maddie: Caesar, August and Tiber. Maddie's the only one I let in the hut.'

'How long have you known Ludo Wilkins?' asked Tony.

'All my life. We've got the same birthday. We started school together.'

'Just a moment,' said Kate. She left the room and met Sophie Taylor in the corridor. 'We've got a solid ID. Get everything you can on Ludo Wilkins, date of birth, 26$^{th}$ August 1996.' Sophie looking excited, hurried off. When Kate returned, Logan was drawing diagrams on a piece of paper to show Tony how to get to the best fishing spots on the Pākuratahi River. Tony thanked him and tucked the paper into his folder while she sat down.

'Eight days ago, a man was murdered in Martinborough,' he said.

'Doc Scott. I know. I've got Starlink.'

'Your friend Ludo was seen outside the Scott house the day before the murder and on two more occasions this week. You can understand why we'd like to speak to him.'

Logan frowned. 'I knew it.'

'Knew what?' asked Kate.

'The idiot stopped taking his meds.'

'What meds?' asked Tony.

'His dad is getting too old to look after him.' Logan looked from Kate to Tony and saw that he'd have to explain. 'We grew up in Featherston, best mates. Ludo's mum skipped out when he was a baby, and his dad brought him up. He was a bushman, ex-army. Right from when we were little fellas, Logan's dad took us hunting. We learned survival skills, how to shoot, fish, and train dogs. By age twelve, we were so good in the bush, we could go off by ourselves.'

'Go on,' said Kate.

'When we were seventeen, he went a bit odd. He'd look at me funny; sometimes, I'd wake up, and he'd be standing over my bed, staring at me. I asked what he was doing, and he'd shake himself and then be as right as rain.'

Logan sighed, hesitating as he worked out what he should and shouldn't say.

'One night, when he was eighteen, he walked down the middle of the road, stark naked, yelling at cars. The next day, your lot had him in the secure ward at Porirua. They told his dad he had Bipolar and would be on medication for the rest of his life.' He paused and shook his head. 'Poor bugger was in there for three months.'

'How was he when he got out?' asked Tony.

'Really quiet. Ludo was fit like me; you have to be in the bush. He'd put on a tonne of weight and sat around all day watching TV.' Logan scratched his beard as he remembered. 'They cut back the medication, and he came around, but it took months before he smiled again. Properly I mean. To cap it off, while he was in hospital, you guys came and took away all their rifles. I understand why, but they don't have much money. His dad used to shoot food for the table, so he was upset.'

'Did Ludo go back to hospital?' asked Tony.

Logan lowered his head, as he thought about the answer, using his fingers to count back. 'The first time was when he was eighteen. That was ten years ago. Then, he was good for about three years. Pissed off about the rifles but okay. Then he went off his meds, and the same thing happened again, and he was back in Porirua for three months. He was really good until three years ago. He was working as a farm hand at the Sumich's on Raupaki Road. He'd been there a year, and we all thought he'd cracked it, but he went off his meds. Hid from the nurse when she came to give him his injection.'

Kate looked up. 'When three years ago? What month?'

'February,' said Logan. 'His dad called Doc Scott, who took him to the hospital in his car. Old man Wilkins was grateful because the doc didn't call the police. He got me to drop off a side of venison afterwards to say thanks.'

Tony cleared his throat. 'Do you stay in touch with Ludo?'

'Course.'

'How often do you see him?'

'Quite often, once a month maybe. If he's having a good spell, I take him up to my hut. It gives his dad a break.'

'That's where he lives? With his father?'

'Mostly. Now and then, he takes a tent and disappears off by himself. He has a cell phone, so his nurse can find him to give him his injection.'

'I thought you said he'd stopped his medication,' said Kate.

'If he's standing outside the doc's house, it sounds like it. He gets all hyped up and doesn't think he needs it anymore. Then it goes pear-shaped, and he's back in hospital. The last time was for eight months.'

'When was that?' asked Kate.

'Three years ago, like I said.'

'Did he ever say anything about hurting Dr Scott?' asked Tony.

Logan reared back, his hands up as if to ward him off. 'No way. Ludo's not like that.'

'He's never threatened anyone when he's been unwell?' asked Kate.

'He gets worked up and says things he doesn't mean. But he'd never hurt anyone.'

'When did you last see him?'

'Two weeks ago, at his dad's place. He was in good form, laughing and joking around.'

'Have you seen him since then?' asked Tony.

"I've been with Gemma, she's my girlfriend. It's my fault, I should have called him.' His brow furrowed, and then he looked from Kate to Tony, suddenly understanding why he was there. 'That's what this is all about isn't it? You guys think he killed the doc.'

# CHAPTER
# TWENTY-SEVEN

KATE SPENT the seventeen-kilometre drive to Ludo's father's house speed-reading the notes Sophie sent through. It was all there, just as Logan had said. The first admission at age eighteen, then the second a few years later. The last one was three years ago, a couple of days after Juliette Bisson was reported missing. No wonder his face hadn't come up in the face recognition software. Ludo had never been formally charged with a crime. He'd always been dealt with under the Mental Health Act.

She scoured her memory for any mention of him in the Bisson investigation and came up with nothing. He was working on the farm next to the cottage where the French girl lived, and no one had told them. Sick at the thought they had missed a potential witness, she forced herself to consider the obvious. That, despite what his friend Logan said, Ludo Wilkins might be involved in two murders.

The first time Tony drove past the Wilkins house, it looked as if no one was home. An old railway workers' cottage, it stood in solitary splendour in the middle of an overgrown section on a street of rundown houses which backed onto the railway tracks running into Featherston. A wooden house, it hadn't been painted for years; its pitched roof, more rust than iron. The solid front door, paint peeled down to bare wood, was flanked on either side by windows, the curtains drawn. A broken concrete path led from the gate to the crooked steps at the door.

Kate pointed to a spot near the corner. 'Park over there, out of sight of the house.'

They had left the station immediately after interviewing Logan, Kate calling on the way for backup to meet them at the address. The street was empty apart from a dog sniffing a lamp post on the corner. Tony turned off the engine and radioed Comms for an ETA.

'There's a kerfuffle in town,' said the operator. 'It'll be another twenty minutes.'

There was no point in protesting. Kate was too keyed up to sit quietly and wait. Ludo was her first and only real lead, and she couldn't afford to lose him. She got out of the car, took off her jacket and vest and tossed them onto the back seat. Then she pulled her shirt out of the waistband of her trousers, undid the top three buttons, ruffled her hair and put on her sunglasses.

'Where are you going?' asked Tony.

'For a look,' she said. 'You wait here for the others.'

'Boss, we should…' A call on the radio cut him short, and when he looked around, she was gone.

Kate settled on a casual, out-for-a-stroll disguise. She dawdled down the street, stopping outside a neighbour's house to lower her glasses and study their garden before pushing them back up her nose as she wandered slowly past the Wilkins' place. She stopped again, bending over to smell a rose draped along the fence. As she straightened, she glimpsed a shadow moving behind a curtain in a front window. Her mouth went dry as her heart sped up. It wasn't a wasted journey after all.

Keeping her breathing steady, she walked to the intersection, crossed, then sauntered back along the other side of the road, taking care not to even glance at their house. Once she was out of sight, she rounded the corner and ran to the end of the block.

Crouched low, she turned left onto the railway embankment, dropping into the dip between the tracks and an eight-foot high wooden fence which leaned crookedly between the rails and the row of houses. Bent double, she ran along in the shadow of the high fence, following it until she reached the back of Ludo's home. From there, she could see the roof, but not the house itself. Most importantly, there was no gate, no way he could get out of the yard. Satisfied she had Ludo where she wanted him, she jogged back to Tony at the car.

Six uniformed officers wearing stab-proof vests and belts were gathered around him when she returned. She gave them a quick rundown of the layout and her plan to get inside. Two of them were to go around to the railway line to guard the back fence. The rest she ordered into position on either side of the front of the house, with strict instructions to stay out of sight. She and Tony would knock on the front door and, if necessary, push their way in, the officers charging in as backup if things turned nasty. Inwardly pleased with her plan, she couldn't hide her excitement about getting Ludo Wilkins back to the station, where she had a whole list of questions for him to answer.

'How far away is Nathan?'

'He's finishing up a job in Daylehurst,' said Tony. 'It's vital we get this guy so we should wait until he gets here.'

Kate did some quick calculations in her head. Daylehurst was on the other side of Masterton—at least an hour away. Ludo's father was ex-army. He would notice anything unusual happening outside the house and alert his son, who was fit, off his meds and a skilled bushman. Unpredictable, Ludo was unlikely to come with them of his own accord.

Her six officers, competent and experienced, could also be called away at any moment, and she didn't fancy the odds of her and Tony taking Ludo into custody without them. Right now, she had the element of surprise. Effectively, she also had him surrounded. There was no guarantee her situation would be the same in an hour. Decision made.

'We're going in.' She did up her vest and checked to ensure she had everything on her belt. Tony turned away to kit up, but not before she saw his eyes roll in disbelief. Or was it disgust? Whatever, it was insubordination. There would be words when they returned.

The gate clicked shut behind them as they walked up the path to the front door. She knocked. They waited, listening for movement. Nothing. She knocked again and then called out. 'Mr Wilkins, it's the police. I'm Detective Senior Sergeant Sutton, and I'd like to talk to your son, Ludo.'

A floorboard creaked, then bare feet soft toeing across a wooden floor. A bolt was drawn back, a lock unlocked. The door opened a fraction.

'He's not here.' A sliver of an older man's face was visible in the gap.

'I'm DSS Kate Sutton. This is DC Tony Hunter.' They held their badges up so he could see them. 'We'd like to come in and ask you a few questions, if that's possible?'

'Ludo's not here, and I'm not answering any bloody questions.' He stepped back to shut the door, but Kate's shoe was in the way. She hard shouldered the door. It rebounded off the man's chest. He staggered back. Behind him, another man, a young, fit, tall man dressed in camo gear, his long hair flying as he hurled himself out the back door. Knees and arms pumping, he sprinted across the backyard, vaulted the fence and landed free and clear in a scrabble of stones on the other side.

Tony groaned, swearing as he elbowed her aside to tear through the house in pursuit. He tried to scale the fence but only made it as far as the top before falling back. His white shirt and clean suit were streaked with dirt. From behind the fence the officers shouted as they ran after the fugitive. Tony, nursing his grazed hands, looked at Kate standing in the doorway, Ludo's father behind her. 'We should have waited,' he mouthed.

———

'You did your best, guys.' They looked so dejected she had to say something to cheer them up. 'He got a lucky break, that's all.'

Tony snorted. She ignored him. On the drive back to Martinborough she listened, as he expressed his unflattering opinion of her judgement. She didn't attempt to justify her decision, knowing that one day, if he didn't piss people off the way he was pissing her off right now, it would be him making the tough calls. Only then would he understand.

'It was sheer luck there was a quad bike parked at the end of the street. Once Ludo reached that, there was no way we could catch him.'

She turned to Tony. 'Even a dog can't trail a quad bike, Tony, so it wouldn't have made any difference if Nathan was there or not. He got away. It happens. We deal with it. We move on.'

He shrugged, busying himself with his phone, his disdain bordering on contempt almost palpable; what was worse, his attitude was contagious. This was her first murder investigation as lead detective. She felt her support from the rest of the team slipping. Ludo had been lucky. Next time, he wouldn't be. She had to drive that message home if she wanted to reinstate their respect.

'Everyone stop what you're doing and listen to me!'

Tony's smirk and raised eyebrows attracted a few sideways looks from the younger officers.

'Ludo got away. It happens. That's an end to it. Next time, he won't. We will catch him.' A slow grumble of agreement filled the room. 'We work as a team. I'm the person in charge of the team. I make the decisions; sometimes, they don't always work. I take responsibility for my mistakes.' She paused. 'And I take the credit for my successes.' Soft chuckles followed. 'I believed June. If I hadn't, we would not be looking for Ludo. I did, and we are.'

Now she stared directly at Tony, daring him to return her gaze. He kept his head down. 'Ludo is a person of interest, but there are other lines of inquiry we need to follow. That's the job. Yours and mine. We work together until we find out who killed Dr Scott.' She could feel it; she almost had them back onside. 'Have I made myself clear?'

'Yes, boss.'

'I didn't hear that.' She cupped her hand to her ear.

This time, the call was louder, more believable.

'Right,' she said. 'You all know what you have to do. Go do it.'

She turned, and with her heart pumping and her chest heaving, she went into her cubicle and sat behind her desk.

———

The story of Ludo's escape reached headquarters before she had time to get on the phone and explain. Not that her pride would have let her do that exactly. Excuses said out loud, always sounded so lame.

Jack didn't hold back. 'The Commissioner isn't happy. Neither am I. The press is delighted at having someone to go after. It's you, in case there was any doubt. There's a video doing the rounds called the Keystone Kops. It shows your guys running along the railway track and some idiot added the Benny Hill theme.'

'I've seen it. I'm sorry. It won't happen again.'

'Damn right, it won't.' She waited, imagining him counting slowly to four before he spoke next. 'Kate, this Ludo guy is clearly dangerous. Next time, get the AOS involved from the outset. They're trained for this sort of thing. You're not.'

'Yes sir,' she said. 'His friend Logan says he's an excellent bushman and suggests we double the search personnel.'

'Then maybe Logan would like to pay for them.'

That hurt. Jack was hardly ever sarcastic, and she felt sorry to be causing him such angst that he would stoop so low. 'His father has been helpful,' she said. 'He's told us the likely places where Ludo might stash supplies. Let's hope we get lucky and find him.'

'Let's, and that the weather holds.' Now that he'd vented the commissioner's displeasure, his voice returned to normal. 'We need a win, Kate. More to the point, if you're going to stay on the case, you need a win.' He hung up without waiting for a reply.

# CHAPTER
# TWENTY-EIGHT

AT THE SAME time as Kate was walking up the path to knock on the Wilkins' front door, Ava Scott took an open bottle of pinot gris out of the fridge. She filled her glass and drank it down, telling herself she needed the alcohol to settle her nerves. Mimi was coming to look at her paintings. Her opinion mattered as she would be the first person to see her work in twenty years. If she didn't absolutely love them, then, as far as Ava was concerned, it was all over. Her life, her work, everything. The long weekends alone in her studio would have been for nothing.

She replayed the words of her art teacher in London on the endless loop track in her mind. 'You're a talentless little fool. You've come from nowhere with nothing to offer the world.' The sneer on his face still haunted her. He was the reason Dan had to come and take her home six months into her three-year scholarship. That man had killed her talent.

Then a year ago, she heard he'd died, and her heart danced a little jig. She looked up the bastard's obituary in the Guardian, and when she saw his own works damned by the faint praise and barbed comments of his former students, it was as if she'd been set free. She found the studio, purchased supplies and there hadn't been a moment since when she wasn't thinking about her work.

But was it any good? The question haunted her just like his words.

Ava had convinced herself Mimi would know. She may have been brought up in small-town New Zealand, but her money had taken her to the best galleries in the world. Born with innate taste, Mimi had acquired knowledge. Most importantly, she had an 'eye' for what was 'good' and what wasn't.

She heard the rumble of the Porsche drive into the carpark then stop. Ava quickly sloshed more wine in her glass and slugged it down. By the time her friend walked in, Ava was relaxed, her jitters gone. They hugged, and Mimi took off her sunglasses and looked around.

'Put your bag down,' said Ava. 'I'll wait, while you look. Promise you'll tell the truth. Don't be nice just because you're my friend.'

'I always tell the truth about art,' said Mimi.

The finished canvases rested in a long line against one wall. Ava leaned against the bench, biting her knuckles as she watched Mimi, one arm hugging her waist and the other holding her chin, as she studied the paintings.

There was a time before she stopped drinking when Ava had known her friend's every expression. The spa had changed everything. Now, Mimi guarded her emotions, and consequently, their relationship changed too. The shared good times were over. Still friends, they were not as intimate as they had once been. There was no more drinking wine to excess and spilling secrets, taking risks and being wild women. They had got away with those behaviours for years, and Ava had had a blast. Then Bruce demanded that Mimi get sober. He threatened her, saying that if she didn't stop drinking, she would never see him, or their girls again.

Ava had been astonished when Geoffrey took Bruce's side. 'It's harmless fun,' she said, waving her glass at him. 'F. U. N—Fun. You're so caught up being the almighty doctor, you don't know what the word means anymore.'

'For God's sake, Ava, grow up,' Geoffrey yelled, thumping the table so hard Louie had skittered sideways out the door. 'You behave like a spoiled adolescent with a booze problem. You should stop drinking, too.'

'Or what? You'll put me on a plane to Australia?'

'If that's what it takes,' he said. The sadness in his voice hit a nerve, making her want to put her arms around him and tell him she loved him. She moved towards him, but he pushed her away and walked out of the kitchen, slamming the door behind him.

On principle, Ava didn't stop drinking. She cut down, and for a time, their relationship improved, but it never returned to how it was when they were first married.

Six months after Mimi returned from the spa, they talked on the one rare occasion when Bruce wasn't around. Or so she thought. It was late afternoon on a cold winter's day, but the blue sky and bright sunshine heralding the spring more than made up for the temperature. Wrapped up in thick cashmere jumpers, they sat at the table outside on the terrace at Mimi's house.

'I miss us,' she said. 'You and me, we were great together, weren't we?' She poured another glass of wine and pushed it across to Mimi. 'One little drink won't hurt. I won't tell if you don't. Go on, you're so boring now. Live a little.'

Ava was never sure if it was accidental or if he'd been eavesdropping, but Bruce overheard their conversation. He burst onto the terrace, his body quivering with fury, and swept the glasses and bottle off the table, smashing them into thousands of tiny pieces on the stone paving. He yelled at Ava to get out of his house and never come back. The colour drained from Mimi's face as she curled into herself, unable to move.

Ava was terrified too, but she stood up to him. And she blurted out the only thing she knew that would stop him from attacking her.

He froze; his laboured breathing caught, then slowed as he unclenched his fists. With his hands locked behind his head, he walked to the end of the terrace, turned, and came back to them. He apologised, and they made a pact, the three of them. Not to ever mention it again. And they hadn't. The uneasy truce lasted.

Ava wasn't banned from their house, she continued to spend time with Mimi, and life continued. But the honesty between them was gone, banished. It was different, but it was okay.

Ava went to refill her glass from the bottle on the bench. It was empty. The room was spinning behind her eyes, but she wasn't scared any more. Whatever Mimi had to say, she could take it.

Her heart rate moved from a steady thump to imperceptible, the dizziness faded and her brain cleared. Criticism would be good for her. It was the only way she would truly grow as an artist. If Mimi said her paintings were trash, or just good—she didn't know which was worse —then Ava would be okay. She would survive and do what she had to do. She would scrape down the canvasses and start again. Excruciating but simple. She braced, waiting, while the seconds passed into minutes.

At the far end of the studio, Mimi bent over to examine a smaller work. Ava recognised Mimi's game face, the one she put on every day to lock in her feelings and keep the world at bay. She was giving away nothing. Why couldn't she hurry up? She either liked them or she didn't; they were either good or they were rubbish. Why didn't she just say that Ava was talented but maybe it would be better if she tried again? They could both live with that. Then, they could wander across the road to the pub where Mimi could have lunch, and Ava could have a proper drink. Or five.

Mimi's heels made a rat-a-tat noise on the concrete floor as she walked back to Ava.

'I'm thinking the McElhinney Gallery in Jamaica Street,' she said.

It took Ava a moment to realise what she was saying. Then, when she did, the purest of pure joys exploded in her chest and flooded every tiny fibre of her being.

'They're too busy, they wouldn't take me.' She was shaking with excitement.

'When Adam sees these, he will. It has to be the McElhinney because it's the only gallery with enough wall space to display such big pieces; their clients can afford the prices you'll charge.'

'You like them?'

'I do,' said Mimi. Her smile was genuine. 'I've known you for twenty years, and I never realised. You're an artist, Ava. You're the real deal.'

Ava doubled over, hugging herself, half laughing, half crying. 'You mean it? You're serious?' She was being pathetic, she knew that, but the critic inside her, the teacher in London, had to check Mimi truly meant what she was saying.

'They are magnificent paintings. I don't understand why you've kept your talent hidden for so long.' Mimi rinsed a glass under the tap, filled it and drank the water in one go. 'Has anyone else seen them?'

'Kate Sutton and her sidekick, Tony, what's-his-name, saw them when they came to check the studio existed.'

'Did Geoffrey see them?' asked Mimi.

'He wasn't interested.'

'I'm so sorry.' The sympathy only worked because it was Mimi who was offering it. Ava walked into her open arms, and they held each other. She warmed to the feeling of Mimi's closeness. It felt as if she had finally come home after years alone in the wilderness.

Mimi leaned back to look at her. 'You're going to be famous.'

'Don't forget rich,' laughed Ava.

'Only with proper management,' said Mimi. She stepped back and adjusted her t-shirt before fanning her face with her hand. 'Phew, it's hot in here. If this is going to be your permanent studio, you'll need decent air conditioning.'

'I was too scared to ask in case Phillip kicked me out.'

'Phillip Marlow? Is he your landlord?'

Ava nodded.

'I know him. Leave him to me, I'll sort him out after I speak to Adam. I'm thinking of an exhibition in two weeks. You'll be ready by then?'

'I'm ready now, but the McElhinney calendar is booked up a year in advance,' said Ava.

'Murphy Enterprises owns their building, and I'm one of Adam's best customers. He can bump someone down the list and make room.'

'Will you be my agent? I'm serious. You do the business. I'll paint. I'll pay you fifteen per cent of everything I earn.'

'Ten per cent, and I'll do it,' said Mimi.

Ava did a double take, then laughed. 'Done. But I'm buying lunch.'

'Deal. As part of my fee, I'd like the little painting at the end. A wall in the library has been waiting for just that piece.'

# CHAPTER
# TWENTY-NINE

BIRDSONG DRIFTED in from the square outside as the uniformed officers took their seats in front of the whiteboard. At the windows the curtains rose and fell with the breeze. Already warm, it was a harbinger of the heat to come. This lovely environment is totally at odds with the task at hand, thought Kate as she walked in, ready to start the day.

After yesterday's tune-up she decided to keep Tuesday morning's team-talk short. Consciously focusing on the positives, she mustered her brightest smile as she listed their achievements to date, then she informed them they were making progress. She turned to Tony and still smiling asked him to update everyone on the search for Ludo.

He rose to his feet and, eyes down, read from his notebook. 'Two drones went up first this morning in the area around Mt McKerrow. A small team has nearly reached the hut his father told us about. That's it. There have been no sightings. In fact, there's nothing to indicate he's even up there. He could be anywhere by now.' One-handed, still not looking at Kate or anyone else in the room, he flipped the cover of his notebook back into place and resumed his seat.

What was wrong with him that he couldn't manage his emotions like a man, she wondered. There were more important things to be getting on with. Forcing a smile, she thanked him and pointed to the photo of Michelle Parker on the whiteboard. 'The practice manager,' she said, tapping the photo with her pen, 'has confirmed she was in a relationship with our victim. He was going to leave his wife once the practice was sold. They had plans to start fresh somewhere else.'

Sophie Taylor raised her hand. 'Did Michelle know he decided not to sell before he was killed?'

'She says she didn't,' said Kate.

'We've only got her word. There's a motive right there. She finds out he's betrayed her and bingo. People have killed for less.'

'Tony, you checked her alibi,' said Kate. 'What did you find out?'

Slouched in his chair one row back from the front, Tony looked up, but not at Kate, directing his answer instead to a spot behind the whiteboard. 'Ms Parker went to the 4:30 PM session of *Anyone But You* at the Roxy in Masterton. According to the cashier, she arrived early at 3:30 PM and bought a glass of red wine which she drank in their outdoor garden area alone. She bought an ice-cream before she went into the movie. *Anyone but You* is one hour and forty-three minutes long, so she left around a quarter past six. It takes forty minutes to drive back to Martinborough, if you stick to the speed limit.'

'Thank you,' said Kate. 'Any questions?'

Disappointed murmurs and shaking of heads followed.

'Okay then, moving along. The tests confirmed our victim was suffering from frontotemporal dementia when he was killed. Ava will be informed this morning. I'm hoping patients will feel more comfortable reporting their experiences with the good doctor after they find out about his problems.' She paused to let this sink in.

'Dr Fraser has provided a PDF about FTD which you can download from the server. Read it so you know what you're talking about.'

'What if someone had a problem but don't want to talk about it?' This was from one of the uniforms from out of the district.

'Good point.' She fingered her lips as she considered the answer. 'Take their name and contact details for now. I'll take advice and let you know.'

'Can we give them the handout?' asked another.

'Yes but print off copies and take them with you. No emails.'

She turned to her DC who she was pretty sure was playing a game on his phone. 'Tony.' She paused, waiting for him to look up, which he did, eventually. 'Go over Ludo Wilkin's movements since his last admission to hospital three years ago. I want to know where he's been living, where he worked, who his associates are. You're an experienced DC. I don't have to spell it out.'

His standing confirmed, he shuffled back in his chair and nodded.

'The rest of you, I want you out talking to his patients. Did our victim hurt anyone, did he make a mistake, did he offend anyone? We need to know. You've got plenty to do. Go do it.'

# CHAPTER
# THIRTY

DAN FORRESTER ARRIVED at the health centre early on Tuesday morning. Well before opening time. He wanted time there alone, without Michelle's interfering presence watching his every move. After speaking with Aiden Cooper last night, he had no idea what he was looking for. He only knew he would know it when he saw it.

The lawyer had called him on his cell as he was putting Ava to bed. Drunk to the point of slurring her words, Mimi had driven her home from the studio, getting back around six. Although she could barely walk, Dan had never seen his cousin looking so happy.

'Two weeks,' she said, fixing one eye on Dan as she slumped into a chair at the kitchen table. An imperious finger rose up and pointed at him. 'Be there.'

'What's she talking about?'

'McElhinney's have agreed to move things around,' said Mimi. 'Ava will have her first exhibition in two weeks. I know it's a bit soon after Geoffrey's death, but let's just say the publicity won't hurt.'

'Are you sure about that? It seems cold-hearted.'

'A positive and brave step forward in the face of overwhelming tragedy is how we're going to play it,' she said. 'Once the public see the paintings, they'll forget all about her being a grieving widow.'

'Hey, let's have a drink,' said Ava. She got up and wove a tricky few steps to the fridge. She opened it and peered inside. 'Where's the champagne?'

'You drank it last night.' He laughed at the pouty expression on his cousin's face. 'How about I get you upstairs so you can take a nap before dinner?'

'Who's cooking?' she asked, slurring the 's'.

'I am, but only if you have a sleep first.' He lifted her left arm over his shoulder and, nearly hoisting her off her feet, walked her up the stairs. In the bedroom, she yanked herself free, tottered a few steps, tripped over her foot and fell face-first onto the bed, her arms spread wide. She reminded him of an upside-down snow angel, in imminent danger of being smothered by her duvet. Grabbing her by her ankles, he manoeuvred her into the recovery position, wedged pillows front and back, then turned her head to one side so she could breathe. Then he pulled the quilt over her comatose body. It was when he was tiptoeing out the door that his phone rang.

'Dan Forrester,' he whispered.

'Aiden Cooper, from Cooper, Collins in Wellington. Sorry to call out of hours. Is this a convenient time to chat?'

'Give me one second.' He put down the phone, fetched a bucket from the bathroom and put it next to the bed. Then he sat on the top stair to take the call. 'Thanks for waiting, What's this about?'

'I'm not sure exactly, but I thought I should let you know that Geoffrey called me six months ago. In a professional capacity. He wanted my advice about something a patient had told him during a consultation.'

'Okay, go on.'

'I wish I could. He refused to tell me who the patient was or what he said. I told him I rarely gave advice on hypothetical situations, but he was adamant that was all he could say. He wanted to know about the rules around breaking confidentiality.'

'What did you tell him?'

'That in certain circumstances, provided he'd notified the appropriate regulatory authorities, he could. He asked me for a list of the circumstances and the names of the authorities. I emailed these to him, but I never heard back. Now I hear he's been murdered.'

'Yes, a week last Sunday,' said Dan.

'You have my sincere condolences.'

'Thank you. How did he sound when he called you?'

'Upset. Maybe a little confused. I think that's why he wanted to see my advice in writing. In normal circumstances, I would have called him back, but my own family matters intervened.'

Aiden paused. 'I thought you should know. He seemed very worried about whatever it was. I suggested he write it all down. Everything he was told, then date it, sign it and put it in a safe place. He said he would. It's why I called you. So, you can look for it if it hasn't turned up already.'

'As far as I'm aware, nothing like that's been found,' said Dan. 'It could be anywhere.'

'If he did write it down, it will be in a safe place. Where a doctor would put something he didn't want anyone to find.'

'That doesn't help,' said Dan.

'Sorry, I thought you might know because I understand you were friends. You went to school together, didn't you?' He paused. 'If this has anything to do with why he was murdered, I'll never forgive myself.'

'What was your family matter?' Dan asked.

'My son died. He was hitchhiking in Turkey and was hit by a truck.'

'How awful, I'm very sorry. It's no wonder you didn't call Geoffrey back.'

'He was a wonderful young man.' Aiden coughed and Dan heard him swallow before he cleared his throat. 'Re Geoffrey, I thought about calling the police, but with nothing definite to report, I'd only be wasting their time.'

'I understand,' said Dan. 'Don't beat yourself up for not calling sooner, will you. I appreciate you phoning now and if I find anything, I'll let you know.'

The call ended. The door between the hall and the kitchen closed quietly, then a few minutes later, the unmistakable rumble of Mimi's Porsche could be heard, as she backed down the drive.

Dan felt a pang of sadness she hadn't stayed. He'd been looking forward to catching up with her without Bruce hanging around. That man didn't like anyone talking to his wife, but he especially didn't like Dan talking to her. It was probably because they'd gone out together a few times in their teens and Bruce, as much as he tried to hide it, was as jealous now as he had been then.

An hour alone at the health centre and he'd found nothing. He'd searched every nook and cranny in Geoffrey's room, then he moved on to look through Alex's room. He was about to go into Michelle's room when he heard a voice.

'Who's there?' It was Lily Baxter and the poor girl sounded scared.

'Only me.' He walked into reception.

'You frightened the life out of me. I thought we had a burglar.'

'I came in early to get on top of my paperwork.' He grimaced. 'Michelle's audit, the bane of my existence. I'm heading across the road to get a coffee. Want one?'

Lily hung her jacket on the back of her chair and leaned across to switch on her computer. 'A flat white would be lovely,' she said.

Her youthful smile instantly transformed the dismal prospect of another day in the consulting room into something bearable.

# CHAPTER
# THIRTY-ONE

AVA SWALLOWED ANXIOUSLY and nodded for Tamsyn to continue.

'Kate told you about the changes I found in Geoffrey's brain at his post-mortem,' she said.

Today, it was Ava who was sitting in the saggy armchair, her short frame swamped by faded floral fabric. Tamsyn and Kate sat on the sofa, and Dan leaned against the wall beside the open French doors. He had come home early to support his cousin, who was more willing to listen to Tamsyn than Kate. Ava was concentrating on everything the pathologist told her.

'I sent a tissue sample to Auckland, and the results confirmed Geoffrey was suffering from a condition called Frontotemporal Dementia.'

'But he was only 48. He was too young to have dementia,' said Ava.

'This type comes on earlier in life than the types.'

Ava's eyes sought Dan's for confirmation, and he nodded.

'It's not Alzheimer's,' Tamsyn continued. 'FTD affects a different part of the brain. It affects the part that plans ahead, assesses situations and people, anticipates consequences. Because people are complex, symptoms such as a loss of inhibition are often excused rather than seen as a cause for alarm.' She rustled around in her bag and brought out a sheaf of folded A4 papers. 'Information for later,' she said, putting them on the coffee table.

'How could he work? Wouldn't the patients have noticed?' Ava, confused, sought out Dan again.

'Memory isn't the first thing to be affected,' he said. 'Sometimes, all that happens is the person goes into themselves, they aren't as talkative. Or they say the wrong thing. We all do that from time to time and don't think anything of it.'

Ava paused. 'I thought he was just being a prick.'

A moment's silence followed this statement before Tamsyn rode to the rescue. 'You wouldn't be the first wife to think that. You said he put on a lot of weight.'

'He turned into a complete pig, eating junk food in his car where he thought I wouldn't see him.' She paused, biting her bottom lip. 'Did he know he had it?'

'Because FTD affects insight, he probably didn't,' said Tamsyn.

'Oh,' said Ava. 'I see.' She leaned back, sinking further into the chair, her knees higher than her hips. Louis took that moment to enter the room. He walked over to Ava and jumped into her lap. She stroked his head, and he settled, his purring interrupting the snatches of sound coming from June's TV next door. 'He kept away from people,' said Ava. 'He was always in his garden when he wasn't at work.'

'You were at your studio most weekends,' said Kate. 'So you didn't spend a lot of time together.'

'We didn't.' A thought occurred to her, and she struggled forward, using her hands on the armrests for leverage. Louis looked annoyed but stayed on her lap. 'The affair with Michelle. That was the FTD, wasn't it? He would never have done it otherwise.'

'Maybe,' said Dan. 'Did you ever ask him about it?'

'Why? I didn't see any point. I just thought it was what menopausal men do. Better that he have his fling and get over it. I mean, look at her. He'd never leave me for her.'

Louie's purrs and June's TV were the only sounds in the room before Kate cleared her throat. 'Has the sale of the practice gone unconditional yet?'

'My lawyer emailed the documents through this morning. The new owners take over in a few days.'

'That was quick,' said Tamsyn.

'Not really. They were all set to buy it before Christmas, but Geoffrey pulled the plug. Now we know why.'

Dan was about to speak when Kate lifted her hand. 'What I'm about to ask is very important Ava. Did Geoffrey ever tell you about anyone he had offended, hurt, or made a mistake treating?'

'No, he didn't,' said Ava. 'But if he had FTD, he wouldn't know, would he?'

She's right thought Kate and hoped the team was having better luck with their inquiries. Ava's interest in her husband's life, either before he died or now, was too patchy to be reliable. She stood up and was followed by Tamsyn.

Ava stayed in the armchair stroking Louie, bending over to whisper in his ear. It was Dan who saw them out. At the door, he paused, and Kate had the feeling he wanted to say something. Tamsyn, who was keen to return to the hospital hurried past them out the door. Kate looked at him expectantly, but he gave her a little shrug as if he had changed his mind.

'If you think of anything…' said Kate, leaving the offer open. 'You have my number.'

She caught up with Tamsyn halfway down the drive. 'What do you think?'

'She's a strange one,' said Tamsyn. 'I can't tell if she's upset about him dying, or if she really doesn't care.'

They had stopped at the end of the drive and Kate dug in her handbag for her keys. She looked up, her head cocked towards June's house. 'Do you hear that?'

'What?'

'June's TV.'

'It is, too. So what?' Tamsyn turned away but Kate put a restraining hand on her arm. 'June always wears headphones when she watches the races. We shouldn't be hearing it. Something's wrong.'

She started running.

# CHAPTER
# THIRTY-TWO

AT EIGHT O'CLOCK THAT EVENING, the noise in the Incident Room was so loud that no one could hear what the person next to them was saying. Despite the open windows and the fans whirring overhead, the room was both hot and muggy.

Warm air laden with moisture coming down from the tropics had swung around the top of the North Island to hit the East Coast, bringing with it the first prospect of decent rain that summer. Moths batted against the lights, then dropped into coffee cups, only to be spat out by officers too busy to check what they were drinking.

There were too many people in a confined space, and with not enough places to work and another murder to solve, it was no wonder tempers were frayed. Irritations, usually brushed off with a smile or a line of cheeky banter, escalated, in one instance resulting in a scuffle, an overturned chair, and the combatants forced apart by colleagues.

It was a relief for everyone when Kate, followed by Jack, emerged from her cubicle and stood at the front of the room. She held her hands up for quiet.

'At 1:17 PM this afternoon, Dr Fraser confirmed the death of June Whittaker at her home in Martinborough.' She turned and pointed to June's photo. 'Seventy-three, a widow, she lived alone. Her relatives in

Australia are still to be notified, so her name has not been released to the press. The cause of death is likely to be blunt force trauma to the back of her head. The weapon, a five-iron golf club, which June kept at the bottom of her stairs for self-defence.'

How many times had she told June to put it away? Shaken by the thought she should have done it herself Kate paused and took a sip of water from the glass on the table beside her.

'Death occurred between 8 and 11 PM on Sunday—that's roughly forty-eight hours ago and fits with the evidence at the scene. Based on the markings in her racebook, June was watching Trackside when she was killed. Paul and his team are still at the house, and we'll get the scene photos up in the morning.'

At the back of the room, Bill Comber, a senior sergeant based in Masterton and now seconded to Kate's team, put up his hand. 'How did the killer get in?'

'June kept a key under a pot of geraniums at the back door. As there was no sign of forced entry, we have to assume the killer gained access to the house using the key.'

There was a collective groan as shaking heads rippled across the room.

Kate held up her hand. 'However,' she paused. 'It doesn't look like this was a spur-of-the-moment thing. June wore headphones when she watched the races, making it easy for someone to come in without her knowing. Blood spatter indicates she was hit from behind. The first blow knocked her unconscious, the second finished her off. The third was for reasons only the killer knows. Blood would have landed on the killer's clothes. Remember that when you are interviewing people tomorrow. Ask about stains, uncharacteristic washing, et cetera.' She stopped to let them catch up on their notes.

'June's body has been removed. The post-mortem is at eight tomorrow morning. I will be attending, and Tony, it would be helpful if you were there too.'

Tony nodded and she continued. 'Detective Superintendent Jack Anderson is here in a support/oversight capacity. I remain in charge of both murder investigations. I'm holding a short press conference when we're done here.'

By now, rivulets of sweat were running down her chest and back, soaking through her shirt and making her want to rip it off so she could tear at her itchy skin in a frenzy of scratching. Judging by the restless shuffling in the room, she wasn't the only one suffering from the humidity.

'There is massive interest in this second murder,' said Kate. 'Bear that in mind when you conduct the house-to-house inquiries tomorrow. Remember, people are scared, so don't discuss any details. Reassurance and evidence gathering are all that is required. We are a professional organisation. We deal in facts, not rumours.'

A hand shot up at the back. It was Bill again. 'That's all very well, Kate, but there's been two deaths in the last fortnight. If we add Juliette Bisson, that's three killings in three years in one small town. It has to be more than a coincidence. What do we tell people?'

An experienced officer, stable and steady, Bill had turned down promotions several times in order to stay working in the community. Kate respected his judgment, but homing in on one killer being responsible for all three killings without any concrete evidence to back it up was premature.

Fixating on one theory had sent inquiries off the rails in the past. She likened it to putting blinkers on a horse, and if his proposition took hold, it could prejudice the investigation. Aware he was only saying what everyone was thinking, it was her job as the OIC to remain open to all possibilities. She focused on his question rather than the statements preceding it.

'What would you suggest?'

Bill flushed at being put on the spot. 'I'd ahh, we have to …' He stopped to gather his thoughts. 'I'd tell everyone to keep their doors locked. If living alone, maybe move in with friends or family for a few days and report any suspicious behaviour to us, no matter how minor. Also, they should keep an eye on their neighbours. Oh, and stay calm and let us do our job.'

'Perfect,' she said. 'Write it up, give it to the media team and have them spread the word. Anyone else with a question?'

'Do you think the same person killed June and Dr Scott?' Sophie Taylor had grown increasingly confident during the investigation, a quality which Kate was keen to encourage in such a promising young woman.

'I don't discount it,' she said. 'June lived next door to our first victim. Perhaps the killer thought she was a risk. We don't know enough yet to say anything definite.' Her answer was greeted with a rumble of concern, and she raised her hands for quiet. 'Hopefully, we'll know more after Paul has finished examining the scene.'

'Perhaps the killer is a psychopath who kills people for no reason,' suggested Tony. This was greeted with a few nodding heads and low mumbles of assent. Kate held up her hands for quiet again and was about to speak.

'What about the search for Ludo Wilkins?' he interjected. 'He's got to be the prime suspect. We let him escape once, and another person is dead. Don't we need a bigger search party?'

The shuffling stopped, the room suddenly quiet. That Tony was out of line was not in doubt. All eyes were focused on Kate to see how she would respond.

'Jack and I are ahead of you on this. Just now, we've sent instructions to increase the size and scope of the search party, first thing in the morning. Tomorrow we're sending a helicopter up to search all the huts in the area for signs of life.'

'About time,' said Tony.

This was greeted with a smatter of laughter. Kate frowned. 'I must caution all of you. It is too soon to make Ludo Wilkins our prime suspect.' She paused, waiting for the protests to settle. 'He remains a person of interest. Unless any of you know something I don't? Tony?'

No one said a word. Slouched in his chair, his eyes fixed on the floor in front of him, Tony shrugged, his desire to make an impression on Jack at her expense, back on a leash.

'No more questions?' She could tell from the tense silence which followed that there were many in the room who felt like Tony. But now was not the time for another morale-boosting speech. June's murder meant they were past that. They wanted results. Stiffening her spine, she scanned the room, noting whose gaze slid away when she looked at them. Sadly, there were too many to count.

'Right,' she said, summoning her most commanding tone. 'See you all bright and early in the morning. You know what to do.' She turned and headed off to the briefing room which had been set aside for the press conference. She hoped the reporters would be kinder to her than her staff.

# CHAPTER
# THIRTY-THREE

THAT NIGHT, Dan lay in bed staring at the darkness through a gap in the curtains, hoping the rain would come. It was needed to clear the air of the dense wraparound mugginess, making him sweat into his sheets. It was nearly four. He'd been awake since one, unable to get back to sleep partly due to the heat and partly because he couldn't stop thinking about June. What was he doing when she was killed? Had he heard her cry out and ignored it? Had he seen someone and dismissed it? The questions piled up inside his head. It didn't help that the house was also weirdly quiet. Ava had left to stay with Mimi and Bruce, saying she no longer felt safe at home even with him there. Quite frankly, he couldn't blame her.

Ten minutes passed. He sat up, done with sleeping, and peeled the damp cotton sheet from his back. Sitting on the side of the bed with his head in his hands he wondered if Aiden's revelations, as vague as they were, had anything to do with the deaths? If it was even faintly possible, didn't that put the onus on him to find the document, before anyone else was killed?

He told Kate about it when they were standing outside June's house. The initial fuss had died down, the ambulance had gone, and they were waiting for the SOCO team to arrive.

'I should have told you before,' he said. 'June might still be alive if I had.'

It was four o'clock in the afternoon, and the stress lines around Kate's eyes had deepened as the hours ticked over. Clearly distressed by June's death, he hoped she wasn't blaming herself.

'What are you talking about?' she asked.

'I got a call last night from a lawyer about Geoffrey.'

'Go on.' She walked across to sit on the low fence and stretched her legs out in front of her.

He told her everything Aiden said about the document. 'Geoffrey must have hidden it somewhere. I've searched the medical centre, but so far, no luck. I'll start on the patient records in the morning.'

'That could take forever, and we don't have that long. How about I get a team in there with you?'

'Before or after you get permission from the courts to search the medical records of people with no relation to the case?'

She swallowed. 'That could be a problem.'

'It's very possible that it doesn't exist,' he said. 'The FTD muddies the waters somewhat.'

'How?'

'One of the early symptoms of FTD is confabulation.'

'What is confabulation?'

'Making stuff up. Convincingly too. I had a patient in St Kitts once, an accountant. Same age as Geoffrey. He was convinced the Mafia were forcing him to launder money because if he didn't, they were going to murder his wife and children. He was so sure of the details, I believed him.'

'He was lying?'

'You can't call it lying because he really believed he was telling the truth. I only found out he'd made it up when he was caught embezzling money from his real clients to buy Bitcoin on behalf of his imaginary clients. It took a year for the neurologists to confirm the diagnosis.'

'Did his clients get their money back?'

'Luckily, the price of Bitcoin tripled that year, so they did.'

'What happened to him?' asked Kate.

'He went into care. I'm trying to say that Geoffrey could have made up whatever he called Aiden about. It could have been part of an elaborate fantasy which he developed as part of the dementia.'

Kate tipped her head back, closed her eyes and whimpered. 'Just one break, that's all I need.'

'Sorry.'

She ran her fingers through her hair. 'It's not your fault.'

The SOCO van rounded the corner at the end of Palmer Grove and drove slowly towards them. She turned to Dan. 'Look, I get it might be a figment of his imagination, but do me a favour, will you?'

'If I can,' he replied.

'Search everywhere. Go through it with the proverbial fine toothcomb. But don't tell anyone what you're doing; the killer might come after you, too. I don't want another murder on my hands.'

'There are limits as to what I can legally look at, you know that, right?'

'Two murders, maybe three if you count Juliette. Frankly, Dan, I don't care what you look at.'

# CHAPTER
# THIRTY-FOUR

IT WAS 10 o'clock by the time Kate got home. She felt bruised and battered after the press conference, which had not gone well. Aside from giving her hell about the botched attempt to take Ludo into custody, towards the end, another reporter had asked her if they were looking for a serial killer.

'There is no evidence to support such a theory.' She tried to sound both firm and dismissive.

'Three killings in the same area in less than three years. Isn't that all the evidence you need?' This came from an earnest slim young man. Kate thought he didn't look old enough to be a reporter.

'No, it's not.' She hoped that he would take the hint and leave it there, but it was not to be.

The reporter stood up, his chin thrust out defiantly as he played to the cameras. 'Doesn't the man you tried and failed to take into custody have links to all three murders?'

Either there'd been a leak, or this guy was fishing. She flushed and stammered out the standard reply she'd been trained to provide. 'I cannot comment on an ongoing investigation.'

'Which means he does.' He sat down to a room full of murmurs, dark looks and a rustle of papers.

Tempted to tell him where he could put his theory, Kate fixed a stony expression on her face and asked if there were any more questions. No one put up their hand, so she thanked them and left.

Too tired to cook, she picked up a bag of Kentucky Fried Chicken on her way home, dumping it on the kitchen bench as soon as she walked in the door. Her hunger, a distant second to the urgent need to dig a set of files out of the boxes stacked against the wall. On the drive back she had explored the possibility there might indeed be a link between the three killings. She had to. Had she ignored what was staring her in the face?

One by one, she ferried the boxes into the living room and made a new stack against the wall until she found the one she wanted. The letters JB were written in biro on the top left-hand corner, and she had to look very hard to see them. All documents relating to Juliette's inquiry were supposed to be in police storage, either behind a firewall on the national database, or locked in the basement archives at the Masterton Police Station.

Three years ago, unable to accept the decision to scale back the investigation, she made copies of everything so she could work on the case at home. Then her marriage had blown up, and she'd put her search on hold.

When she opened the box and saw the files neatly stacked on top of each other, it felt as if she was greeting an old friend. She set them down on the table in the order she wanted to read them. Her tummy grumbled, and she remembered the chicken.

When she looked up later, she was surprised to see that it was not only dark outside but that it was two o'clock in the morning. She'd read everything. A pile of bones lay on the plate on the floor beside her feet. She threw them in the bag. Fast food might taste great, but waking up to the smell the following day was another issue.

It was a clear night, the full moon casting a silvery spotlight on the path as she walked down the side of her house to the bin. Above her, the Milky Way stretched across the black velvet sky. There had also been a full moon on the night Juliette went missing. How much brighter everything must have looked out in the country, far from the lights of town. How beautiful it must have been on her last night on Earth before whatever came to take her, arrived to ruin it.

She dropped the rubbish in the bin, then remembered it was collection day tomorrow. She wheeled it down to the curb and wide awake, she stood on the pavement and looked back at her townhouse, which was silhouetted against the sky. Not in her wildest dreams had she ever thought this would be her future. But that was okay. It was warm, safe, and convenient. It was all she needed and it would do for now.

She wasn't home much. It didn't matter if the housework wasn't done and the lawn wasn't mowed. As she locked the door, it occurred to her that living alone was actually quite nice. It was liberating not having to meet expectations. There was no subtle disapproval when she arrived home late. No one telling her she worked too hard. She could focus entirely on her job, a luxury she hadn't known before. Best of all, it was refreshing to have her mind to herself; uncomplicated by the constant demands of a husband and children.

Collecting a glass of water from the kitchen, she opened the windows to get rid of the fatty aroma of fried chicken. She'd be up again in three, maybe four hours, but it didn't matter. Re-reading the files had been helpful, especially now that she knew Ludo had worked on the farm beside Juliette's cottage. It wasn't clear how the recent murders were related to her disappearance, but the answers to her questions felt tantalisingly close. All she needed was another few days, a few more people to question, and she was hopeful the final pieces of the puzzle would fall into place. This time, she wasn't giving up. No matter what Jack said about resources and overtime budgets. She'd work for free if she had to. When her head hit the pillow, Kate fell instantly into a deep, sound sleep.

# CHAPTER
# THIRTY-FIVE

JACK ANDERSON ORDERED a double espresso and took a seat at a table by the window overlooking the square. It was early, and he was the only customer. The café was brand new; its modern, minimalist style of clean lines and pastel colours set it apart from its more established competitors. He'd been surprised when Bruce suggested they meet here, but now he understood. Nora's still had to attract the locals, so their conversation was unlikely to be interrupted or overheard. His coffee arrived; its pungent aroma tickling his nostrils as he gazed out the window.

The leaves on a few of the trees in the square had begun to fall. Jack figured this was more likely to be due to the dry summer than the approaching autumn. The grass, shaded by the trees and kept watered by pop-up sprinklers, was freshly mown. The woman walking her dog, the white stone war memorial in the centre, and the quiet streets on four sides all combined to create the impression of a peaceful, safe place to live. It was nothing like the murderous image of Martinborough, the press had painted. Recently, Lizzie, his wife, tired of the cold Wellington summers, had been pushing him to buy a weekender here. Until the murders, when she suddenly went quiet.

The door opened and Bruce walked in, greeting the owner with a raised arm and a request for his usual. He looked every bit the big-city Aucklander in his sunglasses, short-sleeved designer shirt, khaki chinos and boat shoes, his presence filling the room with energy. Jack partially rose and they shook hands.

Bruce leaned across the table when he was settled. 'I don't understand what's happening to us, Jack. June's murder is another sign we've lost our way as a society. I listened to talkback radio on my way into town. Some say it's our education system that's at fault. Others, that we don't have enough prisons. Whatever it is, my little town can't bear the brunt of the lawlessness much longer.'

The owner arrived, placed a large flat white in front of Bruce and raised his eyebrows at Jack, who shook his head. His empty cup was whisked away.

'Whatever's going wrong, it has to stop,' said Bruce, taking up where he had left off. 'She was an elderly widow, doing no one any harm. In her own home, for chrissakes. If it's more police we need, let's get them. If the mental health services are understaffed, bring in more professionals from overseas. But we can't afford to keep going like this.'

'I agree with everything you say,' said Jack. He meant it. This uncomplicated acknowledgement was also his way to stop these conversations dead in their tracks. Bruce said nothing, drinking his coffee instead.

'I have a few questions for you,' said Jack. 'Is it a problem if I record this? Saves the hassle of me taking notes.'

'Fire away.'

'Where were you this last Sunday afternoon slash evening?'

'At home with Mimi.'

'Is there anyone with any reason to hurt or kill June Whittaker?'

'No one.' Bruce met his eyes, sipped his coffee again and licked the white foam from his top lip as he replaced the cup in its saucer.

'Ava Scott is staying with you. Did she tell you about Geoffrey's dementia?'

Bruce nodded.

'Were you surprised?'

"Yes and no. Yes, because by all accounts, he was doing a reasonable job as a doctor.' He paused. 'And no, because I had heard a few rumbles. I told Kate about one instance, but there were more.'

'Rumbles?' asked Jack.

'You know.'

Jack shook his head.

Bruce sat up and straightened his shoulders. 'This is one example, but there were others. One of our community board members went to see him about a female problem.'

Jack raised his eyebrows.

'A breast lump,' said Bruce. Jack relaxed, pleased it was nothing below the waist. 'Geoffrey "forgot" to tell her about a suspicious biopsy result.' Bruce did the finger tweaks around the word forgot. 'Luckily, it was all right in the end, but she wouldn't have known if she hadn't called to find out and it could have turned nasty later.'

'Did she complain?'

'She changed doctors.'

'Was he your doctor?' asked Jack.

'Until six months ago,' said Bruce. 'Mimi stayed with him, she's more loyal than me.'

'Why did you change?'

'He brushed me off when I went to him with a problem. He said it was old age, but as you can see, I stay in shape, I'm fit.' He puffed out his chest to demonstrate. 'A friend put me onto a specialist in Wellington, who prescribed tablets which magicked the old age away. I didn't say anything to Geoffrey because we've been friends forever. I explained I was spending all my time in Wellington and asked for my notes to be sent to a practice there. It's the truth. I do spend more time there.'

'He was okay with that?'

'Seemed to be. Never mentioned it. Not that I saw much of him before he died.'

'Why was that?'

'Work. Holidays. Ours, not his, got in the way. If we asked them over, Ava came, not him. Apparently, he had other things to do.'

'What things?' asked Jack.

Bruce looked around and when he was sure the café owner wasn't listening, he leaned across and in a low voice, said, 'Michelle Parker, according to the gossip.'

'They were having an affair?'

'Evidently,' said Bruce. Jack didn't return his chummy smile. Disappointed, Bruce placed his hands flat on the table. 'Three weeks ago, you couldn't get a seat in this place, it was so busy. Look at it now. It's empty. Businesses all over town are suffering. The only customers are reporters and cops, and neither of you are big spenders.' He closed the distance between them again. 'Between you and me, how's your girl really getting on with the investigation?'

Jack straightened his shoulders and met Bruce's gaze. 'I have total confidence in Detective Senior Sergeant Kate Sutton. She is doing an excellent job. Trust me when I tell you she is very close to getting a result. As a prominent member of this community, it would be very helpful if you could get that message out.'

'That's all?' Bruce's tone brought back memories of a similar exchange three years ago when he came to Jack demanding an update on Juliette Bisson's disappearance. It rankled now every bit as much as it had then.

'Didn't you find something when you searched their houses? You were there long enough.'

'I can't tell you about an ongoing investigation, as well you know.'

Like a terrier after a rat, Bruce wasn't about to give up. 'What about that botched arrest last week? Your lot looked incompetent. The reporters at the press conference last night made mincemeat of your girl.' He pushed a copy of that morning's Wairarapa Times-Age across the table. '*The Martinborough Murderer Strikes Again*' screamed the front page headline. 'This is an absolute disaster for the town.'

'There was nothing Kate could do. She can't comment on the details in an ongoing investigation. Headquarters has been in touch with the editor. We're making a formal complaint.'

He might as well not have spoken, Bruce was determined to finish what he had come to say. 'She fumbled the answers to basic questions. Maybe, if she was better at her job, June would still be alive.'

'That's enough,' said Jack. 'Our job is to find the person or persons responsible. It is not to indulge the crazy theories they fired at us last night. And stop referring to DSS Sutton as my girl. She's a highly trained detective, and this is the twenty-first century. Show some respect.'

'Why are you going door to door? Why is Ludo Wilkin's face plastered all over the media with a warning not to approach him? He should be in custody, and you know it. The public has every right to be concerned.'

'Ludo Wilkins is a person of interest. That is all. It's too soon to accuse him of a crime.'

'Ludo has problems with reality and everyone knows it.' Bruce's face turned red as he leaned even further across the table. 'Why aren't you up in the hills looking for him?'

Jack had had enough. He folded his hands and set his expression to pleasant. 'We sent more officers into the bush this morning, along with drones and dogs. We'll find him.'

'Good,' said Bruce.

'Something's been bugging me,' said Jack. 'Whatever happened to the CCTV system which was supposed to be installed around the square?'

'You're referring to the state-of-the-art system which Murphy Enterprises donated to the town?' asked Bruce. 'As far as I know, it was installed while I was in Auckland.'

'No, it wasn't.'

Bruce frowned as he tidied his belongings into a pile. 'That's not good. My apologies. I thought it was up and running. Leave it with me. I'll get onto the council and find out what's happened.' He pushed back the chair, its steel legs screeching on the concrete floor, and stood up. 'June Whittaker was a good woman. She didn't deserve to die like that, Jack. Nor did Geoffrey. I'm serious. You'd better find this lunatic Ludo and lock him up before he kills anyone else. If you don't, I have connections in Wellington, and I'll make it my personal mission to see that you and your girl are fired.'

'Duly noted,' Jack said. His tight smile masked his deep anger at Bruce's half-baked threat. They walked to the door and stepped out into the sunshine. Bruce put on his sunglasses. Jack watched him stroll to the end of the street. There, he climbed into his dark blue Porsche 911 GT Turbo, a car Jack openly lusted after but could never afford. When Bruce had gone, he took out his phone, dialled a number, and hit call.

'It's Detective Superintendent Jack Anderson. I'd like to speak to your CEO.'

# CHAPTER
# THIRTY-SIX

THE MIDDAY SUN blazed through the front windows of the café casting long rectangles of light across the polished wooden floor. Though any heat radiating up from the pavement outside, was more than matched by the arctic blast from the air conditioner directly above Bill's head. It was why he sat at this same table every day; to get a break from the stuffy atmosphere of the police station.

'I knew I'd find you here,' said Kate as she slipped into the chair opposite him. 'I wanted to tell you what a great job you did with the media release.'

He looked at her suspiciously before replacing his cup in his saucer. 'You came all the way from Martinborough to tell me that?'

'I did.' She hugged her jacket around her as she checked the server was bringing her coffee. 'And to pick your brains.'

'Of course.' He cocked his head, a wry smile on his face. 'How was the postmortem?'

She laughed and held up her hands in surrender. 'Okay, you got me. I was here for that too. It showed nothing we don't already know. Blunt force trauma to the back of her head. It meant she didn't suffer, which is some consolation I suppose.' She stopped talking to thank the server for her flat white. It was excellent coffee, hot and strong enough to take away the residue of dead-body-taste, still clinging to the back of her throat. 'If you've got time, I really would like your advice.'

'Ask away,' said Bill. He looked good for his age, which Kate put around the mid-fifties. More than good. His neatly cut silver-grey hair, complimented his green eyes which were sparkling enough to be interesting. The broad shoulders and flat belly; testaments to his daily exercise routine. Like many great-looking, unmarried men in their fifties who look after themselves, he was gay. A fact he neither hid nor widely shared. 'But make it quick because I have to be back on duty in five minutes.'

'What do you think happened to Juliette Bisson?'

'Well,' he said, looking directly at her. 'I think an evil person saw a pretty young girl living alone in the countryside and decided to do his worst.'

'What do you think this evil person did with her body?'

He folded his hands together on the table. 'No one looked for her for five whole days, so he had plenty of time to do any number of things. Cook Strait is only twenty kilometres down the road from her cottage. As we both know, throw something in there, and you'll never see it again. The ocean trench and strong currents don't give back, not to mention the sharks.'

Kate shuddered as she imagined Juliette sinking deeper into the dark blue ocean, her long blonde hair wafting around her pretty face.

Bill continued. 'Jack sent teams into the bush. We had police divers searching the lakes and rivers. It was too dangerous to send them into the strait itself, but we scoured the beaches for weeks afterwards and didn't find her. We had teams searching the bush, and we notified the hunters who are up there every day to keep a look out for her. In the end, we had to give up. If she was alive and being held prisoner, or if her body had been dumped anywhere else, we would have found her by now.'

'I agree.'

'It was the saddest case I've ever worked on,' he said. 'I still get nightmares about it. The empty cottage, her father, the endless searches. I was with him when he found out we were scaling back the inquiry. He was devastated. I couldn't have driven him to the airport. All credit to you for doing it.'

They sat in silence for a full minute before Bill shook himself and finished the last of his coffee. 'I'd better get back. Can't sit here all day reminiscing about old times.'

He half rose when Kate said, 'There was another death on Raupaki Road around the same time.'

'Yes, I forgot about him,' said Bill. He settled back into his seat. 'Ivan Simich died the same night she went missing. Pancreatic cancer. I know the family. Isobel took it very hard. Still does. Ivan died, and five days later, the police are crawling all over their property, asking questions, searching their paddocks and outbuildings, and disturbing their stock. It was a tough time.'

Kate nodded. 'Remind me again, how far it is between their house and the cottage.'

'About a kilometre, but there's a shelter belt of pine trees between them if I remember correctly. That blocks any view of the properties. The Simichs couldn't have seen anything.'

'They must have driven past the cottage on the Saturday and the days after that. They had to go into town to make arrangements and get supplies. Friends and family would have come out to pay their respects. Why do you think they didn't notice she wasn't there? Surely, they used to wave out to her, a young girl living alone in a cottage they owned?'

'You're right. Isobel felt awful about it afterwards.'

So she should, thought Kate. She had a duty of care to keep an eye out for Juliette no matter how she was feeling.

Bill interrupted her thoughts, saying softly, 'Go easy on her. Ivan had just died, and she was in shock.'

Kate wanted to be charitable, she really did, but she found it hard to accept that Isobel hadn't checked on Juliette at least once in those five days. Or asked someone to do it for her. 'Your honest opinion now. Is Juliette's disappearance related to our murders?'

His eyes narrowed. 'The laws of coincidence would say yes. This is a depressing and horrific possibility, but maybe we are looking for a serial killer.'

'Ludo Wilkins?'

'It makes my skin crawl to think about it, but I guess it's possible.' He stared out the window, watching the cars drive by. 'In my experience, innocent people don't run.'

'Scared people do.'

'But eventually, they calm down, see sense, lawyer up and come in,' said Bill.

'Psychotic people can't calm down,' she replied.

'There is that,' conceded Bill. He checked his watch and stood up. 'I should get back. I'm meeting Dave after work. He's in the local Porsche club, and we're driving out to Tinui tonight.'

'What sort of Porsche does he own?' asked Kate.

'One of the old ones from the seventies. A 911 G. White. Guess what I'll be doing this weekend.'

'Cleaning it?' She was rewarded with a laboured nod. 'Does Bruce Murphy belong to the club?'

'He pays the sub but never comes to any meetings. He's too busy. Now I really have to go. It's been nice chatting.'

He walked a few steps then turned and came back. 'For what it's worth, you're doing a fine job. Don't let Tony Hunter get to you. He's ambitious and he's too young and arrogant to know that Will Beveridge is not his friend. You didn't hear that from me.'

He watched her to make sure she understood.

'And forget the reporters. They're jackals. They only care about headlines.'

'Thanks for the heads-up.' Genuinely touched by his words she added, 'It means a lot.'

# CHAPTER
## THIRTY-SEVEN

THERE WAS ONLY one person in the waiting room at the health centre when Kate walked through the door on Wednesday afternoon. She had prepared herself for the usual mix of crying babies, bossy toddlers, and gossiping pensioners she encountered every time she visited her own doctor. She shouldn't have been surprised. The town was deserted. The cafes and shops had closed; their owners, tired of waiting for customers to appear, had gone home for the day. Her own officers conducting their door-to-door inquiries created the only discernible movement.

'It's been like this since June died,' explained Lily. 'They're all too scared to leave home. Either they want the doc to visit them, or they say they'll wait until you've caught the killer.' She paused and looked hopefully up at Kate. 'I don't suppose you've got any news?'

'Not yet,' replied Kate. She felt Lily's wave of disappointment on hearing her answer try to swamp her, but she fought it off. The team was working as hard as it could to find the killer, and they would, she was sure of it. For the sake of their morale, they needed people to stop doubting and start believing. Besides, she thought, what good does hiding at home complaining about the police on social media do? In addition, June and Geoffrey were murdered at home. Logic would dictate, it was better if everyone was out and about, carrying on as usual.

'Tell people we're making progress,' she said.

This had the desired effect. Lily brightened considerably on the other side of the counter.

'I've come to see Michelle if she's free,' said Kate.

'Let me check,' replied Lily. She returned less than a minute later, looking stern. 'She's busy, but if you don't mind waiting, she can see you in ten minutes.'

Kate found a seat in a sunny spot in the waiting room and looked for the magazines. Finding none, she took out her phone and scrolled through her emails, answering the ones she could, leaving the rest for later.

Tony had sent through a summary of Ludo's movements over the last five years as per her request. It was short but, by the looks of it, thorough. The closely typed information was difficult to read on her phone, but she managed to get the gist. That he had underlined the parts he thought important, helped. It basically reiterated everything Logan said. Ludo had lived with his father in Featherston between his spells in hospital. That was until two months ago when he had gone bush, only visiting the family home to get supplies and meet with the nurse who gave him his medication. Then, three weeks ago, he missed his appointment with her and hadn't been seen since.

In the past, he had worked as a labourer, kitchen hand, gardener, and road worker—most of his jobs lasting around three months. The exception was the job as the Simich's farmhand. He'd kept that for a year. The work involved him moving stock, feeding out and fixing the water troughs. He'd also made silage and baled hay in the paddocks adjacent to the Simich homestead and surrounding the cottage they rented to Juliette.

Kate imagined them three years ago during a summer as hot and dry as this one. Two young people, one a loner, the other alone. There was no way they didn't see each other. They must have spoken, at the very least in passing, if not spent time together. Her heart raced as she considered the possibilities. That she hadn't heard of his existence until a couple of days ago was understandable. He had disappeared before they could get to him, quietly admitted to hospital by Geoffrey Scott, the very same week that Juliette was reported missing. Geoffrey, who had a duty of care to his patient, couldn't break patient confidentiality. But why hadn't Isobel Simich said anything? What did she know?

'Excellent report, Tony. Thank you.'

Kate clicked send and watched as *Delivered* popped up under her message.

Next, she checked her voice messages. There was only one. It was from Jack: "I'm checking a couple of things and will see you back at the Incident Room later." She was about to reply when Michelle appeared at the entrance to the waiting room. Kate stood up. 'Thank you for seeing me at such short notice and sorry to interrupt your day. I should have called ahead.'

'No problem.'

Her tone ensured Kate understood that indeed it was a problem. It took her a few moments to work out what was different. It was only when she was sitting across from Michelle in her tiny office that she figured it out. 'Your hair. You've had it cut. It suits you.'

Michelle half-smiled as one hand automatically reached for the base of her neck to touch it. Then she straightened and folded her hands in her lap. 'Tell me what you want.'

'There's a few details I need to get tidied away,' said Kate, keeping her eyes on the blank page in her notebook. 'It's for the form fillers back at the office. Can you confirm for me again where you were on the Sunday afternoon Dr Scott was murdered?'

Michelle sighed. 'I was at the movies in Masterton.'

'What time did the film start?' asked Kate. 'My fault; I should have written all this down properly the last time.'

'Four, but I was there early and had a glass of wine in the courtyard.'

'How early?'

'Around three,' said Michelle.

'And the movie was?' asked Kate, keeping her head down.

'*Anyone But You*. I like Glenn Powell.'

'I like him too,' said Kate. 'I heard they shut down Sydney Harbour Bridge for an hour to film the ending,'

Michelle hesitated for a moment then nodded. 'It was amazing. I needed to see a happy ending.'

'I totally understand,' said Kate. She closed her notebook. 'Have you thought any more about the complaints against Dr Scott?'

'Since the last time you asked?' A short impatient huff followed. 'I haven't had time. Did Ava tell you she sold the practice? The new owners want to come in straight away, which means I'm the one who has to get everything ready for the handover.'

'When does that happen again?' asked Kate.

'Friday afternoon.'

'And you're staying?'

'Actually,' said Michelle. A new light sparkled in her eyes. She leaned forward and whispered, 'I'm leaving. I found a tenant for my flat. I'm off to Australia on Monday. Dan knew someone who knew someone who had a vacancy for a practice manager. We did an interview on Teams, and I got the job.'

'Wow!' said Kate. She was genuinely surprised. 'When we talked on Saturday, you said you were staying.'

'I was, but after speaking to you, I realised that I did have options. Geoffrey's gone. There's nothing for me here. I asked Dan if he could use his contacts to find me something, and he did. The next-door neighbour is only too keen to have Gertie, she spends all day there anyway. And you were right; I do have money put aside for emergencies. If this isn't an emergency, what is?'

She looked happy, younger, maybe even as young as thirty-nine, thought Kate. The put-upon expression was gone, replaced with an excitement she hadn't seen before. Which made what she had to do next, even harder. Kate put her notebook in her bag.

'Michelle Parker, I'd like you to accompany me to the Masterton Police Station for further questioning. This is a request. You are not being arrested; however, you may wish to have a lawyer present when I question you.'

Stunned, Michelle stared at her open-mouthed for a few seconds.

Then she nodded once very slowly, collected her bag from under her desk, stood up and with shoulders back and head held high, she followed Kate out the door.

# CHAPTER 38

A SHOCKED LILY was straight on the phone to her mother, and the news was around town before the two women reached the Masterton station. No one could figure it out. Michelle? Surely she hadn't killed Dr Geoffrey? It couldn't be her. Weren't they looking for Ludo? Wasn't he supposed to be the killer?

Speculation ran rife, not helped by Lily finally revealing that she had known all along about Michelle's affair with Geoffrey Scott. 'Of course I knew. I worked with them. That woman,' she said to her mother. 'She took advantage of that poor man after Mrs Scott took up painting. He was being neglected, and you know what they say about nature filling a vacancy.' It was payback time. It seems Michelle had not always been kind to Lily during her performance reviews.

To say Kate's team was surprised when she radioed ahead to tell them she was bringing Michelle Parker in for questioning was an understatement.

'Do you seriously think she's a suspect?' asked Jack. He and Tony stood crammed together in Kate's tiny office. He kept his voice low so he wouldn't be overheard.

'I brought her in for questioning, didn't I?' asked Kate.

'But you didn't arrest her.'

'Correct,' said Kate.

'She's asked for a lawyer,' said Tony.

'I advised her that might be best.'

'I don't understand. Why is she here?' asked Tony.

'Because she lied about where she was when Geoffrey Scott was murdered.'

Tony stiffened. 'I checked her alibi myself. I spoke to several people who said she was at the movie theatre when Dr Scott was murdered.'

'Correct,' said Kate. 'However, it's not the whole story. I'd like it if you could both monitor the interview. I'd appreciate your input.'

There was a knock and without waiting for a reply, Sophie poked her head around the door. 'The duty solicitor has arrived ma'am. It's Charlotte Grainger. She's in with Miss Parker now.'

Kate thanked her, got up and eased past the men to walk the short distance to Interview Room One. They followed behind, ducking into the observation room.

Michelle, her eyes red-rimmed from crying, looked up when Kate entered. She was sitting at the table. Beside her sat a lawyer Kate had dealt with before. Everything about Charlotte Grainger's appearance screamed big-city lawyer. Which is what she was, until ten years ago when she married the owner of a successful rug factory in town. She could have given up work and lived a nice life as a rich man's wife. Instead, she brought her tailored suits and high heels into service as a defence lawyer for the poor and downtrodden of the district. Admirable but annoying, was how Kate often described her.

'Kate,' said Charlotte.

'Charlotte,' said Kate.

The pleasantries over, she sat down and opened her folder on the table in front of her. 'Have you had enough time with your client?'

'I have. Let's get on, shall we?' Charlotte wrote Michelle's name and the date at the top of a pad of yellow legal paper. She made a show of underlining both words before writing Kate's name on the line beneath.

Kate began by getting Michelle's permission to record the interview, then proceeded to identify everyone present and their roles before explaining that this was an interview, and Michelle was not under arrest. She made sure Michelle understood she was free to go at any stage. Then she waited while Michelle plucked a tissue from the box on the table and dabbed the tears from her eyes.

'Where were you on the Sunday afternoon when Dr Geoffrey Scott was murdered?' she asked.

'I was at home,' said Michelle. Her voice faltered, and Charlotte put a comforting hand on her arm. 'Around two o'clock, I drove to Masterton to see '*Anyone But You.*'

'This has been verified by the cashier and several witnesses who saw you there,' said Kate. 'What time did the movie finish?'

'Five-thirty,' said Michelle.

'And what time did you leave the theatre?' asked Kate.

A gulping sob was followed by more eye-dabbing. 'Before that.'

'Much before?' asked Kate.

'I left as soon as it started. I went to the bathroom. No one was at the desk, so no one saw me leave.'

'What did you do then?'

Michelle turned to Charlotte, unsure what to say next.

'Just tell the truth,' Charlotte urged, her voice gentle.

'I drove back to Martinborough.'

'Did you go home?' asked Kate.

'No. I went to see him. I knew he was there alone. I parked on the other side of the reserve and walked through it, then I ran up the drive staying close to the hedge so June wouldn't see me and tell Ava.'

'Where was Dr Scott when you arrived?' asked Kate.

'In the garden at the back of the house.'

'Where he was killed.'

'Yes. But I didn't kill him. He was alive when I got there, and he was alive when I left. You have to believe me.' The words came out in a pleading rush.

'What time was this?'

'Around five-thirty.'

'Did you speak to him?' asked Kate.

'That's why I went. The day before, we met at the health centre like we always did on Saturday afternoons. He told me he wasn't going to leave Ava. He said I should get another job someplace else. Then he told me he didn't love me anymore.' She collapsed over the table, her head buried in her arms, sobbing loudly. Charlotte reached across and stroked her shoulder, while Kate waited.

Michelle sat up and reached for another tissue. She wiped her nose and threw the sodden mess in the bin. 'I had to talk to him, you see. I knew he didn't mean it. He only said it because he was under so much pressure at the surgery from all the complaints. Plus, Ava was neglecting him. That's why he put on so much weight; she didn't cook him proper meals. I would have looked after him. I told him that. I loved him. I'll look after you…' Her voice faded. She reached for more tissues and blew her nose.

'What did he say?' asked Kate.

'Nothing. He barely looked at me. He just kept digging his garden. I begged him to listen to me and tell me he loved me, but he kept digging his garden. It was as if I didn't exist. It was horrible.'

'What did you do?'

'I left. I couldn't stand him ignoring me. I had to go. Five, ten minutes after I got there, I don't remember.'

'I want you to think about your answer very carefully, Michelle. Did you see anyone else while you were there?'

'No one.'

Kate sat back in her chair and looked at Charlotte, who raised her eyebrows.

'You must have been angry,' said Kate. 'I know I would be.'

Michelle's face twisted, her brows furrowed. 'I wasn't angry. I was furious. Not with him. Her. Ava. He only said he didn't love me because of her. I know he loved me. I could never be angry with him. I loved him. I still do.'

Kate believed her. She sat back and waited for Michelle to settle, for her breathing to slow.

'Where were you this last Sunday night?'

Michelle laughed then, her relief triumphant and obvious. 'I was with Alex and Lily. I took them out to dinner. I didn't ask permission; I just did it, and yes, the practice paid. We went to the Huntsman in Masterton, and we took a taxi there and back.'

'What time did you get home?'

'Around one,' said Michelle, her confidence growing. 'The neigh-bours will tell you because I woke them up.'

'Getting back to what you said earlier about the complaints,' said Kate. 'Originally, you said there weren't many, and they were the sort of complaints everyone gets. Yet now you tell me,' she paused and ran her pen down the page of her notebook until she found the reference she wanted. 'He was under pressure from all the complaints.'

It was as if a heavy burden had been lifted from her shoulders. Michelle, relieved of her secret and no longer feeling she had to protect her lover, let rip. Information gushed from her like water from a newly tapped spring.

There were many complaints about Geoffrey: his rudeness, his lack of discretion, mistakes with drug dosages, and tests not being followed up. So many she had given up counting. Each time he received a letter from the Health Commissioner, he ripped it up and threw it in the bin.

Sensibly, her feelings for Geoffrey hadn't negated her concern about her own role and professional responsibilities. Without him knowing, she had photo-copied the letters before passing them on to him.

'Everything is in a file at home,' she said. 'You're welcome to it.'

'Do the new owners of the health centre know?' asked Kate.

She beamed, remembering what she'd done. 'Where do you think I got the money to leave from? I called their lawyer as soon as I got to work on Monday and told them what I had.'

'I don't understand,' said Kate.

'Let's just say I've been compensated for my silence, and Ava won't be getting as much goodwill as she thought.' She chuckled. 'It's your fault. What you said on Saturday made me see that I wasn't powerless and that if I didn't look after me, no one else was going to do it.'

'I'm glad I was helpful.' She paused. 'I think. When can I see the file?'

Charlotte reached over and put a cautionary hand on Michelle's arm. 'There's the not-so-small matter of patient confidentiality to consider before you get within cooeee of that file Kate, and you know it. In the meantime, Michelle is giving it to me for safe keeping.'

'May I remind you, Charlotte, that two murders have been

committed in as many weeks, and that file may well hold the key to finding the killer.'

Charlotte nodded. 'I understand and I suggest we both take advice from our respective counsels as to what we do next. Now, if that's all?' She nudged Michelle to get up as she stood herself. 'Thank you for your time. We'll leave you to the rest of your day. Always nice to see you, Kate.'

'And you Charlotte,' said Kate. She saw the two women to the door and handed them over to the constable who would see them off the premises.

# CHAPTER 39

'WHEN DID you know she was lying?' Jack asked. They were back in her office.

'When she didn't correct me about the final scene of *Anyone But You*. It takes place on the steps of the Opera House, not the Harbour Bridge.' From the blank looks on their faces she could tell they had no idea what she was talking about. 'Just to be clear,' she said. 'We all agree she's not our killer. Right?'

'Agreed. If you knew that, I don't understand why you brought her all the way into the station for questioning?'

'I didn't think she'd tell me about the complaints otherwise. Nothing like a dose of Interview Room One to flush the truth out of people.'

'What do you hope to find out?'

'This is to go no further than this room.'

For the first time in days, Tony looked directly at her. She saw actual respect in his eyes. It was as if despite everything he'd been told, she might be good at her job after all.

'Geoffrey left behind a document about an issue with a patient. I think Michelle knows where it is. Until now, she denied there'd ever been a problem. I'm hoping this document is in the file, but I won't know until we get permission to examine it.'

The light of understanding bloomed in their eyes.

'How long before the lawyers say we can see it?' Tony asked.

'I'm hoping, it will be in the next few days. I took the liberty of talking to the guys at the PPS before I spoke to her. They're working through the various agencies as we speak.'

'The Health and Disability Commissioner?' Jack asked.

Kate rolled her eyes. 'And the rest. Our lawyer informs me the Crimes Act trumps all the other regulations, but we still have to be seen to go through the motions. If it's as vital as I think it is, I don't want it to get thrown out of court because we obtained the information illegally.'

'What if this mysterious document isn't in the file?' Jack asked.

'That would be gutting. But it's not the only line of investigation we're following up, is it Tony? Any update from the search party yet?'

He reacted as if she'd just favoured him with a winning pass in front of a stadium full of his nearest and dearest. 'Only that there are more wild pigs in the bush than they thought, and Ludo hasn't visited any huts. The search continues.'

'Keep me updated. I'm off to see Isobel Simich this afternoon.'

'I interviewed her when Juliette went missing. Why are you going to see her?' asked Jack.

'Because, three years ago, Ludo Wilkins worked on their farm. He had to have known Juliette, maybe even talked to her. They could have been friends.'

Jack's face fell. 'Why didn't she tell me that at the time?'

'I want to find that out too.'

'Let's disregard the fact she withheld vital information, and I should charge her with perverting the course of justice, for a moment. Do you think Juliette's disappearance is related to the recent murders?' he asked.

Kate took a moment before she replied. 'I think it's possible.'

# CHAPTER 40

FROM THE VANTAGE point in the bay window of her sitting room, Isobel Simich looked onto the road below, and wrapped her arms around her waist. Her stomach tightened as she watched the cloud of dust kicked up by Kate Sutton's car draw closer. It was two o'clock in the afternoon.

She'd been up since dawn—for no other reason than it was light, and because even though three years had passed since Ivan's death, she still hadn't grown used to sleeping alone. She was as ravaged by his loss now as she had been then. Isobel kept her grief to herself. There was nothing else she could do. He was gone. She was left to get on with it.

At the bottom of the rise, the car turned through the gates into her drive, then immediately slowed. It always happened. It was this house. Grand and imposing, it stood alone on its hill, surrounded by gardens and framed by the dark bush-clad range behind. It had been her family's home for one hundred and fifty years, but not for much longer, she thought sadly.

In his will, Ivan had given her sons and their bossy wives the joint power of attorney and with it, control of her affairs. Done with the best of intentions, her dear beloved husband had underestimated the extent of their greed.

No sooner was their father in the ground, than they informed her the estate would no longer fund the upkeep of the house. She was to find a smaller place in town. The old homestead was to be sold, and failing that, torn down.

For the past three years she had fought to keep them at bay, but those years had taken their toll. The gardens were a struggle, and she had all but given up on the housework. She reckoned she could hold out for another year, two at best before she would have to bow to the inevitable and agree to their demands that she leave.

Kate drove her car slowly past the formal rose garden; the hundred different varieties in their second flowering of the summer, were Isobel's pride and joy. She stopped at the bottom of the steps, got out and looked around her.

Isobel checked her appearance in the mirror and adjusted the belt of her sundress. She applied a slash of bright red lipstick and smacked her lips together, then using the tip of her little finger, wiped clear the corner of her mouth. She opened the front door and stepped out to greet her visitor.

'Good afternoon, Detective Sutton.'

'Good afternoon, Mrs Simich,' said Kate.

Once inside, Kate informed her she was a senior detective sergeant but that it was fine to call her detective.

Isobel, who couldn't give a fig about the woman's rank, smiled graciously and invited her into the sitting room. It was a relief when Kate didn't dawdle to gawp at the hall lined with antique furniture, or gasp at the mahogany and marble staircase leading up to the second floor.

'I made tea,' she said. 'And scones. Cheese there, and date there.' She pointed to the plates on a tray on a small table in the bay window. There was a chair on either side.

'Tea would be wonderful,' said Kate. She stood at the window searching the view for a glimpse of the cottage. 'I can't see it,' she said.

Isobel knew exactly what she was looking for. 'It's behind that shelter belt down to the left. We used to be able to see it from upstairs, but the trees have grown so big we can't now. You've reminded me. I'll ask the manager to get them trimmed before winter.'

She handed Kate her tea, relieved when the detective refused the offer of a scone. The fuss with the butter and jam and the plates and the crumbs on the floor was suddenly too much to bear. 'I was surprised when I got your call,' she said. 'What's this about?'

Kate sat down and placed her cup and saucer on the little table. She fished her notebook out of her handbag. 'I have to keep a record, I'm afraid.'

'Of course,' said Isobel. She poured her own tea, added milk and waited.

'Your husband Ivan died in February three years ago. On the same Friday night Juliette Bisson, your tenant, went missing.'

'He died at midnight,' said Isobel. 'Pancreatic cancer. I don't recommend it.'

'You were with him when he died?'

'I was. So was our son, Tim. Frank, our youngest, was asleep. It was hard for the boys seeing their father in so much pain.'

'I'm sorry for your loss,' said Kate. 'You must miss him.'

Meaningless platitudes thought the old lady, but she nodded her acknowledgement, more concerned about where all this was leading.

'Did you see or hear anything unusual at the cottage or on the road that night?' Kate asked.

'No, but my mind was on other things.' Isobel sipped her tea, quietly replacing the porcelain cup on its saucer.

'Of course.' Kate paused. 'What happened after your husband passed away?'

'I cried, if that's what you mean?' She met Kate's eyes. 'Are you married?'

'Divorced,' replied Kate.

The answer didn't surprise her. Kate looked like a woman with her own life. Ivan's sister had been such a person, focused on her career to the exclusion of everything else. Isobel understood the attraction of singlehood, but she also didn't think being selfish was good for anyone. Ivan agreed with her. He called his sister an emotional coward. She hadn't liked that.

The detective was looking at her, waiting.

'We didn't wake Frank,' she said. 'No point. I phoned Bruce to tell him, only because he insisted it was no bother. He said he'd be out first thing. Mimi, his wife, is Ivan's goddaughter. Ivan liked him. I never did. Mimi never said anything, but you know the type. Controlling.' She leaned forward. 'I think he used to hit her.'

Kate looked up sharply. Isobel waited for her face to settle before continuing. 'Tim went to bed. I curled up beside Ivan and said my goodbyes. I must have fallen asleep because it was light when I woke. I had a shower, got dressed, then I called Dr Geoffrey.'

She reached for her tea and sipped it. 'I was appalled when I heard he'd been murdered. He was such a good doctor, and he was so caring. He visited Ivan twice a day towards the end. To make sure he was comfortable, had enough pain relief.'

'He came out on the Saturday morning?' asked Kate.

Isobel nodded. 'He got here around six, filled out the forms, then called Bruce.'

'What time did he leave?'

'Before Bruce arrived which was around seven. We had a cup of tea and finalised the arrangements for the funeral. Ivan had left instructions about what he wanted, which made it easier. He left around eight.'

'With your husband?'

Isobel had stayed in the kitchen for that part. She didn't want to see the man she loved bundled up in a black bag like a sack of potatoes, then loaded into the back of the station wagon.

'I imagine you had a lot of visitors that day,' said Kate. 'People driving past the cottage. Did anyone mention anything?'

'Nothing,' said Isobel. 'Otherwise, I would have sent the boys down to check. Normally, I kept an eye on her, but Ivan was so sick, and he needed me. I talked to Juliette two weeks before he died. She seemed happy. She enjoyed her work at the vineyard and loved being here.'

'Remind me again how she got to work.'

'A van picked her up and dropped her off.'

'Can you remember who came to your house that morning?'

Still staring out the window, Isobel pursed her lips as she thought about her answer. 'The boys were here,' she said slowly. 'Their wives and the children arrived at lunchtime. I didn't want to see anyone else, not then. Carolyn, the courier, delivered flowers. It's beyond me why anyone would send flowers to someone with a garden as big as mine.' Her finger pressed against her lips; she shook her head. 'That's all. No one else.'

'Does Carolyn still do your deliveries?'

'She moved to Brisbane. They have a young family. Her partner was offered a job with more pay and better prospects. You can't blame them for wanting to go.'

'When was your husband's funeral?' Kate asked.

'On the Wednesday. The same day your lot descended on the cottage looking for Juliette.'

'I'm sorry,' she said.

'Of course I understood. The living must take precedence over the dead.' She reached over to feel the teapot under the tea cosy. 'It's still warm. More tea?'

Kate shook her head. She hadn't finished the first cup. 'Ludo Wilkins. I understand he worked for you that summer?'

'Yes.'

'I checked the statement we took from you back then, and you never mentioned him. Why was that?'

'Most likely,' Isobel said, 'because no one asked.'

Kate raised an eyebrow.

She paused, thinking how best to frame her answer. 'I had so much to think about and Ludo had his own problems. I suppose I wanted to protect him. He's a nice boy.'

'How long did he work for you?'

'A year. With the stock, mainly. He fed out, fixed the water troughs when they broke, and did general farm work. Over the summer, he camped out at the reserve at the end of the road. In winter, he lived in the shearer's quarters behind the house.'

'When did you first realise he had his 'own problems', as you put it?'

'The week before Ivan died, he came up to the house to ask if I would mind if he moved the sheep at night. He said it was because the moonlight was gentler on their wool. I couldn't talk him out of it, and because it didn't matter in the scheme of things, I let it go.'

'Your farm borders the cottage, doesn't it?'

'The cottage is on our land.'

'It's possible Ludo would have seen Juliette, maybe even spoken to her?'

Her eyes closed Isobel swallowed. 'I know I should have taken more interest in her welfare. I know that and I feel awful that I didn't. You see before the boys arrived Ludo helped me with Ivan. He was so kind and gentle with him. If he hadn't been here, Ivan would have gone to the hospice. Do you understand? Ludo would never have hurt her.'

'He had problems,' said Kate quietly.

Isobel didn't move.

'Problems with reality,' said Kate.

'I know that. But I'm telling you, he wouldn't have hurt her.'

'Is that why you didn't tell us about him then?'

'I should have. I've thought about it many times since. And when I met her poor father, it was too late. Then, when the police didn't find her body, I assumed she'd run off. Young people do that, don't they? That's what people in the village said. If Ivan had been alive, he would have told me what to do. When I heard how sick Ludo was and how no one could get a sensible word out of him, I knew I should have said something, but it was too late. It was just too late.'

Somewhere deep inside the house, a clock chimed the hour.

'Ludo would not have hurt her,' she said again, more to convince herself than Kate.

'Did Ludo go to your husband's funeral, Mrs Simich?'

'No.'

'When was the last time you saw him?'

'Three days before.'

'To be clear, you're saying Ludo left the day after Ivan died, the day after Juliette went missing,' said Kate.

'Yes. He didn't show up for work on Saturday. Tim was furious because he just up and left, right when we needed him most. We had to get a man from down the road to help out.'

Isobel didn't move when Kate closed her notebook and put it back in her bag. She stayed in her chair, staring out the window when Kate stood up and said she would see herself out. When she watched Kate walk down the steps and get into her car, Isobel suddenly felt very old. As if the strength she had mustered three years ago to deal with her pain had abandoned her.

# CHAPTER 41

SOME MORNINGS, Lily Baxter liked to get to the medical centre before everyone else. With the sun shining through the frosted glass windows, spreading a gentle light over the empty waiting room, it was a lovely place to be.

However, for the past week, Dan Forrester had been there when she arrived, sitting in his consulting room, tapping away on his computer. He said it was routine paperwork, but how could it be? Most of the so-called paperwork was done at the time of the consultation. At least that's how Dr Scott did his.

She liked Dr Forrester, but she was starting to wonder if he was doing something he shouldn't be. Yesterday, if Michelle hadn't been marched off to the police station, she would have said something. Too late now.

On Friday, everything would change again. Miffed that no one had asked her if she wanted to stay or leave, Lily still hadn't decided what she was going to do. She was annoyed that Michelle hadn't said anything when they went out for dinner. The woman never tired of telling Lily she was the boss, so why hadn't she acted like one? Wasn't it her job to look after the staff?

Instead, she gets carted off to the police station to answer questions.

About what? Yesterday afternoon, after she had been taken away, Lily snuck into her office and googled her search history.

That was how she found out Michelle was moving to Sydney. Not that she blamed her for leaving. Dementia or no dementia, Dr Scott had treated her very badly. Didn't she know men never leave their wives? Or maybe she did, and that's why the police wanted to question her. Had Michelle killed Dr Scott? Was that why she hadn't told Lily about the new owners?

These thoughts were whirling around in her head when she opened the door to the tearoom, crying out in fright when she walked straight into Dan Forrester. His body was so hard she practically bounced off his chest. She didn't fall only because he reached out to steady her.

'Whoa there,' he said.

Lily stepped back when he let her go and flapped her hand in front of her face. 'You gave me the hugest fright. I thought you were in your room.'

'I made coffee. Want some?'

'Is there any milk?'

'Plenty,' he said. 'It's still fresh.'

That's when she heard someone cough in the waiting room. The centre hadn't opened yet. She always used the back entrance, which meant Dan must have left the front door unlocked when he came in. Her quiet, peaceful time was over.

'I'll get it after I've seen to this patient,' she said.

When she returned to the front desk, she saw a man standing on the other side of the counter. She thought it was strange that he was wearing an overcoat. People don't need overcoats in summer. With his head down, he didn't move, not when she slammed a drawer, and not when she put on her friendliest voice. 'We aren't open yet,' she explained. 'Would you mind coming back in half an hour?'

He looked up, his dark brown eyes seeing her, but not really; she would tell people later. Also, his hair was different from his photograph; it was longer. But she knew it was him and was about to run back to tell Dan and ask what she should do when he moved faster than she thought anyone could ever move. He reached across the counter and grabbed her by her wrist, bending it back so she was help-less, stuck.

'Where's the doc?'

His breath stank. Like he hadn't brushed his teeth in ages. Lumps of what looked like chewed bread were stuck in the gaps between his teeth. He kept twisting her wrist as he pulled her towards him, the keyboard and edge of the counter digging painfully into her hips.

'He's not here.'

It was the first thing she could think of to say. Habit? For a split second, she wondered if, in another life, she might have been a resis-tance heroine. It's funny, she told people, how time slows down and you think strange thoughts and how they zing through your mind. By then, she'd seen the rifle in his left hand, pointing at the floor.

'You were talking to him,' said Ludo. Lily knew it was Ludo Wilkins, and her heart was pounding because he had a gun, and she didn't want two doctors dead in less than two weeks. 'See how your mind works,' she said to her mother that night when they were sitting in the dark because neither of them could sleep.

'Call him.' He was holding her arm, gripping it so hard she squeaked. Then he pushed her in front of him, shuffling to the door. 'Dan,' she called or didn't, because her lips moved, but no sound came out.

'Who's Dan?'

'The doctor.'

This time, when she called his name, her voice screeched loudly. 'Dan.'

The door at the end of the corridor opened, and Dan appeared, smiling and holding a cup of coffee. 'I'll bring it down.'

He saw the man holding Lily. 'Be there in a second.' He sounded calm and in control as he bent down slowly and put the cup on the floor.

'Seeing him made me feel better,' she told her mother. 'There was something about the way he moved. I relaxed. Even though Ludo still had me by the wrist.'

Dan, his palms up, walked towards them.

'Ludo, isn't it?' he said as he drew near. 'I was hoping to see you today. We've got a lot to talk about.'

'Where's the Doc?'

'Dr Scott isn't here. I'm a doctor too. I can help. Why don't you let Lily get back to work? She's got a lot to do before the patients arrive.'

Ludo gripped Lily's wrist even harder, hurting her, and she cried out. Dan stepped forward. Ludo pulled back, holding her in front of him like a shield as he raised the rifle, and with his finger on the trigger, he aimed it at Dan's stomach.

'Get Doc Geoffrey.'

Silent tears ran down Lily's face, her eyes pleading with Dan to do something.

'I will, but let Lily go first.'

Dan casually moved so he had one leg in front of the other; he dropped one shoulder, his arms hanging loose at his side. Ludo hesitated, his eyes flicking around the corridor as he considered what to do next.

Easing his grip, he unwrapped his fingers from Lily's wrist. She straightened her arm, rubbing the spot where her skin was dented, as the blood returned to her fingertips. Keeping her eyes fixed on Dan's face, she edged away from Ludo, gradually, smoothly, half a step at a time.

'The doc's been called to a car accident on Moana Road,' said Dan. 'You probably heard about it on the radio when you were driving in.'

'I don't listen to the radio. When's he back?'

'Hard to tell with a car accident. How about you put the rifle down and tell me why you're here? I might be able to help.'

Ludo didn't move.

Dan's eyes flicked from Lily to the front door, telling her to run, leave and get help. Bent low, she ran across the waiting room, pushed through the door and was out.

Ludo swivelled, raised the rifle to his shoulder and bending his head to focus down the barrel, he aimed at her shadow through the glass and pulled the trigger. The door and windows shattered as bullets ripped through them, the glass falling to the floor like a dropped curtain. He kept firing, and Lily kept running, zigzagging down the street towards the square, and was gone.

It was quiet now. A soft breeze drifted through the waiting area. Dan smelled the aroma of hot coffee wafting across the square from the café on the corner. He had counted five shots before Ludo lowered the rifle. He recognised the make and model from his work overseas, having used it himself several times. It was a semi-automatic .22 Ruger 10/20 with an internal magazine holding 10 rounds.

That meant there were five rounds left.

'Put the safety on so we can talk,' suggested Dan. He was relieved and surprised when Ludo did just that, flipping the red button out of sight.

'Thank you.' Dan walked over to the nearest chair and sat down, his thighs apart, his hands flat on his knees.

Ludo, his weapon nestled in the crook of his arm, backed against the counter and stared at him.

'Doc Geoffrey isn't at a car accident,' said Dan. 'He was murdered ten days ago.'

The distress on Ludo's face was genuine. 'Nooooo,' he wailed, drawing out the word as he shook his head, his long hair sweeping across his face.

'Who?'

'We don't know.'

In an instant, Ludo's expression changed. He looked furtively around him, as he hooked his hair behind his ear. 'I know,' he said, his voice low. 'I warned him. He wouldn't listen.'

'What did you say?'

'Not me. Her. She said it.' The end of the rifle waved in the air like a pointer. He stopped, his head to one side as if listening. He nodded violently. Then he shook his head, his tangled hair falling over his eyes again as he muttered something unintelligible. Pushing his hair away, his eyes narrowed as if he were measuring Dan up for a suit. His teeth clenched, and then he started to yell. 'JUST. SHUT. UP.'

Dan concentrating on his breathing, stayed still.

'He was going to talk to a lawyer. Leave it with me, Ludo. That's what he said.' Ludo stopped, again listening before nodding vigorously. 'She says we have to find it.'

'What do we have to find?' asked Dan.

'It's a secret,' said Ludo.

'Tell me so I can help you.'

Ludo put a finger in front of his lips to shoosh him. 'She's talking.' He opened his mouth to speak, then stopped, listening again. 'They're coming.'

Cautious footsteps outside the building. He had to keep Ludo talking so he didn't click off the safety, so he didn't raise the rifle and fire at whoever was outside.

'I can't hear anything,' he said. 'Tell me the secret. I want to help you.'

Ludo crooked his finger, beckoning Dan to cross the floor between them. Ludo cupped his hand against his ear, the whispers filling the silence.

A branch cracked outside.

Ludo paused and looked up. Hearing nothing, he carried on. Finished, he pushed Dan away.

Another sound, this time a rock hitting the pavement, then rolling away.

Ludo took up a defensive position behind the reception desk. With the barrel of the rifle supported by the counter, he listened for the next sound. It came. Another rock. A different place.

He aimed and pulled the trigger.

Nothing.

Swearing, he flipped the safety to red and fired two shots in quick succession into the street.

A blur of fluorescent green slammed into the side of Ludo's head, stunning him, knocking him off balance, loosening his grip on the rifle. It slid out of his grasp towards the floor.

In that split second, Dan hurled himself around the counter, dived low at Ludo's knees and wrapped his arms around them, his forward momentum taking them both down.

The rifle clattered to the floor ahead of them. Dan held on, hugging the young man's bucking legs to his chest, as Ludo tried to claw his way across the floor to his weapon. He was a fingertip away from reclaiming it when Kate brought the edge of her tennis racket down on Ludo's outstretched hand.

The sound of a bone snapping in two. Howling from Ludo as Dan lay on top of him, pinning him to the floor before he sat up and yanked one hand around and then the other, holding them while Kate circled Ludo's wrists with zip ties.

Dan reached for the rifle, switched on the safety and unclipped the magazine.

It was over.

# CHAPTER 42

'IF YOU EVER, EVER, EVER,' Jack paused. 'Ever, ever do that again, I'll bust you down to traffic in less time than it takes to blink.'

Conscious of the people listening outside the cubicle, Jack kept his threat strong and his voice low. It was five o'clock on Thursday afternoon, and he was sitting in Kate's chair in her office in Masterton.

Standing on the other side of the desk, Kate's eyes were focused on a spot behind his head. Her back was straight, her arms by her sides. That her shirt was missing a button, was blood-stained and filthy and that her pants were covered in the same dust which ccated her hair was irrelevant. Kate had knowingly breached every step in the police protocol for managing an armed suspect, and she deserved the rollicking.

'I'm not going to ask what you would have done if you'd missed,' said Jack. 'My blood pressure can't cope with your answer. Not now. But be assured there will be a reckoning.'

He pointed one long index finger straight at her. 'You will reflect on today and provide a full and frank appraisal of the stupidity of your actions when this is over.'

Unable to contain himself, he drummed the fingers of his right hand on the desk, a sure sign he wasn't done. 'You couldn't wait, could you? You had to play the hero.'

All ten fingers were now drumming on her desk. Both hands. He looked at her, his eyes wide, his nostrils flared, his face flushed with fury.

'What would I tell your boys if you'd been shot? How would I have told them?' He huffed. 'Being told your mother died a hero doesn't quite cut it when you're standing beside a body bag.'

'He fired into the street. He could have killed a passer-by. He nearly killed Lily. I couldn't let Dan die.'

Jack stopped drumming and shook his finger at her. 'Dan Forrester can take care of himself.'

'I know that now,' she answered. 'I didn't then.'

'So help me,' he said, shaking his head and getting up at the same time. His knuckles on her desk, he leaned across, his face in front of hers. 'Don't you ever do something as ridiculous as that, ever again.'

'I won't.'

Blame it on stress, shock, whatever; she couldn't help the crossed fingers behind her back. It was a silly childish gesture of defiance, but it felt right. It was honest. She wanted to say more, but he didn't want to hear it. Deep inside, she knew that if the situation demanded it, she would do exactly the same again.

'Sit,' he ordered, gesturing to the chair he usually occupied. He fell back into Kate's chair with a thump.

It was strange sitting on the other side of her desk. Still on a high from the afternoon's events, she fought the urge to reach across, switch on her computer and request a status update from the hospital.

'I spoke to Isobel Simich,' she said instead. 'It seems we missed another witness. A courier driver, Carolyn Morton. She made a delivery to the Simich's that Saturday morning. Her family moved to Australia shortly after. Tony is following her up.'

'It beggars' belief she didn't come forward at the time.'

'People get caught up in their own lives I suppose,' she said. 'Isobel felt she had to protect Ludo. Whatever her reasons back then, she's had three years to tell us what she knew and didn't. I blame her more than I do the courier driver.'

'Speaking of Ludo,' he said. 'I googled psychosis while I was waiting for you to get checked over. It takes four to six weeks for the medication to start working.'

'I googled it too. That's only when you're starting from scratch. His medication was working until a few weeks ago. He's only missed one dose so hopefully it won't take as long.'

'Any news on Michelle's documents?'

'Charlotte is being quite helpful for a change. Once we find a suitable independent medical practitioner and tell them what we're looking for, she will release the file. The Privacy Commissioner has recommended someone in town who might do it.'

There was a muffled knock, and Tony poked his head around the door. 'Lucy from the media team says they're ready for you, sir.'

Jack stood up, straightened his tie and readjusted the belt on his trousers. Stomach in, chest out, he turned to Kate. 'How do I look?'

'Very professional.'

'You should be fronting this, not me.'

'Looking like this? Not a chance.'

'Your call,' he said. 'You're happy with the statement media's put together?'

'I haven't seen it.'

He took a card from his inside jacket pocket, put on his glasses and read, 'Today we were able to locate the person of interest we have been looking for in regard to the investigation into the murders of Dr Geoffrey Scott and Ms June Whittaker. He is now in care awaiting a psychiatric evaluation. We hope to speak to him next week. Meanwhile, the investigation is ongoing.'

He looked up, his eyebrows raised. 'I expect there will be a few questions about how you stormed the health centre armed only with your tennis racket. What do you want me to say?'

'Nothing. It's an operational matter; as such, it's on a need-to-know basis, and they don't need to know.'

'They wouldn't believe me anyway,' he said. 'I'll thank the public for their help, praise the quick response of the front-line staff, blah blah, blah! And get out of there.'

'Can I go home now?'

'I'd say well done, but you shouldn't have done it, so I can't.'

'Then, I won't say thank you.'

'One last thing,' he said. 'I spoke to Bruce Murphy before this kicked off. He was under the impression the new CCTV cameras were installed when he was in Auckland. He was very surprised to hear they hadn't been.'

She cocked her head, waiting for him to finish.

'I spoke to the CEO at the council. Apparently, the system arrived two months ago. There's been a miscommunication. He was waiting for Bruce to give final sign-off, but it never happened.' He paused. 'I guess lines got crossed. It's a pity because it would have been useful.'

'He's a busy man,' said Kate. 'Did he tell you about the sculpture park?'

'He didn't. Don't tell me now. You're exhausted. Go home and get some sleep.'

Kate went to get up but stopped midway when every muscle in her body spasmed at the same time. Jack moved to put his hand under her elbow to help, but she waved him away.

'Leave me. I'll be fine. The reporters have deadlines to meet. You don't want to get them riled up or they'll come after you the way they came after me.'

# CHAPTER 43

DAN OPENED ONE EYE, then the other. He was relieved to find the lampshade stayed in one place. He'd jarred his neck as he tackled Ludo. Or maybe Ludo's knee had hit his ear. Whatever, last night and this morning he felt dizzy when he moved his head too quickly. Inching himself up on his elbows, he eased his legs over the edge of the bed and stayed there until he felt ready to stand.

'Ava?'

There was no reply. She'd left him to manage on his own. Moving at a pace that would make a snail proud and making sure he was never far from something to hold onto, he showered, dressed, and made his way downstairs.

The note on the kitchen table informed him she was at the studio. She suggested he pop in later, anytime after three, to help her to crate up her paintings. It was also his turn to cook. A bit harsh, but that was Ava. Her sole focus was on her upcoming exhibition.

Louis meowed pathetically beside his empty dish until Dan found a box of kibble in the pantry and filled it to overflowing. The cat flashed him a grateful look, then huddled over the bowl, purring loudly as he crunched his way through this unexpected feast. Dan made coffee.

Two weeks ago, he'd been in the Northern Territory repairing cut heads and broken limbs, caring for women in labour, and children with chicken pox. It was one of his more peaceful assignments.

His work often took him to the edges of war zones, where he thrived on the constant threat of the unknown. His craving for adrenalin-fuelled chaos; one of the reasons he and Geoffrey had drifted apart over the years. Close when they were younger, their different philosophies pulled them in opposite directions as they matured.

Yet look how they'd ended up. The irony of his risk-averse friend being murdered in his safe suburban garden, was not lost on him.

Then to cap it off, Dan had been held at gunpoint by a deranged man in Geoffrey's tastefully designed waiting room, only to be saved by a middle-aged female cop smashing a tennis ball into the side of the gunman's head. It had to be the cherry on the irony cake. The Geoffrey of old would have appreciated the joke.

Dan had a problem. This wasn't over. Ludo's words replayed in his head. The secret Geoffrey had recorded then hidden was still out there.

Ludo might be psychotic, but he was not wholly divorced from reality. Everything he said tallied with Aiden Cooper's story. Which meant Geoffrey had not been confabulating—this was not a product of dementia.

But where was the document?

Ludo didn't know.

Dan had found nothing at the health centre. With only so many places it could be, Dan figured it had to be where Geoffrey could get to it easily and quickly, but not so easily or quickly others would find it.

There was little point in him going to the health centre today. It would be crawling with glaziers and workmen. Ava was away all day, which meant he was free to search the house without her getting in his way. He drank the last of his coffee, rinsed the mug and put it in the dishwasher. Slowly and carefully he bent down to put a saucer of water on the floor for Louis. His dizziness was better, but it hadn't gone.

The most obvious place for him to start was in the old surgery.

A warm musty smell hit him as soon as he went in; the room had not been aired for days. He pushed back the faded curtains and opened the French doors leading to the terrace, inhaling the fresh air before returning to start his search. The room was coated in a layer of thick dust, except for the smudges left by the police.

Geoffrey had worked here until he moved the practice to the health centre. Then, for sentimental reasons, which Dan totally understood, he restored the room to how it looked in his father's day. The transformation was so complete that Dan half expected to see old Dr Scott sitting at the desk, smoke spiralling up from the pipe resting in the ashtray beside him.

Old Dr Scott's faded but still legible degree hung on the wall between the bookshelves. The antique desk in the middle of the room faced the door. A chest-high metal filing cabinet stood against the wall between the French doors. An examination couch ran along half the opposite wall, its old rubber mattress covered by a sheet now crumpled and grey with dust.

He started with the filing cabinet. Inside, he found paper, alphabetical separators, an old biro, and a tendon hammer. The desk drawers yielded ink, paper clips, random staples, and an ashtray.

Kneeling, he checked that Geoffrey hadn't been inventive enough to stick anything to the undersides of the drawers, running his fingers over the wood, and earning a splinter under his nail for his trouble.

The single drawer in the examination couch rewarded him with a box of disposable gloves and the blade of a metal speculum.

Outside, it was another hot summer's day, with only a faint nor'easterly breeze offering relief. Sunlight reflecting off the concrete terrace raised the temperature in the small room to an uncomfortable degree. Sweat plastered Dan's shirt to his back, the damp fabric clinging to his skin as he sifted through the clutter in search of Ludo's mysterious document.

The bookshelves were his last hope. Lever files contained exactly what their labels indicated: Geoffrey's IRD returns covering the fifteen years prior to his moving to the health centre. Searching through years of invoices was too daunting; Dan was too hot and by now, impatient. He returned the files to the shelf, deciding such a thorough search would be a last resort.

He took down one of the old medical textbooks; its spine faded, but the title, French's Differential Diagnosis, was still discernible. It was lighter than he expected, and he fumbled the book, almost dropping it. The reason was obvious as soon as he opened it. A square hole had been cut in the centre of the pages.

Why hadn't he remembered how much Geoffrey loved adventure books and spy movies? Hiding something in a hollowed-out book was exactly what he would do.

Outside, he heard the sound of footsteps on the drive, and then those same footsteps crossing the lawn to the terrace.

Bruce Murphy poked his head around the curtains, just as Dan was returning the book to the shelf.

'I've come to see how the man who saved Martinborough is getting along,' he said. His tone was light and breezy as he stepped into the room and gave it a cursory up and down. 'If you're up for it, let me buy you breakfast as my way of saying thank you.'

Dan was about to brush him off when his stomach intervened with a loud gurgle.

'You know what? I'd like that. Ava's at the studio all day and there's no food in the house. Let me finish up here and I'll meet you at Nora's in five?'

'Excellent,' said Bruce. He stepped back onto the terrace. 'My treat, remember.'

Dan waited, listening as Bruce walked to the end of the drive. Then he locked the doors and windows, double-checking to make sure he hadn't missed any, before grabbing his stuff.

When he left, Louis was fast asleep on the sofa in the living room, his tummy a taut round barrel of fur rising balloon-like above the cushions.

# CHAPTER 44

TONY LEAPT to his feet when Kate walked into the Incident Room on Friday morning. He actually offered to fetch her coffee. Not from the machine in the kitchen, but from the cafe on the corner. He even smiled.

The turnaround in his attitude wasn't hard to fathom, but it was tiresome. Did she prefer the version of Tony that was the sullen rebel chewing gum at the back of the class, or this version—the suck-up? It was a hard call.

He trailed after her, stopping at the entrance to her cubicle. 'I spoke to Carolyn Morton last night.'

She lowered herself into her chair and tried not to wince. Overnight, her muscles had stiffened into bands of rigid steel. The painkillers, taken before she left home, still hadn't kicked in.Her shoulder was especially sore. If she wanted to play tennis again this season, she would need to see a physio. Her problem? She didn't have time.

'What did she say?'

'She confirmed she made the flower delivery on Saturday morning. And she remembered seeing Bruce Murphy coming back from the house. They had to slow down to get past each other on the narrow road. Doesn't remember seeing anyone else.'

'Talk to her again tonight.'

'Why? She told me everything she could remember. She'll get annoyed if I call her back.'

'It's an old trick Bill taught me when I was a new recruit. The first call dredges it up. She remembered a few things. Today, she'll be going over it all again, and something she'd forgotten about, will have resurfaced.'

He looked doubtful but wrote the reminder in his notebook anyway. She suppressed a smile. The old Tony would have ignored her. 'Is it possible,' he asked, 'that Geoffrey Scott killed Juliette and Ludo found out then killed him for revenge?'

Kate shifted uncomfortably in her chair. 'Anything's possible, I suppose. But why wait three years? And why not come to the police and let us handle it properly?'

'Because he doesn't trust the police. Because he thinks we wouldn't believe him because of his problems and because ... ' Tony's voice faded as the serious flaws in his scenario raised their heads.

'They're good points Tony.' Far be it from her to discourage a fresh approach. 'It shows you're thinking. When Ludo is well enough, we can ask him.'

For a moment, Tony looked deflated, but then he straightened again, his expression brightening in a way that made Kate brace herself for whatever he was going to say next.

'The last investigation focused on what people were doing after Juliette went missing.'

'Yes,' said Kate. 'We were hoping for sightings and failing that, any suspicious behaviour which might lead us to her body.'

'We should find out what were people doing before she went missing?' He nodded meaningfully, as if it was the first time anyone had considered this angle. If it didn't hurt so much to stand up, she would have shown him the door.

'We know what Juliette was doing,' he continued. 'She was working, going home, going to bed, getting up and going to work. So on and so on. She kept to herself because she was saving money. She didn't have a boyfriend or a social life outside her work at the vineyard.'

Tony tapped his pen against his notepad. 'Take Ludo for example. What was he doing? Did they ever meet? Did they talk? Did they have a relationship?' He saw her expression and his face fell. 'That's what you've been thinking since you found out they knew each other, isn't it?'

'It is. As I said, we can't confirm or rule out anything until we talk to him.'

He was undeterred. 'Okay. Dr Scott then. What was he doing? Isobel said he visited her husband twice a day. He must have seen her. Did he ever stop and talk to her? Where was he on the Friday evening after she was dropped off at her cottage by the work van?'

Kate leaned back, considering his words despite the pain which had now travelled from her shoulder up her neck to settle at the base of her skull. 'We can't ask him now. I understand where you're coming from Tony, but your way means we'd have to ask the whole village what they were doing.'

'Not everyone and not all at once,' Tony countered. 'We start with the people we know who were on Raupaki Road the day before and the day after she disappeared, and we go from there.' He stood poised, willing her to agree. 'What have we got to lose?'

'Time. Resources. Sanity.'

'So we can try it?' He leaned forwards, his eyes bright with anticipation.

'It's not a bad idea,' she conceded. 'I'll give it one day.'

'Who do you suggest I talk to first?'

'How about Michelle? I doubt if she'll talk to me again. Ask if Juliette ever met Dr. Scott.'

'On it,' he said, already reaching for his phone.

'And if nothing comes of this approach, promise me you'll let it go.'

'Deal,' said Tony. 'And I promise to call Carolyn again.'

# CHAPTER 45

LUDO'S PSYCHIATRIST, Dr Christine Su, didn't say much when Kate called. Ludo was asleep and didn't need surgery for the one broken bone in his hand.

'When can we talk to him?' asked Kate.

'That depends on how quickly he responds to the medication,' the doctor replied. 'We know which drugs are effective, and he's responded well to these in the past. It could be days; it could be weeks. If there's nothing else?' She paused for a microsecond. 'I have work to do.' The line went dead, leaving Kate staring at her phone, wondering if the doctor was as short with her patients as she had been with her.

Beyond her cubicle walls, Kate heard the visiting officers packing up, their voices buoyant with the satisfaction of a job well done. It was a cheerful noise. The murderer had been caught, and a celebration at the nearby pub was planned for later that afternoon. The press corps was gone. Yesterday's media conference had finally satisfied their appetite for sensation: the Martinborough serial killer had been captured, their stories filed, they were on to the next headline.

That morning under a threatening sky, Kate confronted Jack in the car park after her meeting with Tony.

'One more week, I need the extra staff for one more week. Tony's come up with a new angle on Juliette's murder. I think he has something, Jack. What if Ludo isn't our killer?'

His expression hardened. 'Look at the evidence. We have him on camera outside two of the victims' houses around the times they were murdered. We have him in the vicinity of Juliette's cottage before she vanished, and, in case you've forgotten, he took a rifle tc the health centre and opened fire. I'm fairly confident we've got our man.'

'That's not enough for a conviction, and you know it,' she countered, her voice steady.

'Granted.' He pointed his finger at her. 'It's your job between now and when the case goes to court to find the evidence and bridge that gap.' He sighed then; fatigue etched in the lines around his eyes. 'Meanwhile, crime doesn't stop while we're twiddling our thumbs waiting for a confession. Those officers are needed back in their own districts.'

'But—'

He sliced through her objection with a firm hand. 'I don't want to hear it. There's a mountain of paperwork waiting for me in Wellington.' He tossed his overnight bag into the back seat of his car. 'You've done a great job, Kate. You got your man. Now find the proof to put him away for a very long time.'

She nodded numbly as he drove away, his hand waving a farewell through his open window. Across the square, Nora's café hummed with life, the tables on the pavement full of customers. There was a buzz in the air which hadn't been there yesterday. Life in Martinborough was almost back to normal. So why did she feel as if some vital piece of the puzzle was still missing?

Seated at her desk in her cubicle, her shoulder ached. Her neck ached and so did her head. If that wasn't enough to crash her mood, then her own mountain of paperwork loomed unwanted and unloved in front of her.

The public never got to see the sheer number of forms and statements generated during an investigation, each one needing careful scrutiny before sign-off. Cases crumbled in court when evidence chains weren't meticulously preserved. She began by sorting files into boxes for transport back to Masterton when a crash followed by startled cries and toppling furniture shattered her concentration.

'Settle down, you lot,' she yelled.

Shushing and stifled laughter rippled through the room. The noise subsided to a more tolerable hum. There was no point in asking them to do anything now. These officers had already checked out: if they were anything like the crew, she'd gone through police college with, they were only marking time before a final celebration at the pub this afternoon.

The ache in her shoulder, like an annoying toothache, wouldn't go away. She reached into her bag, found her painkillers and swallowed more tablets.

Something about Tony's theory nagged at her—there was a loose thread she couldn't quite grasp. What was she missing? Another crash reverberated through the Incident Room, followed by the sound of breaking plates and raised voices. Enough. She wasn't going to find the peace she needed to think clearly, in this circus. Gathering up her phone and bag, she escaped to her car.

Without understanding why, she drove towards the hills and Featherston. Heavy clouds pregnant with the promise of rain massed behind the Remutaka Range like an invasion force preparing to sweep across the plain. By the time she parked outside Ava's studio, the temperature had dropped.

It was still warm in the studio. Ava didn't look up when Kate walked in. She moved between her paintings with a zen-like focus; in her denim overalls, striped t-shirt, and her red polka-dot scarf tied, with the knot at the front, around her head, she looked as if she had stepped out of an eighties rock video. Not at all like a grieving widow, thought Kate. She pulled up, reminding herself that grief assessment was best left to the experts. Her job was to find the killer.

'Packing up?' Kate asked and pointed to the timber stacked beside her paintings.

'Crating up,' corrected Ava. 'The truck's coming tomorrow to take the paintings to the gallery for my exhibition next week. You're welcome to come if you like. I've already invited Matt and Carla.'

The casual mention of her husband's new relationship landed with a punch to her heart. Still. She took a moment for herself, wondering how long it would be, before she could hear their names without reacting. Without feeling as if she had been gutted, sliced open, her shame at being replaced by another woman, laid bare for all the world to see.

Ava's words jolted her back to the reason for her visit. 'As you can see, I'm busy. What do you want?'

'You're okay if I record this?' asked Kate, holding up her phone, her thumb hovering over the screen.

Irritation flickered across Ava's face, but she nodded her consent.

'Simple question. What were you doing on the Friday night before Juliette Bisson went missing?'

Ava's hands stilled. 'Why are you asking?'

'Scene building,' said Kate.

'I mean, why are you asking me?'

'Does it matter?' Kate countered.

'To me, it does.'

'If it helps, we're asking a lot of people. Not just you.'

Ava turned away to hunch over the stack of wood, her back to Kate. 'You've spoken to Mimi?'

The question caught Kate off-guard, though she nodded affirmatively. It wasn't a lie as such because she had spoken to Mimi, just not about that particular Friday evening.

'She told you we went out for dinner then. Just us. No husbands.' Ava looked around and watched Kate's face for confirmation.

'That's right. Stupidly, I forgot to ask her which restaurant you went to.'

'It was The Huntsman in Masterton,' replied Ava. Straightening with her hands on her hips, she arched her back before turning to face Kate. 'I don't understand what this has to do with Geoffrey's murder. Don't you have the killer in custody? I hear you were quite the hero Kate.'

'We have a person in custody. Yes. Getting back to that Friday night, remind me again, what time you were at the restaurant?'

Ava rolled her eyes. 'We arrived around seven. Mimi had to get the girls' dinner before she could leave. Usually, we were home by ten.'

'Usually?'

'Didn't she tell you? We went out to dinner together every Friday night. It was out treat to ourselves.' She paused, her brow furrowed. 'Are you sure you spoke to Mimi?'

Ava was getting suspicious. She was also running out of what little patience she had left. Kate pivoted to a safer topic. One of Ava's favourites.

'Congratulations for getting into the McElhinney. He only takes the very best. It's the perfect place for your work.' She meant it. It was the second time she'd seen the paintings and they were stunning. If she hadn't just been informed that Matt and Carla had been invited, she would have gone to the opening, just to see them properly displayed.

Ava brightened. 'Thanks. Dan's coming later to help me crate them up. Otherwise, I'd be here all night.'

'When does he leave again?'

'After my exhibition. He's going to a job in Mauritius for eight weeks.'

'I've always wanted to go there,' said Kate. 'The mix of cultures, the beaches, it sounds like paradise.'

Ava wasn't listening. Her attention had drifted back to her work. She picked up a hammer, a nail, and a piece of wood. With her back to Kate, she positioned them together, then aimed a solid blow at the nail, driving it home with a single strike.

'You don't mind if I get on, do you?'

Kate took the hint and left.

The first raindrops, fat and heavy, splattered across the windscreen as she reversed out of the carpark. Within moments, the promised deluge transformed deep gutters into raging torrents. Lightning flashed across the sky, followed seconds later by the low rumbles of thunder. The windscreen wipers couldn't keep up and unable to see the road ahead, she pulled over to wait for the storm to pass through.

The Huntsman's manager answered straight away. Kate explained why she was calling, raising her voice so he could hear her over the downpour pummelling the car. With the phone set to speaker, she listened to what he said, the call ending just as the storm moved away.

# CHAPTER 46

'I'M CALLING MARTIN. Say nothing. He'll meet you there.' Bruce yelled this from the front door as Kate led Mimi out to her car. He didn't wait to see her open the door, nor did he wait to witness her protective hand guiding Mimi's head as she settled her into the back seat.

When Kate looked back, his phone was clamped to the side of his head, his urgent call to his solicitor already underway as he disappeared inside the house.

The interview with the Murphys had started pleasantly enough. Mimi welcomed Kate with her usual grace as she ushered her again into the library. There Kate remained, cocooned in silence for ten minutes, before finally the door opened.

'Apologies for the wait,' said Bruce. 'I was in the middle of something when you arrived and couldn't get away.' He shepherded Mimi to a chair on the other side of the table from Kate and they all took their seats.

From the outset, it was obvious Bruce intended to manage their conversation. Kate, not yet sure exactly what she had come to find out, decided to let him.

He smiled at her as if she'd just won a golf tournament for the club they both belonged to. 'Firstly, on behalf of the Martinborough Business Association, may I say how grateful we are to you for solving the case so quickly and for locking up Geoffrey's killer.'

'And June's,' added Mimi. 'You really did a marvellous job, Kate.'

'You did,' he said. 'We can all return to normal and put this nasty business behind us.'

He didn't wait for her response, instead briskly transitioning to the next item on his mental agenda. 'You will be delighted to hear, that the council has approved the sculpture park. This time next year, the public will be focusing on our wonderful park and not these awful murders. Mimi and I are very excited.'

He held up his hand in a gesture of magnanimity. 'It won't be cheap, but after everything this town has done for us, we believe in giving back.'

'We do,' echoed Mimi.

He reached across, covered his wife's hand with his own and gave it a gentle squeeze. Kate thought he looked very pleased with himself and his little world. 'That's our news. What can we do for you? Why are you here?'

She swallowed, taking a moment to lose the energy from his rah-rah speech and gather her thoughts. 'It's nothing really,' she said. 'I've come to ask you what you were doing on the Friday before Juliette Bisson went missing. That's all.'

It was as if she had farted in church. Bruce froze for a full two seconds then shifted in his seat while Mimi stared at some invisible point in the middle distance. Bruce recovered first, his brow crinkling as he made a show of seriously considering his answer.

'Now that's a long time ago. I bet you don't remember what you were doing three years ago.'

'I might if something memorable happened,' said Kate. 'There can't be many young women going missing in Martinborough.'

'Didn't the police take five days to respond?' asked Bruce. 'Five days until the rest of us found out she was missing.'

'You're correct,' said Kate. 'However, once we knew when she disappeared, we let people know fairly quickly.' She offered a measured smile. 'What were you doing that Friday?'

He cleared his throat and turned to his wife. 'Wasn't that my night to stay home with the girls?'

Mimi stared at him for a beat longer than was comfortable, then turned and met Kate's eyes. 'That's right, it was.'

'What about you? What were you doing?' asked Kate

'Ava and I used to go out to dinner on Friday nights. Just the two of us.'

'Where did you go?'

'The Huntsman in Masterton. Yes, now I remember, that was the place. Is it still there? I don't know. If Bruce and I go out, we usually go to one of the Martinborough restaurants. To support the locals, but also because the ones here are very good. '

'They are. The pub does an excellent set menu on Friday night if you're looking for a place to eat,' added Bruce. 'If you get the chance, go. Fifty dollars for three courses and a glass of wine. Can't get better than that.'

'What time were you there?' Kate asked.

'Where?' asked Mimi.

'The Huntsman.'

'I would have left here around six—the girls needed their dinner—and was home around ten.' She pivoted in her chair to look at her husband, her eyes searching his for support.

'Sounds about right,' he said.

'You were home all night?' Kate directed this question to Bruce.

'I was. The girls had sport in the morning, netball in Featherston. It was the beginning of the season, and they were up for regional selection. They needed an early night.'

'Did they get selected?' she asked.

'Not that year,' said Bruce. 'They were the year after though.'

'And for the ski team,' said Mimi, suddenly brighter. 'They're both instructors now. They're in Canada for the season. We went over and had Christmas with them, didn't we?'

'We did.'

'Did you have anything to drink with dinner?' asked Kate.

'I stopped drinking after I went to the spa. It was the best thing I ever did.'

Kate persisted. 'That night?'

'We probably had a glass of wine with dinner.'

'Who drove?'

'Sometimes we arranged a taxi.'

'That night specifically?'

'You know, it's silly, but I can't remember. Perhaps one of us did drive.'

'I can always ask Ava,' said Kate. 'Plus, there are only three taxi companies in the district so it's easy enough to check with them.'

Bruce leaned forward. 'Why are you asking questions about something which happened so long ago?'

She ignored him, keeping her focus on Mimi. 'After I talked to Ava this afternoon, I contacted the manager of The Huntsman. The two of you made quite an impression on him and on his staff.'

'What do you mean?'

'He forwarded me a copy of your bill.' Kate held her phone up briefly, just long enough for Mimi and Bruce to glimpse the Huntsman's letterhead and an itemized list below.

'Three bottles of champagne,' said Kate reading from her phone. 'Two gin and tonics before dinner, both doubles and a bottle of Riesling with dessert.'

The silence in the room grew longer as Mimi's cheek flushed crimson. She lowered her head. Outside, the clouds opened again, and more rain began to fall.

Kate rose to her feet with deliberate calm. 'I'm asking you to come to the station with me, for questioning. If you do not accompany me voluntarily, then I will arrest you. Do you understand?'

Bruce and Mimi stared at her—their expressions locked in identical masks of shock.

Bruce got to his feet. 'Wait outside,' he ordered. Kate had no choice but to follow him to the door. She could have brazened it out but decided things might be easier if she complied. The door closed firmly behind her. She waited, sheltering from the rain under the veranda, hoping her gut feeling would prove her right and that she hadn't just made a terrible mistake.

A few minutes later the door swung open. Mimi emerged first followed closely by Bruce.

'I have to say, I'm disappointed in you Kate. Be assured I will be taking up the matter of your harassment of myself and my wife, with your superior officers.'

Kate nodded and silently handed him the list of senior staff and their contact details she kept in her folder. Then, with gentle firmness, she led a subdued Mimi to her car and helped her inside.

# CHAPTER 47

MERCIFULLY THE RAIN HAD STOPPED, but water still gurgled down the drainpipes. The thunderous percussion on the iron roof had bordered for a time on the unbearable.

Ava stepped back, her critical eye sweeping across the packing crates piled high in the middle of the warehouse. She was almost done, save for three oversized canvases that were too big to manage alone. It would be a relief when Dan finally arrived so she could get them into their crates along with the others.

The truck to take them over the hill was due at seven the next morning, so everything had to be ready. She glanced at the time. Five-thirty. It was late and he should have been here by now. The repairs at the medical centre meant he couldn't work today, so where was he?

As she was wrestling a crate into position, she heard the door behind her swing open. 'Give me a hand, would you?' she called out, stopping midway through the manoeuvre. 'It's heavier than I thought.'

When there was no response, she kept one hand on the crate, so it didn't crash to the floor and turned to see why Dan hadn't rushed across to help.

'Bruce!' The crate wobbled. 'You gave me such a fright. Dan's not here yet. Help me, would you, I can't manage it by myself.'

'Sure.' He elbowed her out of the way, gripped the crate firmly on both sides, then carried it effortlessly to the wall, where he dropped it unceremoniously on the floor—wood colliding with concrete and iron in a jarring discord.

'Careful.'

He dusted off his hands. 'It's only a painting. It'll survive.'

'Or not,' she muttered. She'd seen him in moods like this before. He was standing much closer to her than she liked, and it didn't pay to rile him up.

He stepped even closer, almost closing the gap between them to nothing so she was forced to hip her head back to look up at him. 'What did you tell the police?'

'About what?' Standing on tiptoes, she glanced over his shoulder, hoping to see Dan in the doorway. They were alone.

'You said something to her. Why else would that Sutton woman take Mimi in for questioning?'

'I didn't say a word.'

She attempted to slip past him, but his hand encircled her upper arm, his grip tightening as he lifted her off her feet.

Memories of her art teacher holding her in the same place, hurting her in the same way, flooded back. Flipped straight into fight mode, she used her free hand to beat on his chest. 'You're hurting me. Let go.'

Caught off guard, he loosened his grip, and she wrenched free. She dodged past him and fled to the kitchen where she seized the small vegetable knife she kept for peeling fruit. Legs apart, she stood and faced him, the knife brandished in front of her.

'You haven't got the gumption,' he sneered, but he stayed back. 'Kate Sutton came to the house and asked Mimi about that Friday night. You must have said something to make her so curious? Tell me your exact words.'

'I told her we went out to dinner and were home by ten.'

'I don't believe you. Why did she call the manager?'

'That's all I said. My exact words.' She held his gaze, the knife steady in front of her, refusing to blink or look away. 'Now piss off!'

'If you're lying, if you've put Mimi in danger, I swear, I will make your life a living hell.'

'Like you have hers, all these years?' The question was out of her mouth before she had time to stop it. The words hit home, puncturing his bravado so dramatically she almost couldn't bear to look at him.

'Is that what she told you?'

'No, it's not. Forget I said it. You know me, I say things without thinking. Mimi would never say that. She loves you.'

His eyes cleared as he ran his hand back over his hair, smoothing it into place. 'I know she does. She loves me, because she knows I love her. No matter what she's done. We're happy and don't you ever forget that, you little bitch.' He walked to the door then turned to look back at her. 'We made a deal Ava. Remember.'

'I didn't mean it, honestly I didn't.'

She didn't put the knife down until she heard the roar of the Porsche's engine starting up, followed by the crunch of its tires on wet gravel as the car reversed out of the parking lot.

She still felt shaky when Dan finally turned up ten minutes later. He gave her an odd look when he came in. She returned it with a wonky smile. Grateful that he didn't pry, she set him to work. There was no reason to burden him with the details of her eventful afternoon. Better to say nothing, she decided. She offered up a silent prayer that Mimi would do the same. For all their sakes.

# CHAPTER 48

MARTIN WEDGWOOD HAD BEEN the Murphy family solicitor for eleven years. Privately educated and a graduate of Auckland University, his father and grandfather had been solicitors before him. Independently wealthy, intelligent, discreet and with impeccable manners, Martin personally selected his clients from the small pool of wealthy Wairarapa families who could afford to pay his considerable fees without flinching.

By rights, the Murphys should never have crossed the threshold of his attention. But his hands were tied when an Auckland business associate arranged an introduction.

At their first meeting, Martin, hoping to gracefully deflect their interest, explained that he specialised in family law, particularly the management of inter-generational wealth and succession planning.

Bruce understood immediately. He wrote a number on a piece of paper and slid it across the desk. He explained that he expected that number to double every three years for the foreseeable future. He said he hoped that Martin would consent to oversee his family's needs, as he had come highly recommended. They shook hands there and then.

Within a year, Martin had put in place an intricate system of trusts that devolved income to an assortment of local and offshore accounts in countries known for their tactful banking practices. Tax matters were outsourced to a colleague who had spent a decade with Inland Revenue. After that, Murphy Enterprises pretty much looked after itself.

Thus, it was a very surprised Martin Wedgwood who found himself sitting next to Mimi Murphy behind a table in Interview Room One at the Masterton Police Station late one Friday afternoon.

His clients were generally law-abiding citizens. Occasionally some of the younger family members required assistance, and his junior associate would be despatched along to calm the waters. If this proved impossible, Martin mounted an automatic campaign for name suppression while calling in the necessary favours to ensure an appropriate outcome.

To be contacted on his personal mobile and hear Bruce Murphy order him down to the police station to meet Mimi when she arrived, was highly irregular. It was also a bit rich, and words would be said.

But that was then, and now Martin, ever the pragmatist, was trying to reassure the dejected Mimi that he would find out what was going on. Then he'd put a stop to whatever it was. In the meantime, she was to say nothing and let him do the talking. 'This won't take long,' he said. 'We'll be out of here in no time.'

Half an hour passed. Interview Room One was not a large space, and the air conditioning wasn't working properly. One minute, an Antarctic blast; the next, a tropical breeze. The furniture was old-fashioned, the chairs uncomfortable, and the dark oblong mirror at the end of the room was unsettling. For all Martin knew, they were being observed even now, sitting side by side in silence. Not speaking.

The door opened and Martin got to his feet.

'I'm Detective Senior Sergeant Kate Sutton.' They shook hands, Martin waiting until she was seated before sitting down himself.

'My apologies for keeping you waiting.'

He didn't believe her apology was sincere, but being a gentleman, he nodded. 'We understand you must be very busy.'

'Indeed,' she said. She opened her folder on the table, making the blank page of her notebook visible to both Martin and Mimi. 'Do I have your permission to record the interview?'

'You do,' said Martin. He waited for Kate to flick the necessary switches and check the camera was on before proceeding.

'My client tells me she is here voluntarily. She does not understand what you want to know. Perhaps you can enlighten us.'

'I am grateful for Mrs Murphy's cooperation,' said Kate. 'Three years ago, Mrs Murphy and her friend, Mrs Ava Scott, drove in Mrs Murphy's car from their homes in Martinborough to a restaurant, The Huntsman, in Masterton. The manager of the restaurant has confirmed they arrived between six and seven pm. They had dinner and returned to their homes in Martinborough around ten that same evening. That is correct, isn't it?' she directed this to Mimi.

'Yes,' said Mimi. Martin regretted not having instructed his client to sit up and look the detective in the eye, but it was too late for that now.

'It has been three years, but the manager of The Huntsman still remembers you and Mrs Scott. He has provided us with a copy of your itemised account.' Kate slid it across the table. Martin left it there, peering at it over the top of his glasses.

'One of you had the steak, and one the chicken,' said Kate.

Mimi nodded.

'The dessert. Chocolate mousse for two.'

Mimi nodded again.

'Two gin and tonics, then three bottles of champagne, followed by a bottle of Riesling. Of the two of you, who would you say drank the most?' asked Kate.

'I don't remember,' Mimi whispered.

'The manager remembers offering to call a taxi, but you refused. Who drove home?'

'I don't remember,' said Mimi, louder this time. She looked up, her eyes focused on Kate. 'It could have been me. It could have been Ava.'

'Did you drive Mrs Scott back to her house?'

'I don't remember.'

'That's enough, don't you think?' interjected Martin. He paused, holding her gaze; the drama of the moment was not lost on Kate. 'My client not remembering a dinner which took place three years ago is hardly a crime Detective Sutton. And you have provided no evidence regarding what may or may not have happened that night other than this.' He pushed the invoice back across the table. 'The recollections of a manager who remained in the restaurant and so did not see what my client did or didn't do is not evidence. Correct?'

'That is correct,' said Kate.

'Tell me,' he said. 'When did going out for dinner with a friend become a chargeable offence?' His eyebrows raised, an amused twinkle in his eyes; he waited for her response.

Kate obliged him with a tight smile. There was nothing she could say.

'I fail to see the point of this interruption in my client's life. If you don't mind, we will be on our way.' He nudged Mimi gently, and they stood up. Standing back to let her go first, he guided her to the door and out of the room.

'Interview terminated at 6:30 PM,' said Kate. She flicked off the switches, and the light on the camera turned red.

# CHAPTER 49

TONY LOOKED up as Kate walked past him to her office at the far end of the CIB room. 'It's Saturday, your day off. What are you doing here?'

'The Incident Room in Martinborough is closed, so I thought I'd work here.' She knew it wasn't what he meant, but she couldn't be bothered explaining. Paperwork—the job sheets, reports, USB sticks, and notebooks from every officer seconded to the investigation—was either piled high around Tony's desk or sat in cartons in Kate's tiny office. It was all waiting for her signature before either being uploaded to the database or consigned to the basement archives.

As of Monday, being the only two working detectives in their team, they would return to regular duties: pursuing the ever-present gangs and general ne'er-do-wells across the district. Serious crime it might be, but it lacked the intensity and thrills of an active murder inquiry.

She saw his querying look and took pity on him. 'I don't want to come back with this hanging over me.' She gestured at the paper tsunami engulfing their workspace. 'I'd rather put a dent in it before Monday.'

'Yeah well,' he grumbled. 'You make the rest of us look bad.'

'Call me a tragic,' she replied with a half-smile.

She couldn't tell him the truth—that being here was infinitely better than sitting at home, staring at four walls and listening to the sound of her breathing. Earlier that morning, while loading her breakfast dishes into the dishwasher, she'd actually considered getting a cat for company. In the end, she decided she didn't like them enough to become a stereotypical single lady with cat.

She was in her happy place, she was at work. She cleared an island of space on her desk and powered up her computer. 'Any news from the courier?' she called out, on the off-chance Tony might be listening.

There was a long silence. 'Sorry boss I forgot to call her.'

'Come in here. We'll call her together.'

Carolyn Morton must have recognised the country code, as picked up almost immediately.

'Hey Tony.' Judging by the background noise, she was driving. It was seven o'clock in the morning in Brisbane, two hours behind New Zealand. 'How's the weather on your side of the ditch?'

'A bit cooler, we've had some rain which helps,' said Tony. 'Hey, I'm with DSS Kate Sutton in her office.'

'Good morning, Detective Sutton,' Carolyn replied cheerfully.

'You made a delivery to the Simich house on the Saturday morning,' Tony prompted.

'Yeah. I've been thinking about that, and there are a few things I forgot to mention.'

He ignored Kate's told-you-so smile. 'Like what?'

'Okay,' she began, as an indicator clicked rhythmically in the background before falling silent. 'It was my usual Saturday run apart from the flowers. I got to Raupaki Road around eight-thirty. Bruce Murphy was coming towards me, so I pulled over so we could pass. My windows were up because of the dust, so I didn't get a proper look, but it was him and he was alone.'

She must have stopped because the engine noise changed from driving to idling.

'I drove past the cottage. I remember the front door was open, but I didn't think anything of it. It was a hot day, and lots of people had their doors open.'

'You didn't say that before,' Tony noted.

'I only remembered last night. After dropping the flowers at the Simich's, I was heading back to town when I noticed it.'

'Noticed what?'

'Rubbish. Scattered all over the road and caught in the verges.'

'Rubbish?'

'From the cottage,' Carolyn explained, as if Tony was a bit dim for not getting what she meant.

The engine revved, sped up then sounded as if it had settled into a line of traffic.

'When she first arrived, that French girl—Juliette—waved me down to ask where to put her rubbish. She didn't want to bother Mrs Simich, what with Mr Simich being so ill. It took a while to understand her accent, then I showed her the collection spot straight across from her front gate. It's normally collected on Friday mornings. There was a breakdown that week. They told everyone the collection would be on Saturday instead.'

'I'm not sure what you're getting at,' said Tony.

'There was no bag at the collection spot. Just rubbish all over the road.'

'And?'

'I remember it. That, and the open door.'

'Anything else?' he asked.

'Only what I've told you before,' she replied.

'DSS Kate Sutton here, Carolyn. Thank you—that's extremely helpful.' She paused briefly. 'I'll ask the Queensland Police to arrange for you to visit your nearest station to make a formal statement. Would that be all right?'

'Fine by me.'

'Excellent, then we'll let you get on with your day. Goodbye.'

'Give my love to Martinborough. Miss you all.' The call ended.

Kate leaned back in her chair. 'The thing is, when we arrived five days later, there was no rubbish littering the verges and no bag at the collection spot.'

Tony frowned. 'I don't understand.'

'Someone must have gathered it up and re-bagged it, ready for the collectors to take away.'

'You think her killer did it?'

'Who else?'

'Why?'

'To stop people wondering where she was. To stop them checking the cottage. Think Tony, what does this tell us about the timing?'

Kate's phone rang, interrupting her before she could explain what she meant. Frustrated, she checked the caller ID. She recognised it and answered immediately. 'Dr Su? I hope it's good news?'

'Ludo has responded remarkably quickly to the additional medication. He's slightly sedated and there are some residual delusions but they're manageable. What I'm trying to say is that he's not out of the woods yet, but I know how important it is that he talks to you. In my opinion, he's psychiatrically fit for you to interview him.'

Kate exchanged an excited glance with Tony. 'Now? I mean, could we speak to him today?'

'You can,' Dr Su assured her. 'Come whenever you're ready.'

# CHAPTER 50

'STOP ASKING me what I said. I've already told you.'

Morning light streamed through the windows, catching the steam rising from the water in the pot on the hob. Across the granite work-top, Bruce sipped his orange juice, watching her in a way which she'd told him several times already was very annoying.

'You're sure?'

'I'm sure. I said I didn't remember. Just like we agreed.' She cracked the first shell with a knife and tipped the egg into the roiling water, tossing the shell into the compost chute before reaching for another.

'Martin confirms it,' he said, glancing up from his phone.

'I don't believe you did that. You checked up on me. You're impossible.' She jostled the pan to send the water over the tops of the yolks. Next, she took the bread out of the toaster and put the pieces on two waiting plates, passing them to Bruce for buttering.

It was same routine every day.

Early in their marriage Bruce had shown her the kitchen and told her to cook whatever she liked, but for breakfast he always had two poached eggs—with runny yolks—on buttered toast. Other than that, the menus were up to her. He promised he'd never complain: nor help, as it turned out. With the girls away at university, he had recently taken to buttering his own toast. It was a big step forward in their marriage.

When the eggs—organic because Bruce insisted—were ready, she ladled them onto the toast and deposited the pan in the sink.

'It's important you get it right,' he said.

'I know.' She handed him his cutlery and a linen napkin. She remained standing on her side of the bench to eat. Experience had taught her there was little point in sitting down. He'd only ask for something, and she'd have to get up to get it. This morning had been more stressful than usual. His interrogation of her about the police interview had begun the moment she opened her eyes, and she was heartily sick of it.

'They've got nothing,' he declared. He dipped a piece of toast into the yolk. 'No witnesses. No body. No evidence of any kind. Martin was astonished that Kate brought you in on such flimsy grounds. He suggests we make a formal complaint.'

'I suggest we leave it.' She smiled, softening her tone to make him listen to her. 'It's done. Please, let's just get on with our lives.' She paused, then changed the subject. 'Charlotte rang while you were in the shower. The girls arrive home next Wednesday. Would you like to collect them or shall I do it? I have to be in Wellington anyway to check the gallery is hanging the paintings in the correct order.'

'You meet them. I won't be back from Auckland until Thursday.' He speared another piece of toast with his fork, dunked it in the second yolk and put it in his mouth. 'I'm interviewing for the sculpture park job.'

'I thought you'd asked Ava to do it?'

'I decided not to. She's busy with her exhibition and won't have time.'

'But she's perfect for the role.' Mimi was about to launch into a list of reasons why he should ask her, when she noticed his knuckles whitening around the handle of his fork. 'Probably for the best,' she said. 'Whatever you decide is fine with me. You saw the paintings, I hope. I bought the little one for the library. One of the larger pieces would look amazing by the front door.'

'Most were in crates, but I saw a couple and I don't like them.'

'Seriously?'

'Seriously,' he said, laying his hands flat on the bench or either side of his plate. 'I think you should suggest she finds another agent? Not right away. After the exhibition will do. Ava is not your friend, darling.'

'Of course she is. She's my only friend,' Mimi protested. She laid down her cutlery and stared at him.

'What happens to her will come back to bite you,' he warned.

'Nothing's going to happen to her.'

'Are you sure about that?'

'Why are you so down on Ava all of a sudden?'

'It's hardly sudden. She's a liar Mimi.'

'No she isn't.'

'You're being naïve,' said Bruce, shoving his plate away so forcefully that his fork skittered across the bench and clattered into the sink. 'Think about it. What if the police don't let this drop? Who do you think she'll say was driving the car?'

'But she wouldn't,' said Mimi. Her voice faltered. 'We agreed.'

Bruce abandoned his stool and rounded the kitchen island to stand in front of her. He gripped her shoulders with his hands forcing her to look at him. 'She will sacrifice you to save herself.'

'What if it was me who was driving?'

'You weren't.' He squeezed her shoulders for emphasis. 'How do I know? Because it was Ava who was behind the wheel when you got home that night.' He pulled her against him and wrapped his arms tightly around her, so tightly she couldn't breathe.

She listened to his steady heartbeat through the thick cotton of his t-shirt.

'There is no doubt about it.' He continued, talking into her hair. 'I couldn't risk anything stopping you from getting on that plane. It took six months to get a place, and the spa refused to hold the reservation if you didn't turn up. I paid Ava to drive you home.'

Thub-dub, thub-dub, thub-dub. The reassuring regularity of his heart beating against her ear. Steady and dependable, as Bruce had been throughout their marriage. Once she understood his rules. She relaxed against him, the tension ebbing from her shoulders as he loosened his hold.

'How much did you pay her?'

'Two hundred.'

'Cheaper than a taxi,' she murmured.

'I thought so.'

'I really don't remember,' she whispered. 'I wish I did, but it's simply not there.'

'I know, my love. Ava is counting on that gap in your memory. If the police go after her, do you know what she's going to say?'

'What?'

'Whatever she has to.' He leaned back and hooked a finger under her chin, forcing her to look up at him. 'She's a cold, calculating little bitch and if it looks like things are getting rough, she will say anything to save her own skin. Including that it was you and not her who hit that French girl.'

Mimi jerked back breaking free of his embrace. 'What?'

'You heard me.'

'But that's awful. I mean she couldn't have. I couldn't have. I'd surely remember if I did something so dreadful.'

'Of course you would. That's why it wasn't you. It was her.'

'Why would she blame me? She's my friend.'

'What have I always told you?'

'That I'm too good for her.' She breathed the words and leaned against the bench for support. 'What am I going to do?'

'Say exactly what you've said all along.'

'That I don't remember?'

He smiled encouragingly. 'That's it. Remember, there no witnesses. No body. The police can't prove a thing.'

'You're positive it was her who was driving and not me? You'd tell me if it had been me, wouldn't you?' Tears welled up in her eyes.

'Of course I would. It was Ava. Besides,' he said, reaching for her again. 'do you seriously think I would let anyone hurt you or our girls?'

'No,' she whispered.

'That's right.' He hugged her against him, his head resting against hers. 'Keep saying you don't remember, and everything will be all right.'

They stayed in each other's arms until Mimi took a deep breath and pulled away, disentangling his arms from around her body with her hands. 'You'd better go, or you'll miss your flight.'

'You'll be okay?' he asked.

'Of course.' Her smile was shaky and he could have kissed her, she looked so brave.

'I don't remember,' she said. 'Because I don't.'

'That's my girl,' said Bruce. 'We'll get through this like we get through everything. Together.'

# CHAPTER 51

THE FORENSIC PSYCHIATRIC Unit occupied an unmarked building tucked away inside the hospital complex. For obvious security reasons, conceded Kate, but the absence of signage did nothing to improve her already fraying patience.

There was nowhere to ask for directions, and her call to Dr Su disappeared into voicemail limbo. Eventually, after they'd wasted another twenty minutes circling the grounds—passing one rundown building after another, she tried again. This time, mercifully, the psychiatrist answered her phone.

Five minutes later, a nurse appeared outside the very first building they'd passed. He waved them down, directed them to a parking space, then escorted them through a series of doors, each with its own security camera. Another two sets of locked doors and they arrived at the room where Dr Su and Ludo Wilkins were waiting.

Ludo nodded as they walked in. He was wearing a loose grey tracksuit and dressing gown. The splint on his finger was barely visible inside the sling supporting his arm. His hair held off his face by a headband, had been washed, and he'd brushed his teeth.

Dr Su looked tiny, perched on the chair beside him, her neat frame dressed in a deep-blue shirt buttoned to the neck worn over ankle-length bright pink pants and white Birkenstocks. Her black-framed glasses, too big for her face, highlighted her brown eyes.

Kate had allowed two hours for the interview, but Ludo didn't need that long to tell them what he'd witnessed that night. Despite his drug-induced drowsiness that occasionally closed his eyelids and slurred his speech, he made perfect sense. Kate was in no doubt he was telling the truth.

For the first time in three years, she knew what had happened to Juliette. That her father wasn't alive to learn what was done to his daughter only intensified the emotions which overwhelmed her as she listened to Ludo's testimony.

Still reeling after they left the unit, she tossed the keys to Tony. 'You drive,' she instructed. 'Drive fast.'

He needed no further encouragement. Reversing out of the car park with a spray of stones, he swung the vehicle around before Kate had fastened her seatbelt.

Lights flashing and siren blaring, he sped towards the nearby shopping centre, executed a classic, sharp right at the roundabout and accelerated towards the motorway. His knuckles white from gripping the wheel, his eyes were locked on the road ahead. He swore under his breath whenever slower drivers got in his way, hammering the horn to force them to pay attention and clear the path.

Bracing herself, with one hand gripping the overhead strap, she used the other to call Bill Comber. 'Take a team to the Murphy residence. Bring them in for questioning. Separate cars. If they refuse to come voluntarily, arrest them.'

'On what charge?' asked Bill.

'Obstructing justice will do for now. We'll handle the paperwork afterwards,' she replied. 'No sirens, no lights—nothing to warn them you're coming.'

'What's this about?'

'I'll fill you in when we get back to the station, which should be in an hour.' She paused as Tony swerved onto the motorway, then accelerated across three lanes, while a logging truck braked sharply behind them, its horn blaring in protest. 'Bring Ava Scott in too. Make sure they see each other. Put them in separate rooms, with a uniformed officer in each room, and maintain silence until I get there.'

'On it,' he confirmed. 'I need to—'

She cut him off. 'Ring me when you're on route. I want all three waiting at the station when we get back.'

They'd just reached the notorious bottleneck at Hayward's Hill: a winding, two-lane section under perpetual roadworks between Porirua and Lower Hutt.

With little room to manoeuvre, Tony did his best: siren howling, alternately braking hard when drivers didn't pull over in time, then hitting the gas and tearing past them when they did.

Now clutching her seatbelt for stability, she phoned Jack. He answered on the second ring.

'Hey Kate.' Hearing the siren, his tone shifted to urgency. 'Speak.'

'We interviewed Ludo Wilkins this morning. He was there the night Juliette was killed. He saw the whole thing. Bill's team is heading to collect the Murphys, and another unit is bringing in Ava Scott.'

'Where are you?'

'We're almost in Lower Hutt. Another forty-five minutes, and we'll be at the station.'

'I'm on my way. Don't start until I get there, okay?'

'Roger that,' she replied, struggling to contain her excitement. 'Another call, sorry.' She hit the key to speak to Bill, the background road noise almost drowning out his voice.

'Dan Forrester is at the station with something he's insisting you need to see.'

'What is it?'

Tony navigated the next roundabout practically on two wheels, plunging down the offramp onto State Highway 2 and settling into the outer lane, where traffic at least parted to allow them to get past.

'He wouldn't say.'

'Okay, I think I know what it is. Call whoever and tell them to put him in a separate room. I don't want the others to see him when you bring them in. And Bill—' The line went dead before she could finish.

She tapped in Sophie Taylor's number. Her call went straight to voicemail, but as soon as she hung up, her phone rang.

'Sorry boss, I was on another call. How can I help?'

'You're not a detective, but I think you can do this, so don't let me down. I'd like you to contact the relevant telcos and get the Murphys' phone records for the last month. Go through them line by line so we know who they've been talking to. Also ask them to triangulate the locations of both phones on the Sunday that Dr Scott was killed and the Sunday—'

'Mrs Whittaker was killed,' finished Sophie. 'I guess you want that yesterday.'

'Correct, go as high as you have to, just get the results ASAP. Have one of the others draw up the warrants for the searches and get them sent off to the duty magistrate for signing.'

'Will do.' Sophie ended the call.

Tony executed a violent swerve to avoid a car emerging blindly from a side street, turning directly into their path. Another two-lane road through suburbia threatened to slow them down. 'You should drive like this more often,' Kate remarked.

His focus on the road ahead, Tony merely grunted in response, then spotting a gap in the traffic accelerated into it.

Kate gazed out the window her body instinctively leaning into each curve. The pain in her neck and shoulder forgotten, as she mentally rehearsed the upcoming interrogations. That one of their suspects had killed Juliette seemed certain—but which one?

When Ludo told her about the vehicle which sent his 'angel' flying into the paddock, her wings, the white nightgown lit by the full moon, she believed him.

He had described the same angel to his treating psychiatrist three years earlier. She was there in black and white, documented in the admission notes Dr Su shared with them. Back then, his recollection was dismissed as another one of his delusions.

While the medication banished his other fantasies, this one persisted, but Ludo wasn't stupid. Aware that his freedom depended on him appearing sane, he stopped talking about her. He never mentioned his angel again and consequently he was allowed to go home. His freedom depended on him keeping the secret, so Ludo kept the secret.

She looked up the record she'd made regarding his description of the vehicle.

'It was a Porsche 911 GT with mag wheels. Red. The latest model.'

Kate asked him how he knew.

'I love cars, especially Porsches and I know a lot about them,' Ludo replied. 'Ask me anything.' She hadn't, she knew he was telling the truth.

'Tony?'

'Yes ma'am.' He pulled out into a passing lane and sped past a Honda Jazz crawling up the initial ascent of the hill road. Its elderly driver, oblivious to the queue forming behind him, looked visibly startled when they roared past.

Another sharp bend appeared, the ground on the passenger side dropping away, as Tony accelerated through the corner, driving straight towards another steep bush-covered incline, before turning into the next corner then braking hard to avoid colliding with the oil tanker labouring up the hill in front of them.

'When we get back,' said Kate, secretly revelling in the fact that he'd addressed her as ma'am for the first time, 'find the details of every vehicle the Murphys have owned over the past five years. Focus on the Porsches registered to Bruce, his wife, and any companies they control. Include leased vehicles. I want complete histories, including whether they still own them and if not, what happened to them. Begin with the car Ludo described.'

'Understood,' said Tony.

The hillside fell away again leaving nothing but open air and a magnificent view beyond the passenger window. In the distance, spread out below them lay the painted patchwork of the Wairarapa plain glowing soft yellow in the midday sun. In the distance the silhouettes against the blue sky, of Nga-waka-o-Kupe (the canoes of Kupe) the hills shaped like canoes, to the east of Martinborough.

Kate leaned against the headrest, grateful for this being one of those rare moments when the stars aligned and the universe functioned as it should. When so often, it didn't.

Frustrated by their position behind the tanker, Tony muttered to himself as he pulled out over the centre line, flashed his headlights aggressively and whipped up the siren. Taking the hint, the driver reluctantly engaged the air brakes and eased into the next passing bay, allowing them to surge ahead.

The next stop: Masterton.

# CHAPTER 52

BILL STOOD by the back door, his face creased with worry, as Tony swung their vehicle into the station's last parking space.

'What is it?' Kate asked, as she squeezed her body sideways to fit through the narrow gap between the parked cars.

'Sorry boss, Bruce Murphy was gone by the time we got there. His wife said he was on his way to Auckland. I alerted Wellington and they sent a cop to the airport to stop him getting on the plane, but he never arrived. He checked in but didn't show up for the flight.'

'That's not good,' said Kate. 'Put out a 10-1 and a border alert. Tell them there's a warrant out for his arrest.'

'Already done,' said Bill.

They walked down the corridor to the CIB room. 'Have you told Mimi he didn't get on the plane?'

'Not yet.'

'Let's keep it that way, shall we? Where are they?'

'Ava Scott is in Interview Room Two. Mimi Murphy is in One, her solicitor, Martin Wedgewood is with her. Both have been cautioned. Charlotte Grainger is on her way to be with Ava, and I've put Dan Forrester in the tearoom because there was nowhere else.'

'Does Dan know we brought Ava in?'

'No. I kept them apart as instructed.'

'She didn't call him?'

Bill swallowed, flushing as he ran his hand around the back of his neck. 'I'm fairly sure she didn't.'

'But not absolutely certain?'

'Correct.'

'No matter, it won't make a difference in the long run.' She thought for a moment. 'I'll speak with Dr Forrester first.' She glanced up to see Tony hovering in her office doorway. 'Well done re the driving by the way. Get onto the vehicle search before you do anything else.'

'What vehicle?' asked Bill.

'Tony is researching the Murphys' Porsches.'

'I can do that. Remember, my partner is a member of the Porsche Owners' Club. I've picked up a fair bit listening to him and his mates.'

'Good idea. Tony, brief Bill on the details. That frees you up to observe the interviews.' She paused, fumbling in her bag for her wallet. 'Before we start, would you mind nipping down to the café and getting us all a coffee? Flat white for me. Large. Bill?'

'Same. Also, large.'

She handed Tony the money. 'And whatever you're having.'

He left, and Bill stared after him, then leaned towards her. 'What was that?'

'Put it down to my irresistible charm and winning personality,' she replied. She flicked an imaginary lock of hair over her shoulder.

Bill snorted. 'You might be charming on a good day but irresistible? Give me a break.' He walked away. 'I'll get back to you about the Porsches.'

Dan Forrester rose to his feet when Kate entered the room, his eyes lighting up when he saw her.

'I found it,' he said. He reached into his messenger bag, took out an envelope, and put it on the table. 'I would have brought it in sooner, but I had to make sure it was legally all right to show it to you.'

Kate picked up the envelope. Inside, were several pages of typed, double-spaced text, each page bearing two signatures at the bottom: Ludo Wilkins and Geoffrey John Scott. It was dated six months ago.

Her heart rate quickened as she read the first page. She turned to the second page. It was a laboratory report: a lithium level test requested by Geoffrey John Scott. The specimen receipt date and the results, dated three days later, were all highlighted with fluorescent pink.

'The result's in the normal range,' said Dan.

'Meaning?'

'It confirms that Ludo was taking his medication properly when he made the statement. His psychosis was effectively in remission. The next page shows cognitive function testing, which is also normal.'

'Sorry to be dim, but so what?' she asked.

'It means Ludo was mentally competent when he made the state-ment,' said Dan. 'A defence psychiatrist could try to contest it, but I doubt the jury would buy it.'

'Let's leave the legal stuff to the lawyers.' She re-read the statement, skimming past the identifying details to the part which she hoped would tell her who was driving the car that struck Juliette Bisson. Word for word, everything Ludo had told her this morning was there in black and white. As she finished, she felt tears welling up in her eyes. Not bothering to wipe them away, she looked at Dan. 'Where did you find it?'

'Hidden inside a book buried in Geoffrey's strawberry patch: the same one he was tending when he died. I found it the day after Ludo shot up the health centre.'

Tony opened the door, and she nodded for him to come in. She swapped the documents for her large flat white and took a sip while he skimmed through them.

'I checked the legality of me giving it to you,' said Dan. 'Both to protect myself professionally, and because I wanted to make sure it would be admissible in court. It was given to Geoffrey as part of a medical consultation, so there are privacy implications. I'm still waiting on the final opinion but decided to give it to you anyway.'

'Why?'

'Because Bruce knows it exists and probably knows that I have it.'

Kate's heart skipped a beat. 'How?'

'I suspect Geoffrey told him. He also saw me putting the book where Geoffrey first hid it, back in the bookcase. I put a marker in the book. When I checked for it after we came back from the studio, it was on the floor.'

She frowned. Surely markers in books belonged in spy novels? For a moment she wondered what Dan actually did overseas. There was no time for that, maybe when this was all over, she'd ask him. 'So why did you search the garden?'

'Because there were only two places Geoffrey loved to be and where in the last six months, he spent the most time. I searched the health centre. It wasn't there. It had to be somewhere in his garden.'

Dan's smile was quick. 'I know where you can find Juliette's body.'

Kate stared at him, not moving, letting what he'd said sink in. A few moments later, she smiled. 'Of course,' she said, shaking her head. 'I'm such an idiot. That's why he's not on the plane. He's there now. Quick, Tony, we need cars! As many as you can, but no lights. No sirens. He can't know we're coming.'

'Where do I say we're going?' asked Tony.

'Martinborough, of course. The cemetery.'

Sophie appeared in the doorway.

'What?' Kate asked.

'You'll want to see this. Read the top sheet.' She handed Kate a sheaf of papers. A quick glance at the letterhead told her it was a report from Bruce's telco. It looked too complicated to absorb now. 'I'll look at it when I get back.'

She passed them back to Sophie, then turned to Dan. 'Thank you,' she said, and was gone.

# CHAPTER 53

THE MARTINBOROUGH CEMETERY lies halfway along Puruatanga Road, and is sheltered from passing traffic by a dense wall of cypress hedging. Scattered along the remainder of the road at random intervals are lifestyle blocks, and commercial vineyards, some with and some without restaurants.

In summer, at the weekends, people come to lunch at the rustic tables placed beneath mature trees or amongst the rows of vines. Today, being warm and sunny, the restaurants were packed.

Kate swallowed when they turned the corner and she saw the number of cars and bicycles parked haphazardly beneath the Acer trees lining the grassy verges of the long straight road. She prayed it wasn't this busy the whole way along.

The last thing they needed was an intoxicated punter alerting Bruce —or worse blundering into their operation. Thanks to Tony's driving, they'd arrived before the others. A small comfort arrived in the form of a uniformed officer who appeared beside her as soon as she stepped out of the car.

'We secured both ends of the road as soon as we heard.' She pointed into the distance, down the empty road. 'Bridget's manning the checkpoint at the other end. We've liaised with the restaurants on either side of the cemetery and the owners are on board. They'll keep everyone in place until we give the all-clear.'

'Good work,' said Kate. She checked the officer's name. 'Susan, I owe you and Bridget a drink when this is over. Have you seen anything?'

'Nothing,' said Susan. Her eyes flicked away to a small van which had stopped at the blocked-off intersection. She sauntered over, bending down to speak to the driver.

Kate left her to it. She took out two sets of body armour from the back of the squad car and passed one to Tony before securing her own. Then she methodically checked that the necessary equipment—torch, retractable baton, pepper spray, Taser, handcuffs and plastic ties—was in their designated pouches.

She thought about the Glock pistols in the lockbox and decided they wouldn't need them. Bruce wasn't a registered firearms owner so had no legal access to a gun. The alternative was unlikely. A man of his standing would be a fool to have an illegal weapon in his possession— the penalty if he was caught with one, too great.

'Ready?'

Tony scanned the road behind them for the cavalry. 'Shouldn't we wait for the others to get here first?'

'And give Bruce time to destroy the evidence?' Kate's voice hard-ened. 'Not on my watch.'

When he glanced back, she was a hundred metres down the road, crouched low, barely visible in the shadow of the trees. Cursing under his breath, Tony did the only thing he could. He ran after her.

On the drive over from Masterton, Kate had studied then memo-rised the cemetery's layout.

The grounds formed a perfect rectangle, bounded by the road on one side, with vineyards on the remaining three, effectively separating it from nearby restaurants. The dense hedge meant the roadside provided the best cover for her approach.

The only gap in the hedge was the main entrance, twin wooden gates which were always left open. She paused there to peek over the gates, scanning for any sign of Bruce while she waited for Tony to catch up so they could plan their next move. Directly ahead she saw no sign of Bruce.

When she looked behind her, she saw only a deserted road and trees, grass, and sky. Tony had vanished. She couldn't afford to wait; the stakes were too high. She returned her attention to scrutinising the layout of the cemetery.

Two narrow dusty pathways intersected at right angles in the rectangle's centre, dividing the grounds into four quadrants, each filled with headstones in neat, orderly rows.

She ran to the crossroads where a white hexagonal structure, more reminiscent of a croquet pavilion than a cemetery's equipment shed stood, its doors open. A climbing rose adorning the walls was studded with late-flowering, butter-yellow blooms whose fragrance intensified as she edged closer. It was empty except for a row of wall-mounted spades, waterproof clothing and a compact refrigerator. Corrugated tracks in the dust led away to her left.

Sheltering behind a door, she looked across to the far side of the cemetery where a dust cloud billowed around a small digger near the boundary. Was it a digger or a back-hoe? The name didn't matter because the nerve-jangling screech of metal rasping against compacted dirt cut through the afternoon quiet just the same.

Her phone rang, and she scrabbled to silence it.

Jack's voice was terse. 'Where are you?'

'At the cemetery,' she whispered, though she needn't have bothered. The noise of the digger was loud enough to mask a two-tonne truck driving by, let alone her voice.

'Stay there and wait for back-up. That's an order.'

'But—'

'Wait!'

She ended the call and powered down her phone. If he knew what she knew, his instructions would be dramatically different. But he didn't know. How could he? Which why ducking low, she zigzagged between the gravestones to get closer to Bruce and the digger. All the while, she was acutely aware that if he looked up, he would see her.

The machine convulsed each time its blade struck the earth, then trembled as it withdrew, releasing metallic shrieks against the sun-baked clay as Kate manoeuvred into position.

Then, before she could make a run at him, the hollow thud of heavy steel impacting wood. It was the sound she had been dreading. She unclipped her Taser, switching it on as she sprinted into the gap between the digger and the hole.

Planting her feet wide, arms extended in front of her, she aimed the Taser at Bruce's chest, her finger hovering over the button.

'Kill the engine. Or I swear Bruce, I will shoot you.'

Bruce stopped. His hands still gripped the controls, the digger's blade suspended ominously over the grave, only a few feet from Kate's head.

'Turn off the engine and get out slowly,' she shouted.

His gaze swept the area. She was alone. A cold smile spread across his face and he leaned forward, resting one arm casually on the dashboard. 'I can't do that Kate.'

He pushed a lever forward; the digger's arm swung towards her, viciously striking her in the flank, knocking her off her feet into the open grave. With a bone-jarring impact, she landed face-down on the coffin, spitting dusty clay from her mouth, her Taser useless beside her.

Panic surged through her as she rolled onto her back. She moved to stand up, but mindful the coffin lid could collapse at any moment, only got as far as her knees. She had to spread her weight as much as she could so as not to go through the lid.

Above her, the blade reared back, its jagged teeth hanging over her. One push of a lever and she would be crushed. There was nowhere for her to go—the grave too deep for her to reach the edge. Its walls too sheer to give her any purchase.

The engine's pitch intensified, the machine rocked backwards as overhead, the blade quivered. She scrambled desperately onto her side, sliding across the coffin's polished surface, compressing her body against the dirt wall, shrinking her outline to its smallest dimensions all the while sending up silent prayers.

'Stop, or I fire.'

An electrical sizzle punctuated the air. Stopped. Silence. Five excruciating seconds passed. Another crackling burst. The unmistakable sound of a convulsing body hitting metal before tumbling onto hard ground. Guttural groans and teeth grinding against involuntary spasms.

Kate couldn't see anything other than the dirt walls rising on four sides to the rectangle of blue sky above. The engine died, the ensuing silence broken by the metallic snap of handcuffs engaging.

'Tony, I'm down here.' There was no one else it could be. 'Hurry, get me out of here; I'll ruin the evidence if I fall into the coffin.'

Kate lifted her arm skyward, crying with relief as his warm grip enveloped her hand. Anchoring himself on the edge of Ivan Simich's grave, Tony hauled her upwards to safety and the land of the living.

# CHAPTER 54

'DO you have any questions or comments before we finish?' Kate directed her question to Charlotte Grainger, who had been observing the interview from her position behind Ava.

The solicitor shook her head, her dark curtain of hair swinging across her face, as she leaned forward to touch Ava's elbow gently. 'Is there anything you want to ask?

Ava shook her head once, her gaze fixed firmly on the table.

'Give me a minute,' said Kate rising to her feet. She stepped into the corridor, making sure the door was closed behind her.

'Any suggestions?' she asked Jack, who had been monitoring the interview from the adjacent room.

Dirt from the grave had worked its way inside her clothes and had been chafing at her skin throughout the hour-long interview. The sensation was both irritating and revolting—she couldn't decide which was worse. What she needed was a long, hot shower, clean clothes, food, industrial-strength coffee and a couple of paracetamol tablets for her increasingly painful bruised ribs.

Jack gave her a grim smile. 'You're doing a good job.'

Returning to Interview Room Two, she flicked the switch to halt the recording before carefully removing three DVDs from the machine. She labelled one 'Master' and the others 'Working Copy' and 'Disclosure,' then completed the necessary forms, obtaining signatures and dates from Ava and Charlotte before handing 'Disclosure' to Charlotte for her records. This crucial phase of the investigation, at least, was now complete.

'Will I have to go to court?' asked Ava.

'Probably,' said Kate.

'But you haven't charged me with anything yet?'

'You've been very helpful. I'll let you and your solicitor know the specific nature of the charges in due course.' Kate handed them each a card.

'My exhibition opens on Friday,' said Ava. 'If the press found out I was involved … ' Her words faded into silence.

'I can't predict what the press might do,' said Kate.

Any sympathy she might have had for Ava evaporated during the interview. She opened the door and stepped aside to let them pass, nodding to the constable who would see them off the premises.

Back in her office, Kate found a note on her desk asking her to call Bill Comber. Before she could dial his number, Jack appeared in her doorway. His expression telling her he was eager to discuss Ava's statement.

'Two seconds,' she said, holding up one hand while she keyed in Bill's number. Jack settled into the chair in his favorite position, one one giant foot resting atop his opposite knee.

'I think we've found the car,' said Bill. 'One of my mates at Wellington Central is on his way there now to check it out.'

She hung up and grinned at Jack. 'We might have found the car.'

'Where?' he asked.

'In Wellington. One of theirs is on the way now to get a visual and confirm.' She reached behind to scratch a part of her back she had to strain to get to.

When the itch was gone she called out to Tony. He popped his head around her door. 'Has the doctor given Bruce the all-clear yet?' she asked.

'He's still got to stitch his face.'

'Has Toby dropped off my clean clothes?'

'Right there.' He pointed to the shopping bag hanging on the hook behind her door.

'Give Bruce food and drink if the doc says that's okay. When he's ready, put him in Interview Room Two. You're sitting in with me when I interview Mimi, so get something to eat while I take a shower. I've got dirt in all the places I never, ever want to have dirt again.'

# CHAPTER 55

MARTIN WEDGWOOD HAD BEEN at the station since noon. It was now past seven o'clock in the evening and his mood had soured considerably by the time Kate and Tony walked into Interview Room One.

The veneer of urbane sophistication had given way to barely concealed irritation—a shift in composure which did not bode well for his client. He sat directly behind Mimi, out of her line of sight, frowning, as Kate apologised for the delay. Noting his frustration, she spelled out the requisite cautions and identifications for the video recording.

'Tell us again what happened after 5:00 PM on that Friday night in February three years ago,' said Kate.

Mimi turned to Martin, unsure how to respond. He waved his hand dismissively, signalling her to comply.

'I picked up Ava and we drove to Masterton.'

'Describe the car you were driving,' said Kate.

'It was a Porsche 911 GT. Red. Bruce gave it to me for my birthday.'

'You have a very generous husband.'

Mimi's smile was sad. 'Don't I.'

'Do you happen to remember the registration number?'

'Funnily enough. I do. It had a personalised plate. It was KAH 282. KAH for car, and my birthday is on the 28th of February.'

'Thank you. Sorry, I interrupted you. Go on.'

Mimi closed her eyes momentarily. 'We ate at The Huntsman, then we went home.'

'Back to Martinborough?'

'Yes.'

'You didn't go anywhere else? You drove straight home?'

'I think so,' said Mimi. 'I don't actually remember. I had a bit to drink.'

'Who drove?'

She shrugged. 'It could have been me. It could have been Ava. I don't remember anything after leaving the restaurant.'

'What is the next thing you do remember?' asked Kate.

'Waking up.'

'Where were you?'

'In the spare room next to the garage. I'd been sick. The door and window were shut. The smell woke me up.'

'What did you do then?'

'The door was locked. I couldn't do anything. I'm ashamed to say this now, but Bruce used to lock me in there, so the girls wouldn't see me drunk.' Her voice had dropped to a near whisper.

'Let me get this straight. You remember going to the restaurant, but not how you got home.'

'Yes,' said Mimi, her gaze fixed on the table.

'You remember waking up the next morning and not being able to leave the room?'

'Yes.'

'Was there a bathroom you could use?'

Mimi shuddered. 'No.'

'What did you do?'

'I can't.' She turned to Martin, distressed. 'Do I have to say?'

'I think we can surmise what happened next, don't you, Detective?' He straightened in his chair now that he had something to contribute.

Kate nodded. 'You don't have to answer that. How long were you in the room?'

'After I woke up, you mean?'

'Yes.'

'Three hours. The girls went to netball training. I'd arranged for a neighbour to take them because I knew I might not be able to. When Bruce unlocked the door at nine-thirty, he told me that Ivan had died. He was my godfather.'

'This is Ivan Simich?' asked Kate.

'Yes.'

'Were you close?'

'Sort of. My father worked on their farm before I was born. That's the only reason he agreed to be my godfather. He used to send me birthday and Christmas presents, and they came to our wedding. I invited them to our housewarming and to dinner a couple of times.'

'Did you see him before he died?'

'No, and I feel so guilty,' she confessed, her voice catching. 'And I never went to see Isobel either.'

'You didn't drive out to see him that Friday night?' Kate asked, watching her carefully.

'Did Isabel say I did?'

'I'm interested in what you have to say.'

'I could have, I suppose. I used to do terrible things when I drank too much.' Mimi's hand went to the flush creeping up her neck. 'I don't remember though. I told you.'

'Thank you.' Kate closed her folder, then stopped. 'What happened after Bruce let you out of the room?'

'I had a shower and got dressed,' she said. 'That's when he told me I was going to the clinic. We say it was a spa, but it was a proper clinic for alcoholics because that's what I was.'

'When did your husband book you into this clinic?'

'I'm not sure. All I remember is he said that if I didn't go, he was going to divorce me and stop me from seeing our girls. He really would do that.'

'Did he say anything else?'

'He said he hadn't worked as hard as he had for me to drink it all away.'

'How did that make you feel?'

'Like I had no choice. But,' she said smiling wistfully, 'it was the best thing I ever did.'

'What happened to your car?'

'Bruce told me he sold it. He said I deserved the latest model for giving up drinking. He met me at the airport, and we drove home in it.'

'You didn't think that was odd?' asked Kate.

'No,' said Mimi. She summoned what was left of her self-esteem and looked Kate directly in the eye. 'We're rich. We could afford it.'

Kate met her gaze. 'You might be surprised to learn that we think we've found your car in Wellington. The one you drove to the restaurant.'

'As I've said many times, I remember driving to the restaurant,' said Mimi. 'But I don't remember driving back.'

'If the Vehicle Identification Numbers check out when we inspect this car, then the forensic evidence team will examine it for fingerprints.'

'But it was three years ago. My fingerprints won't be there now.' A note of defiance entered her voice.

'Actually,' said Kate. 'This particular car hasn't been driven for three years. It was trucked to its current location and it's been in storage since then.'

Alarmed, Mimi swung around to Martin. 'You didn't tell me that.'

'I didn't know,' said Martin,

'What do I say?'

'My advice remains the same,' he said. 'Tell the truth.'

She swung back to Kate, her features contorted with distress. 'I can't,' she said, then added in a voice barely above a whisper. 'I can't remember.'

# CHAPTER 56

MARTIN WEDGWOOD LOOKED VISIBLY RELIEVED, when Jack declared they were finished for the day. 'The district can't afford the overtime. Go home, get a proper night's sleep and come back ready for business at eight tomorrow morning.'

When Kate arrived at seven, she was relieved to see that overnight cleaners had been through the office; the rubbish bins had been emptied, a cursory vacuum had relieved the carpet of dirty footprints and the lingering odours of stale food were nearly gone, replaced with the manufactured scent of a commercial air freshener. She'd come in early to prepare for her interviews with the Murphys while it was still quiet.

She cleaned off one of the whiteboards and wrote the word PEACE lengthwise down one side. Then, beside each letter: Planning, Engagement, Account, Closure and Evaluation. She was under no illusions that this was going to be easy. With one shot to get it right, the acronym served as a valuable framework to order her thoughts. Next to each heading, she added the bullet points she'd been working on throughout the night because she'd been too wound up to sleep. Stepping back to assess her work, she felt she'd addressed every essential angle of questioning.

The printer was still churning out a copy of her plan when Tony arrived bearing coffee. Refreshed, he looked smart in a crisply ironed shirt and a well-cut suit. Jack arrived a few minutes later. He was unshaven, his rumpled appearance a testament to him having spent the night in the clothes he'd arrived in yesterday afternoon.

Nodding his thanks to Tony for the coffee, Jack examined her plan.

'Have I missed anything?' she asked.

'No. It's all there. I spoke to the station sergeant on my way in. Bruce slept well last night. Mimi, not at all. He managed breakfast, but she couldn't face food. Also, Martin Wedgwood telephoned to say he'll be delayed.'

'But I'm ready to start now.'

'He won't be here much before ten,' said Jack.

She looked at her watch. It was eight o'clock. 'That's two hours. What's he doing?'

'Patience, little grasshopper,' said Jack, wagging his finger at her. 'The value of moving slowly is that one can always see the way ahead.'

'Star Wars?'

'The Clone Wars.'

'Never heard of it.'

'Irrelevant,' he said. 'How are your ribs?'

She eased herself slowly into her chair. 'The drugs help.'

Tony poked his head around the door to her office. 'Dr Fraser is starting the postmortem at nine. I said I'd be there, so I'd better make tracks.' He drained the last of his coffee then tossed the cup in the bin. 'Good luck with the Murphys.'

'Thanks, call me when you have news.'

Jack watched him go, a thoughtful expression on his face. 'He's changed his tune. What did you do?'

'I had a chat,' she said.

'With Tony?'

'No. With Will Beveridge.'

He thought about it for a moment, then nodded. 'Nice.'

'I thought so.'

'What have you got for me?'

On her desk were the telco reports Sophie had thrust in front of her, yesterday. On top was a new page, a concise summary of the findings.

She skimmed it then handed it to Jack. When he'd finished, he laid it on the desk and smiled.

'Sophie Taylor's work,' she said. 'Bright girl. She'd make a good detective.'

'It wouldn't hurt to have another clever young woman in the CIB. Are you going to let Martin see it before you question them?'

'As I don't have to, I won't.'

'Fair enough. Any updates on the car?'

Kate turned on her computer and refreshed her inbox; a new message popped up and she read it to him.

'The VIN's been verified. It's definitely our vehicle—a Porsche 911 GT. There's an attachment.' She downloaded a set of photos and sent them to the printer.

'Is it all there?' asked Jack.

'Looks like it,' she said and passed him the printouts.

He scrutinised a shot of the front of the car. 'Including this large dent in the bonnet.'

Kate relayed the rest of the email to him. 'It's in a car yard in Miramar and the owner is singing like a songbird. He bought it cheap from Bruce Murphy on condition that he file off the VIN then sell the parts before crushing the rest. But he's a car nut and couldn't bring himself to do it. It's been sitting under a tarpaulin for the last three years.'

'Excellent.'

'The vehicle forensic team is checking it over. You know what this means, don't you?'

'I do, and I'm so goddamned proud of you.'

Determined not to get ahead of herself, she held up both hands. 'Don't jinx it. You know what they say about the fat lady and singing.'

'I don't, because that would be discriminatory against fat ladies.' Jack's grin almost split his face in two. 'Or is it discriminatory against thin ladies? Actually, I don't care who it discriminates against.'

Suddenly, it was all too much. After days of nothing happening, the information was coming in thick and fast. She needed time alone to get it all straight in her head. She pushed back her chair and stood up. 'I'm going for a walk. Call me if Martin shows up, I've got my phone.'

This morning the relentless sunshine was just plain annoying. She was tired of the heat, the cloudless blue skies, the parched grass, and hot tarmac, the trees wilting on the side of the road.

What she wouldn't give for a week of solid rain. To cleanse the world and everything in it. She started towards the café on the corner then remembered it was Sunday and it was closed. Not that she needed another coffee. Better to walk, she decided. Anything was better than twiddling her thumbs at the station for the next two hours while she waited for Martin Wedgwood to grace them with his presence. Anything was better than reliving the nightmare of seeing Juliette's body wedged into the coffin beside that old man.

# CHAPTER 57

THEY FACED each other in Interview Room One. Mimi sat opposite Kate, her head bowed as she smoothed her pants and t-shirt, now hopelessly crumpled after a night in custody. Dark shadows circled her red-rimmed eyes; her hair, pulled back into a ponytail, looked greasy. Without her makeup, she was pale, older. Martin sat behind her as he had yesterday, silently watching.

'Shall we begin?' Kate asked, keeping her tone professional yet trying not to be unkind.

'Not until I know how the girls are. They moved their flights forward.' She twisted in her chair to look at Martin, her expression pleading for information.

'Margaret, my PA, met them at the airport,' he assured her. They are on their way to Christchurch. As per your instructions, they will stay at their apartment until we know what's going to happen. They asked her to give you their love.'

'Do they know where we are?'

Kate's heart clenched hearing the fear in Mimi's voice. 'When we're finished here, I'll make sure you have access to a phone so you can speak to them.'

Mimi studied Kate's face, searching to see if her offer was genuine, then seeing that it was, relaxed. 'Thank you.'

'Tell me again what happened on the Friday night when Juliette Bisson went missing,' Kate prompted, steering the conversation back to the investigation.

'This is getting ridiculous. How many times do I have to tell you? I remember everything until we left The Huntsman. I don't remember who drove back to Martinborough. I remember waking up the next morning locked in the room next to the garage.'

'Where was Ava Scott when you woke up?' Kate asked.

'Not with me.'

'Did you know she stayed the night at your house?'

'Now that you mention it, yes.'

'How do you know?'

'After Bruce unlocked the door, I went upstairs to get cleaned up. She was in the kitchen having breakfast. She told me.'

'She could have gone home and come back. To see how you were?' suggested Kate.

'I changed her sheets myself, so I know she stayed the night,' said Mimi. She ran her tongue over her lips, picked up her glass of water and drank.

'Did she often stay the night?'

'She did when Geoffrey was at a conference.'

'Only then?'

'And some Friday nights,' Mimi admitted.

'The Friday nights when you went out to dinner?'

'Yes.'

'Did Ava ever drive your car on those nights?'

'Sometimes,' said Mimi.

'Did she drive that night?'

'I. Don't. Remember.' She slapped the table as she said each word.

'Do you remember arriving at your house?'

'No.'

'Ava getting out of the car?'

'No.'

'Or you driving away after she got out of the car?' asked Kate.

'If I don't remember getting home or her getting out of the car, how could I possibly remember driving off?' Mimi turned again to Martin, her hands raised in exasperation as she expected him to intervene. He responded with a subtle shake of his head.

'Did you tell Ava you wanted to see your godfather before he died?'

Mimi's eyes widened. 'Is that what she told you?'

'I'm asking whether you remember telling her you had to see your godfather, Ivan Simich. He lived on Raupaki Road—the same road where Juliette Bisson was living.' Kate deliberately picked up her pen and wrote something unnecessary in her folder.

'I don't remember,' said Mimi. Her shoulders sagged, her voice a whimper.

Kate waited, using the silence to unsettle her.

'What?' Mimi finally asked. 'I said I don't remember going to see my godfather. What else can I say?'

'If I were to tell you that your car was observed speeding on Raupaki Road that night, what would you say?'

'If I don't remember there's nothing I can say. Is there?'

'We have a witness who saw your car, registration number KAH 282, hit a young woman and send her flying into the air. The witness saw the car, your car, stop, turn around and drive away without checking to see if the young woman was alive or dead. The driver didn't even call for help.'

There was a long gap before Ava finally spoke. 'I don't remember.'

The silence in the room grew oppressive, almost suffocating in its intensity. It continued, unbroken, until Mimi's composure finally crumbled. A sob escaped her lips, followed by another, and then another. Mimi didn't stop crying.

# CHAPTER 58

'ARE you sure you don't want to take a break?' asked Jack. He had been monitoring the interview on the screens in the tech room, watching every nuance of the tense exchange. 'That can't have been easy.'

'No break. I can't stop now. We still don't know exactly what happened. Until we do…' Kate left the sentence hanging, her determination obvious in the set of her mouth.

'Okay, but he will be a harder nut to crack. He's cunning. He'll have thought this through.'

'As long as the doctor says he's well enough to be interviewed, I'd like to carry on, said Kate, her voice steady despite her fatigue. 'Has Tony called?'

'Not yet,' said Jack.

She paused, collecting herself. 'I'm ready.'

'Take it slowly. Stop if you find you're heading in the wrong direction or if he's gained control. Leave the room and take a break. I'll be watching. If I think there's a problem, I'll send someone in. Okay?'

'Okay.'

When she walked into Interview Room Two, she found Bruce and Martin sitting together at the table, their heads bowed over a slew of documents, each marked with yellow sticky tabs bearing the words

'Sign here'. The officer minding them, acknowledged Kate with a nod before leaving the room.

'We're just finishing up,' said Martin. He straightened and recapped a gold fountain pen. It looked expensive. Then he gathered the papers into an untidy pile and bundled them into a battered leather satchel, its flap stamped with his initials in fresh gold leaf.

'Business,' explained Bruce, with a thin smile. 'It's like rust—it never sleeps.'

'If you say so,' replied Kate. She sat down opposite him. 'How's your face?'

'Tender, but it'll heal.' He gently fingered the stitches in his cheek. His unshaven grey stubble made him look older, derelict. His eyes, however, remained as bright and alert as usual, reminding Kate of the bird she'd seen on her lawn that morning, with its head cocked, listening for the sound of its next meal.

She opened her folder in front of her. 'You've seen the doctor. Do you feel well enough to be interviewed?'

'I have, and I do.'

'Mr Wedgwood has advised you of the charges against you?' she continued.

'He has.'

'You understand them?'

'I do.'

'For the record, will you state what these are?'

'I've been charged with Sections 116 and 117 of the Crimes Act, perverting the course of justice, blah, blah, blah. And Section 150 of the Crimes Act. Misconduct in Respect of Human Remains. Is that right Martin?' He directed his question over his shoulder without bothering to turn around.

'It is,' Martin confirmed.

Bruce gave a short laugh. 'Misconduct in Respect of Human Remains,' he repeated, his tone flippant. 'That won't go down well with my colleagues.'

'They're not your colleagues anymore,' reminded Martin with a slight chuckle. 'You've sold the business. Murphy Enterprises is no more.'

'Let me stop you there Mr Wedgwood,' said Kate. 'I want to remind you of the seriousness of the charges against your client and advise you that you are here in your capacity as his solicitor, and as such, you are not to introduce irrelevant matters. Do you understand?'

'My apologies, Detective Senior Sergeant Sutton. It won't happen again.' He replied, as if suitably chastened. 'As his solicitor, I have advised my client that he has the right to remain silent in this interview.'

'Regardless, there are some matters which I will put before Mr Murphy. For his comments.'

'Go ahead,' said Martin.

'Where were you on Friday evening three years ago when Juliette Bisson went missing Mr Murphy?'

Bruce responded with a smirk, his lips sealed tight as he shook his head. The gesture reminded Kate of a defiant, rather silly schoolboy.

'Never mind. I have two witnesses who place you at your home that evening. They tell me you were babysitting your daughters, Charlotte and Jessica.'

She paused, giving him space to respond. When he didn't, she continued. 'Your wife and her friend Ava Scott were seen having dinner at The Huntsman in Masterton between seven and nine-thirty that evening. They consumed several bottles of wine between them. They were offered a taxi but refused. One of them drove back to Martinborough in your wife's Porsche.'

Bruce merely shrugged his shoulders, affecting indifference.

'Later that same night, Juliette was hit by a car. We now have a credible witness to the accident.' She emphasised the word 'credible', allowing it time to register. 'That person will also testify the car they saw hitting Ms Bisson was driven by a woman who matches your wife's description.'

He shrugged again, his eyes fixed deliberately on a point above Kate's head.

'Is there anything you would like to say?'

'You're telling the story.'

'If only it were just a story,' she countered. 'The witness reports that the woman made no attempt to help Juliette. Instead, she turned the car around and drove away.'

From her folder, she extracted a photograph of the rear view of the Porsche and slid it across the table. 'Do you recognise this car? Take a good look at the number plate and tell me if you or your wife owned this vehicle on the night in question?'

His eyes dropped to look at the photo, his brow furrowing briefly before he pushed it away with barely concealed irritation. 'Anyone can slap a number plate on a car.'

'We've checked the VIN, and it matches the car registration documents completed by the dealer when they sold you the car.'

He shrugged again.

'The car is in the same condition it was when you sold it. It wasn't broken up for parts as you instructed and it hasn't been crushed. Thank you for trucking it to the car yard, by the way. You made our fingerprinting team's work much easier.'

Bruce remained motionless, still fixated on that distant point behind Kate's head, although his breathing had become noticeably shallower and more rapid. Behind him, Martin's expression betrayed growing concern.

'We have spoken to your wife, Mr Murphy, and she has confirmed our witness's statement. That she was indeed driving the car.'

Still, he didn't move. Kate could almost see the calculations running through his mind; whether to speak now or allow the situation to unfold even further and let the whole ghastly mess play out to its inevitable conclusion. He turned briefly to Martin who responded with a slow, measured nod. 'My client has the right to remain silent,' the solicitor stated.

'Indeed he does.' She reached for her water, took a small sip, and replaced the glass on the table.

'It would have saved considerable time and money for us—the police and, by extension, the taxpayers, if either you or your wife had come forward and reported the accident. More importantly, it would have provided solace to her father to know what had happened to his daughter.' She paused again. 'Your wife came home and told you what she'd done. Didn't she?'

Bruce shifted his gaze to the floor and sighed loudly as if bored.

'You didn't panic,' Kate continued. 'You didn't achieve your business success by panicking.'

A corner of his mouth twitched in reluctant acknowledgement.

'It wasn't just that you didn't panic. Luck was on your side.'

She paused, then pressed on. 'Ivan Simich died at midnight. That's when Isobel called you. She will testify to the precise timing of her call, in court. Calmly and coolly, you worked out a plan. You went to Raupaki Road in the middle of the night to search for Juliette.'

She waited, feeling his tension.

'It was a full moon. She was wearing a long white nightdress so she was easy to find. You see, she was putting out the rubbish and was about to call her father when Mimi hit her. You found her lying in the paddock beside the cottage. Her phone wasn't far away. You carried her to the roadside and placed her in the ditch, covering her with a blanket so she wouldn't be seen.'

Behind Bruce, Martin lowered his head, unable to look her in the eye.

'You knew you were returning later, to collect Ivan's body. After that, it was a simple matter to put Juliette in the same body bag as Ivan and transport her back to the funeral home.'

Staring at his hands, Bruce sighed again. Kate fought back the urge to seize him by the shirt and shake a confession out of him.

'You collected up the rubbish, re-bagged it and put it out for collection the next morning. That way no one would see it and be suspicious.'

Bruce still looking at his hands, gave a minute smile, but didn't look up.

'The stroke of real genius was what you did with her phone,' she said. 'You disabled it and put it in the rubbish bag collected five days before we started looking for her. Probably buried so deeply in the landfill by then we had no hope of ever finding it.'

When he looked up, and met her eyes, he as good as confirmed her guess was correct.

Martin leaned forward. 'I'd like time alone with my client Detective.'

'Certainly,' said Kate. 'One last question before we terminate the interview.'

Bruce met her eyes again, his expression curious.

'Was Juliette dead when you found her in the paddock?'

He flinched. The first genuine reaction he'd shown. 'She was,' he said, his voice hoarse from disuse.

'Interview terminated at 3:15 PM.' She switched off the equipment.

# CHAPTER 59

'MAY I HAVE A WORD DETECTIVES?' Martin Wedgwood stood in the doorway of the main office, unsure whether to enter or to wait for them to come out. It was the first time Kate had seen him look anything other than sure of himself. Jack rose and ushered Martin into Kate's office, where he offered him a seat.

When they were settled, Kate behind her desk, Jack sitting next to their guest, Martin spoke. 'Like you, I'm conscious of the time, Detectives.'

He made a show of looking at his watch, smiling collegially as if they were all on the same side. 'It's late, and my clients have had a stressful day. If you charge them, I can arrange for them to appear in court first thing in the morning. This will give me time to prepare the relevant bail applications. I don't anticipate any opposition as neither of the Murphys are a flight risk, nor do they present a danger to the community at large.'

'That sounds like a plan doesn't it Kate?' asked Jack.

'It does.' She steepled her fingers in front of her lips while she considered it. 'Remind me Jack. Have we finalised the charges?'

'Hmmm,' he said. 'I don't think we have.'

Martin, his lips pressed together into a thin white line, tensed. 'In that case,' he said, getting to his feet, 'I will inform my clients. What time do you plan to start in the morning?'

Kate looked at Jack. 'Is eight-thirty good for you?'

'It is,' he replied. Then swivelled his head to look up at Martin. 'If we start early, there's every chance you'll get your clients in front of the judge by the end of the day.'

'Indeed,' said Martin. A tight head bow followed, first to Kate, then to Jack. Martin said goodnight and left.

When Kate was sure he was out of earshot, she leaned forward. 'For a minute, I thought he might click his heels.'

'I hadn't figured out the significance of the rubbish before you brought it up. It explains why we never found her phone.'

'And never will,' said Kate. 'I'd like to say I worked it out before I went in there, but it just came to me.'

The look on his face was enough. 'Well done.'

Exhausted, Kate wanted to share his enthusiasm but she wasn't done. Tomorrow she'd be questioning Bruce again and so far, his no-comment strategy was working. The same charges applied now, as they had before the interview. What she needed was a cup of tea and a lie-down to take her mind off the case. Maybe a Glenn Powell movie, with a ridiculously happy ending to lift her spirits.

'Where are you staying?' she asked Jack.

'Lizzie's here and she booked us into an Airbnb in town. We're trying that new restaurant near Gladstone. Urlar, I think it's called. It's had very good reviews. You're welcome to join us.'

'Thanks, but no thanks,' said Kate. 'I need to check on a few things before tomorrow. You go.'

He was hardly out the door when Tamsyn's name came up on her phone. 'I've got news,' she said. 'I can tell you on the phone, but it will be easier if I tell you in person. Where are you?'

'In my office at the station.'

'I'm outside. I'll be right there.'

Tamsyn was flushed and slightly short of breath when she walked in a few minutes later. She collapsed into the chair Jack had just vacated. 'Where's Tony?' she asked. 'He was going to meet me.'

'Here.' He sat down next to Tamsyn, his eyes sparkling with suppressed glee.

'Considering Juliette died three years ago, it wasn't an easy post-mortem. Bodies decompose at different rates, depending on size, temperature, exposure to the air, that sort of thing. Two thin bodies jammed together in a small space plus the hot summer when they were buried helped to preserve both corpses.'

'Tell her,' said Tony.

Tamsyn held up her hand as if to hold him back. 'In short, Juliette's body was mummified. She sustained multiple fractures; some were caused by landing on the ground, rather than the car hitting her. There were no internal organs left to examine, so I can't say if she sustained any damage to her liver or spleen, though both are likely. I won't know until the tests come back.'

'Tell her,' urged Tony.

Tamsyn rolled her eyes. 'We had time, and the machine was available, so I arranged a full-body CT before I did the PM.'

Kate shuddered. 'On a dead person?'

'Don't look like that. It's not unusual in a case like this.' She took out her laptop, placed it on the desk, turning it so Kate could see the screen. Two images appeared side by side. 'This is Juliette's,' said Tamsyn, pointing at the screen. 'Now, compare it to this.'

Kate studied the images in turn. She understood exactly what the pathologist was showing her. She looked first at Tamsyn, then at Tony.

'Good work,' she said.

# CHAPTER 60

THIS TIME, when Kate and Tony walked into Interview Room One, both Bruce and Martin rose to their feet, a courtesy Bruce had not extended earlier. They remained standing until Kate sat down. Tony turned on the recording equipment before settling into his chair beside her.

'Interview resumed at 08:55.' She then formally identified those present and repeated the usual precautions.

'My client wishes to make a statement,' Martin declared.

'Go ahead,' Kate replied. She leaned back in her chair to listen.

Bruce cleared his throat and began, his voice steady but subdued as he read the typed, double-spaced statement in front of him. 'I was at home asleep on the Friday night when I heard the car on the drive. Upon opening the door, I found Ava Scott sitting behind the wheel and my wife, Mimi, unconscious in the passenger seat. I helped Ava into the house and took her to the guest room, where she usually stays when she's had too much to drink. When I returned for Mimi, she had regained consciousness and moved to the driver's seat.'

He paused, to steady his wavering voice, before continuing. 'I tried to stop her. She insisted she needed to see Ivan before he died and drove off. I couldn't leave the girls. Ava was in no state to look after them if there was an emergency, so I waited for Mimi to come back.

The thing is, Mimi had driven drunk so often and never had an accident I wasn't that worried. While I was waiting, Isobel phone to tell me that Ivan had died.'

Kate shifted in her seat. Bruce lifted his eyes and briefly met her gaze before looking back down at his statement.

'She told me what she'd done as soon as she got back. I put her to bed and locked the door. I drove to where she said but by the time I arrived, there was nothing I could do. The girl was dead.'

His voice faltered momentarily. He looked up, away from the prepared script. 'You're wrong about me staying cool; I was panicking. If it got out it would have ruined everything: my business, Mimi's life, our daughters' lives, everything we'd worked so hard to achieve. Contacting the police would have brought it all crashing down. Mimi would go to prison, but what would that achieve? She was already booked for treatment in Australia. It wasn't like it was going to happen again. I did what I had to do to save my family.'

'And Juliette's father?' Kate asked. 'Did you consider what your deception meant for him?'

'Of course, I felt bad. But I couldn't bring her back. I could, however, save my family. That's why I did what I did.'

'Go on,' she prompted, keeping her voice steady, her face composed. She heard Tony shifting beside her and silently willed him to stay still.

Bruce shook his head, apparently having nothing more to add.

'You concealed Juliette's body virtually in plain sight. After all, who would question an undertaker going about his lawful business?'

'Correct,' said Bruce.

Martin leaned forward. 'My client has provided his statement. The next appropriate step is for you to charge him formally. He's entitled to be brought before the court as soon as possible.'

'All in good time,' replied Kate. 'We've yet to address the murders of Geoffrey Scott and June Whittaker.'

'How are those relevant?' Martin demanded. 'You've presented nothing connecting my client to either of those unfortunate incidents.'

'I agree,' said Kate. 'Allow me to remedy that.'

She distributed three copies of phone records, offering one to Bruce and one to Martin while retaining the third. 'Mr Murphy, would you kindly read aloud the name, phone number and service provider displayed at the top of these documents?'

His face darkened. 'Bruce James Murphy, 0223 798 6430, One New Zealand.'

'And the dates?'

'Read them yourself.'

'These records correspond to the days on which Geoffrey Scott and June Whittaker were murdered.' She said this calmly, keeping her gaze fixed on Bruce. 'You'll notice two distinct intervals, each approximately thirty minutes in duration when your phone was powered off.'

'It's not illegal to turn off your phone,' Martin interjected.

'No. But it is most unusual for Mr Murphy to turn his off. The analysis of his records revealed no similar occurrences except these. Perhaps you'd like to read out the specific times?'

Martin responded reluctantly. 'On the first Sunday, between 4:15 and 4:45 PM. On the second Sunday, between 9:45 and 10:15 PM.'

'These times closely align with the estimated times of death of our two victims.'

Martin leaned forward and put a cautionary hand on Bruce's shoulder. 'My client declines to comment.'

'Your service provider triangulated the signals from your phone both before it was turned off and after it was turned on. This provided us with your locations. Shall I remind you where you were on each occasion Mr Murphy?'

'My client has nothing to say,' Martin repeated firmly. 'None of this is relevant, Detective. My client has been more than cooperative. He has acknowledged responsibility for the offences which you intend to charge him with, and accordingly, I must insist he be brought before the court without further delay.'

He began to rise when Kate posed another question. 'Do either of you know what a hyoid bone is?'

Martin shook his head. 'Should we?'

Bruce remained silent, but he turned his body away from her, crossed one leg over the other, and folded his arms in front of his chest as he stared at the floor.

'It's a small bone located in the throat, just below the jaw. We all have one. It sits here,' she said, indicating the area above her larynx. 'Juliette wasn't embalmed, was she?'

Bruce shook his head almost imperceptibly.

'Dr Fraser is a specialist in the field of body decomposition. She says bodies break down at different rates depending on factors like the environment and body shape.'

'I fail to see what this has to do with my client.'

'Bear with me, Mr Wedgwood. This is important.' Kate paused. 'Have you heard of mummification?'

'Yes,' snapped Martin.

'In her preliminary report, Dr Fraser states the mummification of Juliette's remains was quite advanced. Which explains the almost pristine state of her bones. Even the little ones, like her hyoid, for instance.'

'It is my belief Mr Murphy you were aware this might be the case. It explains why wanted to destroy Juliette's remains with the digger two days ago. You had to destroy the evidence of your crime.'

'My client has already admitted to the Section 150 charge,' Martin reminded her.

Kate extracted a photograph from her folder depicting a tiny bone beside a measuring tape. She turned it around for them to examine. 'Note that it resembles a stirrup sitting backwards, with a solid section at the front and two delicate wings running backwards on either side.'

'Yes,' said Martin. 'But—'

She raised her hand for silence. 'This is a normal female hyoid bone,' she explained. Then she overlayed a second photograph on the first. This image showed the same distinctive bone structure, but one wing was completely detached from the solid middle section. 'This is Juliette's hyoid bone. Do you see the difference?'

'Obviously it's broken,' said Martin.

'There are two ways to break a hyoid bone. The first is by hanging. The second is strangulation.' Her voice was deliberately quiet.

The colour drained from Martin's face as he turned to look at his client.

'Juliette didn't die when she was struck by the car, or even when she landed in the paddock.'

She waited to let her words fully register with the solicitor and his client.

'She was still alive when you found her, wasn't she Mr Murphy? If you had called an ambulance, she might have lived. But you didn't do that, did you? You wanted the whole sorry business over, so you strangled her.'

No one moved.

'Then three years later, when it was apparent Geoffrey Scott was going to reveal what you'd done, you killed him too. Then you killed poor June for no reason other than you were afraid she might let something slip, that would link you to his death.'

Kate rose. She reached across the table and deliberately placed her hand in Bruce's shoulder. 'Bruce Murphy, I am arresting you for the murders of Juliette Bisson, Geoffrey Scott and June Whittaker.'

# CHAPTER 61

THE MCELHINNEY GALLERY, situated on Victoria Street in Wellington stands as one of New Zealand's premier art galleries. Adam McElhinney had cultivated a reputation for his uncanny ability to identify emerging trends and artists as well as for the eye-watering prices commanded by their works. Invitations to the exhibition openings were as carefully curated as the artists.

With over three decades of experience in the art world, Adam excelled at generating genuine excitement around new works by blending high-net-worth individuals and influential critics with a smattering of colourful eccentrics with extensive social networks. His fifty-five percent commission, he imperiously informed any artist who dared to question his fee, represented excellent value—worth every penny for the privilege of bearing the McElhinney stamp of approval.

Ava was having none of it. She beat his commission down to forty-seven and a half percent for the first exhibition and forty percent for each subsequent showing. Adam only relented on condition that he retain the exclusive right to sell her work, domestically and internationally, for the next five years.

Shaking her head, she exuded a manufactured disbelief and biting her bottom lip, signed on the spot without reading the small print. An oversight she was now regretting.

On, this, the afternoon of her first exhibition, she sat in her car parked one block away from the gallery, eaten up by anxiety that Clause 53 might end her artistic career before it had properly begun.

The clause specified a requirement of good character. It was followed by Clause 54, which obligated her to immediately disclose anything which might bring her work or the McElhinney Gallery into disrepute.

The paintings had been professionally hung. The full-colour catalogue was itself a work of art and had been distributed to a select group of potential investors throughout the country. Such was the excitement generated by the works and Adam's skilful promotion of Ava that all but three paintings had sold before the doors officially opened.

Tonight, when sufficient witnesses were present to appreciate and later communicate the drama, red dots would appear beside the works and the desire to own a genuine Ava Scott would begin.

The thought, that everything she had so hard worked to achieve might come crashing down, was unbearable. If she was charged with perverting the course of justice, then Adam could and would— knowing him—invoke his contractual protections: Clause 53 and Clause 54. Her paintings would be consigned to the abyss.

Kate had promised to tell her if the charges were going ahead this morning, but it was nearly noon, and she still hadn't called.

After enduring a week of nightmarish revelations, Ava was relieved to be connected to the Murphys only by association. But what if her silence had contributed to her own husband's murder? Worse, what if that became known? Charlotte Grainger was doing her best to manage the press, who had detected that something was amiss. So far, she had quashed speculation with threats of defamation litigation, and the cash-strapped media organisations had backed off. For now.

Only this morning, Adam had looked at her warily and asked her if there was anything she wanted to tell him. She looked him straight in the eye and she lied. He said he believed her, though she suspected he might have recorded her response on his phone.

'Ring, dammit,' she said, slapping her phone against her palm, then nearly jumped out of her skin when it actually rang. Heart racing, her throat dry with fear, she answered.

'Ava Scott.'

'Ava, this is DSS Kate Sutton. Apologies for the delay. We've discussed your case with the crown prosecutor and we've come to a decision.'

'And?'

'We've decided not to prosecute—'

'Oh, thank you! Thank you! Thank you! Thank you! You don't know what this means. You have literally saved my life,' she exclaimed, gulping back a sob.

'I haven't finished,' said Kate. 'We have decided not to prosecute… for now. The charges remain pending. We will make a final decision after the conclusion of the Murphy trial.'

'What do you mean?'

'Just that. I have informed Ms Grainger, who will contact you with a full explanation. Meanwhile, you are not to leave the country, and you must keep us informed of your whereabouts.'

'But I don't have to go to court?'

'No,' Kate confirmed.

'And no one will know about me not reporting Mimi for driving under the influence?'

'Not unless you tell them yourself.'

'Does Dan know?' she whispered.

'Not unless you've told him.'

'I haven't.' Ava took a slow, deep breath. The sick feeling in her stomach faded. 'Are you coming to my opening?'

'No,' said Kate firmly. 'I'm not.'

At five o'clock, the McElhinney Gallery opened its doors, and by quarter past five, the last three paintings had been sold.

'I told you they were good,' whispered Dan. They stood side by side in a corner, away from the crush of people crowding the gallery. Ava's height meant no one could see her, so they were left alone. Soon enough, Adam would insist on introducing her to the influencers in the room, forcing her to engage in what she dreaded most—small talk.

Dan leaned closer. 'Adam tells me you're the most exciting new artist to emerge in the last decade.'

'He just wants you to buy a painting,' she replied.

'I have.' He pointed to an enormous canvas, prominently displayed near the gallery entrance. 'He's keeping it in storage for me until I have somewhere to put it.'

'My poor baby, it might be years before it sees daylight again,' she murmured, signalling to a passing waiter for another drink.

'Probably.' He put down his glass and kissed the top of her head. 'I should leave soon, or I'll miss my plane.'

'Keep in touch,' she said.

'I do.'

'A text twice a year is hardly staying in touch.'

Adam appeared smiling broadly and a little intoxicated. He manoeuvred between them and put a proprietorial arm around Ava's shoulder. 'Your fans are eager to meet you,' he said. 'To tell you how much they adore your work.' He steered her into the crowd.

Dan watched her go until she disappeared among the bodies. He retrieved his bag from the storeroom and stepped onto the street, where he waited alone for the Uber that would take him to the airport.

# CHAPTER 62

TOBY PRESSED enter and gave Kate her phone back. 'Show some restraint Mum. Don't swipe right on the first good-looking man you see. Read a few profiles and get a feel for the app first.'

Exasperated, Kate busied herself at the kitchen bench. 'I told you. I'm quite happy being by myself.'

He cocked his head and studied her, amusement crinkling the corners of his mouth. 'Are you, Mum? Really? Reuben and I don't think you are.'

'Move please.' She gently nudged her eldest son aside and opened the oven door. The rich, mouthwatering aroma of roast lamb filled the kitchen, accompanied by clouds of steam which fogged the window.

She had invited the team for dinner; they were due to arrive any minute. Salads needed dressing, glassware required retrieving from cupboards, and she certainly didn't need her son ruining her concentration with explanations about the dating app he'd installed on her phone—without her permission!

A quick peek beneath the tinfoil revealed the lamb needed another twenty minutes. Carefully re-sealing it, she closed the oven door and began grating carrots for the salad.

'Reuben and I are leaving tomorrow, and we don't want you to be lonely.'

'I'm fine as I am.'

'Promise me you'll at least look at it. Check out the ones who think you're cool, read their profiles, and when you're ready, start chatting.'

She stopped grating but didn't look up. 'What if no one likes my profile?'

'Don't worry, I've set it up so they will. I found photos that actually make you look hot. I even made you interesting and I didn't mention your job. You're an ex-homemaker.'

In the living room, he touched the test panel of duck egg blue she'd painted on the wall. 'That will look good,' he said.

'I think so.' She made sweeping movements with her hands. 'Go. They'll be here in ten minutes, and I need to get organised.' She waited at the front door while he walked to his car.

'You need to buy a bike,' he called.

'Why?'

'Mountain biking is top of your list of interests.' He laughed out loud when he saw the expression on his face. Then, he climbed into his car and drove away.

Two hours later, dinner was over and everyone—with the exception of Tamsyn and Paul, who had family obligations and couldn't be there—was sitting comfortably in the living room. Her first proper gathering in her new home had gone off without a hitch. The empty plates returned to the kitchen reassuring her she hadn't lost her touch.

It was a warm night and the doors to her back garden were open. From where they were sitting they could watch the stars emerge as dusk settled into night. Kate lit the candles she'd found when she unpacked the boxes. The washing up could wait; they needed to talk. Jack topped up their wine glasses, and they sat in silence for a few minutes, reflecting on their recent experience.

Sophie was the first to speak. 'How is Ludo?'

'Dr Su says he's making good progress,' said Kate. 'He'll be home soon and should be well enough to testify at the trial provided he stays on his medication.'

Tony sipped his wine. 'If he doesn't, will his statement to Dr Scott be enough?'

'That's for the judge to decide, but the prosecutor believes there's a good chance it will. Everything combines to provide a compelling motive.'

'Do we know yet how Bruce found out about the statement?'

'He won't say. I suspect Geoffrey's dementia played a role. Maybe he dropped a clue without meaning to. Maybe he told Bruce he was going to the police. Whatever, Bruce knew that if the truth came out, then everything he'd worked for would be gone. He had to silence Geoffrey to conceal Juliette's death.'

'I still don't understand why he killed June,' said Tony.

'He was terrified she'd seen him at the house,' said Kate. 'I blame myself for that. I mentioned June saw more than she first said. I was referring to Ludo, but Bruce didn't know that and got scared. He couldn't take the risk.'

Jack sat up. 'He killed June, not you. Remember that.'

'I'll try,' she said.

'Imagine how relieved he must have been when Ludo shot up the health centre,' said Tony.

'Relieved and vindicated. He believed he deserved his good fortune, no matter what he did. His sense of his own superiority grew even stronger.'

'If only he had stuck around and supervised the car getting taken apart. He messed up bigtime when he left it to someone else.'

'He'd got used to people following his orders.'

Jack held up an unlit cigar. 'Do you mind if I smoke?'

'Go ahead,' said Kate.

He got up, moved his chair closer to the open doors, sat down and snipped the cigar's end with a cigar cutter, then lit it. Several puffs to get it going, and a cloud of aromatic smoke slipped into the night air.

'You have to hand it to him. He came from nothing. He's a shrewd businessman and he worked hard to get where he is. But I agree with you,' said Jack. 'He made the cardinal error of believing he was untouchable. I've heard that even now, he's in jail and he still thinks he's better than everyone else.'

'If he'd just called an ambulance when Juliette was lying in the paddock, none of this would have happened,' said Bill. He was lying on the floor, his wine glass balanced on his stomach, his legs out the door. 'What's the penalty for dangerous driving causing injury? Three months in jail, disqualification from driving, a fine. It's nothing. Certainly not worth three lives.'

'Calling an ambulance would have meant the whole world finding out what Mimi had done. He couldn't let that happen. He killed Juliette to preserve the illusion of his perfect family.'

'Surely,' said Tony, refilling his glass from the bottle which was doing the rounds, 'Mimi could have put her big girl pants on, fessed up the day after it happened, and taken the consequences.'

'She was locked up remember,' said Kate. 'He put her on the plane to Australia, the same day Juliette's disappearance was made public. Maybe she knew, maybe she didn't? But he told her that if she wanted to see her daughters again she had to stop drinking. It was months before she came home, and by then it was all over. People had moved on.'

Jack, resting his head on the back of the chair, popped off a stack of perfect smoke rings. 'Martin Wedgwood played a blinder. The business assets were transferred into a trust before Bruce was formally arrested and there was nothing we could do to stop it. If he'd done it afterwards, he'd have got nothing like their true value. He's a beneficiary and so are his daughters. That's how he can afford to retain the country's most expensive King's Counsel for his defence.'

'Did Mimi get anything?' asked Tony.

'She got the blame for destroying the family.' Kate looked grim. 'And the house and her car. Not that she'll be able to drive it. Whether the girls will support her when her money runs out remains to be seen.'

'She will go to prison, won't she?' asked Sophie.

'She will,' said Jack. 'Most likely for the charge of perverting the course of justice. She'll get out after serving twelve months if she behaves herself.'

The candles flickered, and moths flew in from the garden to bat against the light in the kitchen.

'You're forgetting the one person who could have prevented this whole tragedy,' said Jack. 'Ava Scott. She was there. She knew what happened.'

'But did she?' Kate asked. 'She denies any knowledge of what happened after they got back to the house. She maintains she fell asleep and didn't wake up until the next morning, then didn't learn that Juliette was missing until the following Wednesday.'

'I don't believe her,' said Sophie.

'Neither do I,' said Kate. 'But a jury might.'

Bill, who was enjoying the wine and wondering if his partner would come and collect him, so he didn't have to drive home, suddenly spoke up. 'I saw her on the news last night. Ava Scott. Her exhibition sold out. She's the art world's new sensation.' He paused. 'It doesn't seem fair, does it? Not after everything that's happened.'

'It isn't fair,' said Kate. 'We'd be out of a job, if the world was fair.'

'Pass the wine,' said Jack. 'Too much reality is killing the mood.'

When they'd all gone home, and after she'd finished the washing-up, Kate's curiosity got the better of her and she checked her phone.

A small green circle overlapped the logo of the app Toby had installed. She had no idea what it meant but tapped anyway. And there it was. A photograph of a man holding a fish. Then another of a man standing in front of a smart new car. It clearly wasn't his car because the For Sale sign was in the window, but still, he looked pleased with himself. She scrolled down. Photo after photo of people unafraid to put themselves out there, all hoping for an encounter, a connection, a few words to calm the loneliness.

A world of possibilities was there on her screen, waiting for her to summon the courage to go out and explore it.


The End.

# MARTINBOROUGH, FEATHERSTON, MASTERTON AND THE WAIRARAPA

Martinborough, Featherston and Masterton are all towns in the South Wairarapa, a province in New Zealand occupying the eastern half of the southern isthmus of the North Island.

This book is a work of fiction. In the interests of the story, I have taken liberties with the descriptions and layouts of places mentioned.

For those of you who know the area, I beg your indulgence for these necessary adjustments.

For those of you who don't know the area, I can recommend the Wairarapa as a place to visit. The wine, especially the Pinot Noir, is excellent. The restaurants serve wonderful food, the scenery is gorgeous, and the people are friendly.

# ACKNOWLEDGMENTS

My immense gratitude goes to those early readers who have provided invaluable feedback through several iterations of the book.

Josie, your keen eye for what works and what doesn't is appreciated as always. Felicity, Vanessa and Georgie, your insightful comments are reflected in the final work. Harry, you nailed it.

My gratitude to Brenda Channer for her insight, and for putting me straight on several police matters. Any errors of fact are entirely my own. My gratitude also to the senior members of the legal profession whose pithy answers to my naïve questions were very helpful.

Happy 70th Birthday Phillip. I have used your name, your diction and your deep voice, but otherwise the man in this book is entirely a product of my imagination.

To the people of the Wairarapa, you are a fantastic bunch; kind, funny, practical, civic-minded and welcoming. As far as I know, there is not one serial killer amongst you.

As always, I would like to thank you, the reader, for reading my latest work of fiction. If you have enjoyed it, please take some time out of your day and post a rating and/or a review.

I get a huge kick out of hearing from my readers. Feel free to contact me either on my Facebook page or on my website.

www.facebook.com/rosyfenwickeauthor

www.rosyfenwickeauthor

# ALSO BY ROSY FENWICKE

A DSS Kate Sutton Murder Mystery.

## The Secret of the Fallen Woman

Pre-Order NOW for
22/02/2026

**The Secret of the Fallen Woman**

A DSS Kate Sutton Murder Mystery #2

The Secret of the Fallen Angel

When CCTV cameras record the shocking murder of reclusive Bonnie Smith, CEO of one of New Zealand's largest companies, Detective Superintendent Kate Sutton knows this is no ordinary case. The footage shows a man disguised as a tradesman throwing Smith to her death from the balcony of her secluded country mansion—a brazen act that seems almost like a taunt to law enforcement.

The killer has left his calling card in the most public way possible, yet remains frustratingly anonymous behind his disguise. For Kate, it's as if the murderer is playing a game, challenging her to catch him despite the evidence literally being caught on camera.

On the surface, Bonnie's husband seems genuinely devastated, his alibi watertight. But as Kate digs deeper, she uncovers shadowy connections between him and an ambitious property developer with a reputation for cutting corners—and silencing opposition.

Meanwhile, the victim herself becomes increasingly enigmatic. Who was the real Bonnie Smith behind the corporate powerhouse façade? With each layer of her past that Kate unravels, new questions emerge. What secrets was this reclusive executive hiding in her countryside retreat? And were those secrets worth killing for?

# ALSO BY ROSY FENWICKE

**COLD WALLET**

*'An expertly constructed story with those important little details that really do make it something special.' Reviewer: Chris Reed NZ Booklovers.*

Cold Wallet

'You have kind eyes.' The last words Andrew said to Jess just before he died on their honeymoon. Grief stricken, she returns to New Zealand and to the cryptocurrency exchange he left her in his will. Knowing nothing about cryptocurrency, Jess, a physician, turns to Andrew's associate, Henry, someone she has never liked, for advice.

The solution to her problems may be in the Cold Wallet but without the passwords what can she do?

'An exciting thought-provoking thriller set in the world of cryptocurrency.'

www.ingramcontent.com/pod-product-compliance
Ingram Content Group UK Ltd.
Pitfield, Milton Keynes, MK11 3LW, UK
UKHW010755090625
6297UKWH00038B/395